OF
SHATTERED
DREAMS

Nilesh Rathod is a businessperson, writer and poet. Co-founder of Ensemble Infrastructure India Limited, Nilesh's company currently employs over 2000 people.

Destiny of Shattered Dreams is his debut novel. Nilesh is currently working on his second novel. He lives in Mumbai with his wife Preeti and sons Shloak and Parv. You may reach him at Nilesh@nileshrathod.in or http://www.nileshrathod.in

DESTINY
OF
SHATTERED
DREAMS

Nilesh Rathod

RUPA

Published by
Rupa Publications India Pvt. Ltd 2016
7/16, Ansari Road, Daryaganj
New Delhi 110002

Sales Centres:

Allahabad Bengaluru Chennai
Hyderabad Jaipur Kathmandu
Kolkata Mumbai

ISBN: 978-81-291-3975-7

First impression 2016

10 9 8 7 6 5 4 3 2 1

The moral right of the author has been asserted.

Printed at Parksons Graphics Pvt. Ltd, Mumbai.

To the only person I ever could love.
That is, you

Chapter I

'Your client must go to jail tonight,' the judge said, as he picked up his pen to formalize the pronouncement cancelling Atul's bail. Atul's heart skipped a beat, the blood rushing about in anguish as he sank down on his chair, discredited and shamed. Atul hadn't been as prepared for this; so when reality struck, it did so with a paralyzing force.

Atul Shyamlal Malhotra, thirty-five years of age, chairman of the board and founder CEO of Transmech Telecom Limited (TTL), a billion-dollar enterprise, was now in judicial custody on charges of corrupting government officers, violating the Foreign Exchange Management Act (FEMA), and for other economic offences.

A frenzied media scrum blocked the road, scrambling to capture a glimpse of the man being pushed into the vehicle. With pleas falling on deaf ears, the police were forced to resort to a mild lathi charge so that the cavalcade could move. Atul was on his way to serve time behind bars.

Soon enough, they were inside the prison gates and he was told to get down. Emerging from the vehicle, he saw the bulky iron gates close behind him. Then, escorted by a few police officers, he walked into the main building. There, he was asked to place his belongings on a table so that they could be listed on a Panchnama.

A Patek Philippe Nautica, a Cartier ballpoint pen, a Mont Blanc wallet, some cash and a bunch of credit cards were duly noted and carelessly stashed in a plastic bag. The shirt, chinos and shoes that he was still wearing were duly listed as well. He was issued two sets of prison clothes, a mug, a plate, a pillow and a blanket—all that he would own during his time here—and told to follow an officer to the shower area, where a little green soap was thrust into his hand.

'You get one a week, use it carefully. No replacements!'

It wasn't long before Atul reappeared from the shower, naked and deloused. Tall and broad-shouldered, adorned with a shining mantle of dripping water, muscles curving at just the right places, Atul shone in the bright vapour lights of the shower hall. His sharp nose and high cheekbones, peppered by an unkempt stubble, stood out against his fair colouring, his hazel eyes still intense as ever—circumstances might have changed, but the man refused to be intimidated. He donned the blue and white striped uniform with a cloth badge that read 2393.

This would be his home for a while, maybe a week, maybe a year, maybe more. He hoped a day, but that was not for him to decide. The officer who'd handed him the soap intoned, 'You will share a cell with two other inmates. Your belongings go with you.'

The officer droned on, 'You are allowed to buy a few essentials; the list of permissible items is placed in the lunchroom. You get no more. 6 a.m. headcount. And unless you are dead, you present yourself for headcount or miss seeing the sun for the day. You miss it three times; you won't see the sun for a week. That is what we call solitary confinement here. 7 a.m. breakfast, 12 noon lunch, 5 p.m. supper. Those are the only meals you get. You lose your plate, you miss a meal; you lose your mug, you miss your tea. Replacements cost. 6 p.m. you are back in the cell. 7 p.m. lights out.'

As they walked down the ground floor corridor, he saw cells on either side, each with three or four inmates tucked inside blankets similar to the one he carried. A pungent stinky odour, akin to a heap of old rotting grapes, filled the air. He reached his cell walking up a rusting metal staircase to the first level lit by faint yellow light from bulbs suspended from the roof. Three levels of cells, fronted by a narrow passage each, looked down on an atrium that provided the guards a clear view of all the cells.

The officer unlocked the door to Atul's cell. It was a small room with two stone platforms on either side, and a third at the far end; each seemed too small to hold a human frame, yet two thin-framed men, presumably fast asleep under blankets, huddled on two of the platforms. A foul smelling WC was built into one corner and was filled with human waste. Fortunately, Atul was allotted the platform at the entrance of the cell. He didn't get much of the stink, at least not from the shit-filled pot.

He put his belongings on his platform. The metal door slammed shut and the realization that he was here for real hit him. He watched as the officer disappeared and then looked around. The run-down walls boasted a lot of small and large posters, some of Gods, some of women, and the others of just about anything. The muck-filled pot and leaking tap made the place a perfect breeding ground for mosquitoes.

The silence sent his heart racing and fear began to set in. He could see a high rise in the distance with a few lights still glowing through a small grilled window of his cell. He tried to see what he could spot out there—nothing other than a man smoking on a balcony; soon, he was gone too.

Memories of all that had led up to this day rushed in. His lost love; his daughter Ananya; Aditya, his childhood buddy; Anil, Prem, Rakesh and Qazi, his partners at work. He thought of anybody and everybody he could get his mind to recall. Times like these could drive a man crazy. Atul knew that. A sliver of hope still held him in its thrall and he knew that he had to get through this. Getting used to these walls was now a necessity, not a matter of choice.

Slowly his mind quieted and the night began stretching on endlessly, hour after hour; he had no way of knowing how much of it was left to pass. A few rats kept him company, scrambling across the passage, smelling and nibbling anything they found, retreating into holes he discovered only when they vanished into them. All he had in the world was time. And when he wanted it to pass, it stood still. The night dragged on. Thoughts raced through his mind and vanished, replaced by armies of unknown fears. The battle ended somewhat when a weak predawn light crept in through the window. He was thrilled. Birds began to chirp. They sounded like award-winning music, and soothed his racing mind. Just as Atul began feeling settled, the peace was shattered by the shriek of a deafening alarm, shocking the hell out of him. His cellmates awoke and looked at Atul like he was a ghost out of nowhere.

'Qasim,' said one of them, extending his hand.

'Krishna,' said the other, lying with his head within inches of the muck-filled pot.

'Atul Malhotra,' he replied with a smile. They didn't recognize him.

★

That first morning began a new chapter in Atul's life. One that he never thought existed in his wildest dreams.

He would begin the day by queuing for the shower room, where he got on with his morning tasks—the big job, the small job; he never used the shit pot in his cell for that. Once back in the cell, he kept mostly to himself, hardly ever speaking to Qasim or Krishna. He spent his days observing the way things were done here. Atul liked learning the ropes in any new situation. He would learn some here too.

Meanwhile, under continued media and public pressure, the courts decided to fast track the case. Soon, Atul found himself spending most days at court as the trial continued. During this time, on 18 November, the love of his life married someone else. He had learnt about it shortly before he was jailed, but that didn't lessen the misery. Frantic, miserable and raging, he missed the morning headcount on the day of her marriage. He refused to believe the sun still shone. The warden awarded him solitary confinement for that small misadventure.

Walking to solitary took him down a narrow and hitherto unseen passage to the basement of the jail. The room, just about as wide as its iron door, was moist and full of fungus. The door shut, locking him into near absolute darkness. Some light trickled in from the pores between the door and the metal frame. The room hadn't been cleaned for ages and the stench made him feel he was in a gutter full of sewage.

But none of that mattered to him. To be stuck here in such abject misery, while the love of his life left him to his fate and plighted her troth with another—that was more unbelievable and agonizing than any pain the world could inflict upon him. He felt helpless, maimed and robbed of the last vestiges of his identity. Passing that one day proved harder than his first night in jail.

All day, he alternated between crying inconsolably and drifting off to sleep exhausted, unable to find solace within, since all that he had been felt irrevocably lost. There was no one within him to answer his call. Lines from Qazi sahib's couplets reverberated in his mind.

Waqt masiha haeh, har gham ko samaa lega,
Lekin waqt haeh, waqt lega.
Tab tak kaun mujhe dava dega?
Yuheen chalta rahega yeh gham ka silsila umr bhar,
Kabhi yeh dard ko hawa dega,
Kabhi yeh dard ko dava dega.

Pareshan baadal kitni der apne aap ko rok sakega?
Garaj garaj, falak mein aag lagaa dega,

Barasne se pehele woh bhi isi tapish ko hawa dega.

Kismat kise kehte hain, ham nahin jaante,
Shakal badal badal kar woh bhi mere haal ka hi mazaa lega.

Shola sa bhadak utha, socha ab to mujhe samaa lega,
Aag hi aag haeh, magar qazaa se pehele woh bhi kahan khaakh dega.

Time is a messiah, every sorrow it shall contain,
But time it is and time it shall take.
But who will heal my wounds till then?

Just so will continue sorrow's shackle all life,
Sometimes the pain it shall bluster,
At other times, pain it shall heal

For how long will the distraught cloud contain itself?
Bellowing, bellowing, it shall set the firmament on fire,
Afore bursting it too will set fire to the same desire.

What do you call destiny, this I do not know,
Transforming, altering forms it too shall my extant relish.

Something like the spark did leap, I thought that
now at last it will absorb me,
Fire fire all the way but how shall it give cinders
before destiny's decree.

Chapter 2

Around six months and eighty hearings later, the High Court was ready to pronounce its verdict. The prosecution had been able to prove only some of the charges. There was a hush in the packed courtroom as the judge pronounced the sentence: 'There are three charges against the chief promoter and ex-chairman of Transmech Telecom Limited.

'On the first count of destruction of evidence, the court finds him not guilty. The court discharges him on insufficient evidence.

'On the charges of corruption and suborning government officers, the prosecution could not find any direct evidence; however, the corroborative evidence presented in the matter cannot be sheer coincidence. The court finds the accused guilty.

'This court sentences the accused to two years' simple imprisonment. The court also bars the accused from holding office in any company incorporated in the territory of India for a period of ten years. Additionally, the Rs 1,250 crore deposited by the company in lieu of the equity received from Luxor investments is forfeited.

'The accused is also fined an amount of Rs 2,500 crore. All assets of the accused, including his holdings in Transmech Telecom Limited, will be attached till such time the penalty is deposited.'

The curtains were finally drawn. Atul would spend another eighteen months in prison. He had already served six months by the time the court reached this verdict.

★

With time, Qasim, Krishna and Atul started to have supper together. Approaching fifty-five, Qasim was way older than most of the inmates. He was swarthy, had high cheekbones and well-contoured thick lips blackened by excessive smoking. His short hair stood up straight, like quills on a porcupine, and the craters on his nose extended to other parts of his face. There was something very mature about him. He was respected within those walls and an influential friend to have around.

On the other hand, Krishna was a brat, with a long scar that had been knifed across his right cheek. He was around Atul's age and always ready to pick up a fight. And the bully that he was, he got into brawls often and frequently sported a bruised eye, chin or nose.

The remainder of Atul's days in jail were uneventful. Other than Qasim and Krishna, he made few other acquaintances and kept a low profile. Once in a while, a prisoner or two would approach him as if he were a celebrity. The media did portray him as a political scapegoat, garnering some sympathy for him.

'What are you in for? You don't look like a criminal, you seem like those officer types,' said Qasim, one day.

Krishna butted in proudly, 'I was working for someone in Dubai, he used to supply currency to me in Mumbai. Fake money. I used to circulate it for him. Everything got busted in a police raid. The motherfuckers are in Dubai, I got seven years for it.'

Atul looked at Qasim, 'What about you?'

Krishna intervened again, 'Qasim bhai, tell us. I asked you so many times, you never talk'. 'Qasim bhai never speaks about himself,' he added, turning to Atul.

Qasim looked blank for a while, clearly pondering where to start from.

'What is it, Qasim bhai? Share it with us, we are friends after all,' said Atul.

'I was convicted for killing my three-year-old daughter. I am serving life for that crime.'

'Did you?' asked Atul.

'It was 13 May 2000. The same month that Bill Clinton visited Mumbai. I was thirty-eight then. Worked as a security guard at the docks. I had a wife, Sabina. She loved me, only I didn't have the eyes to see it. She nagged me for attention but I loved my freedom. After work, I would drink, play cards and come home whenever I felt like. The only time I needed her was when I wanted her. Other times, she was a pain.

'With all the money I lost gambling and drinking, she had to work as a housemaid. With our daughter's growing needs, even that was never enough. She worked double shifts, fed me whenever I came home, let me have her at my will, and looked after my daughter too. All that she pleaded for was a bit of affection. Even that became too much for me to part with. The pleasures of life blinded me. The more resilience she showed, the more arrogant I became.

'One night, I came home around 1 a.m., as usual, drunk. She laid out a meal for me. I was happy, I had won some good money at *Teen Patti* that night. But she started preaching: "Stop drinking! Spend time at home, take interest in our little girl's needs..." One thing led to another. I pushed her out and asked her to get lost with her daughter. I wanted nothing to do with them. The quarrel continued on the verandah of our chawl and the neighbours watched us fight. I slapped her hard. Our little girl slipped from her hand and fell three floors to her death.

'My world collapsed in a split second. It was an expensive realization. As if that was not enough, Sabina jumped after her. The demon in me vanished, but not before consuming everything I ever had.'

Atul heard the story in absolute silence. A thousand thoughts filled his mind. Hadn't he done the same to his five-year-old daughter Ananya and his wife Roshni?

'Do you have regrets?' asked Atul.

Qasim looked at him, 'Not a moment goes without regret. And you know what is more painful than the regret? Guilt.

'Fourteen years have passed, but the guilt refuses to leave me. I want to meet them, tell them how I feel, ask their pardon. But they are gone. The pain of having to live with that burden is way more than any conviction any court could give me.'

The story played on Atul's mind and never left his conscience. Not a day passed when he did not think of what Qasim had revealed.

'What about you, Atul?' Qasim asked. A momentary silence prevailed before Atul began to speak.

'Mine is a long story and inconsequential at that. My ambitions and dreams cost me my conscience. I could never stop seeking. That seeking landed me where I am today.'

Atul drifted down memory lane. How time had changed the man he had been—a powerhouse of dreams, overflowing with ambition and energy...

His story, he mused, was a straightforward one. Passion and ambition, deceit and drama.

Chapter 3

It was way past midnight on a balmy Mumbai winter's night in 2010. Atul and Roshni, his wife of eleven years, sat arguing in the back seat of his bulletproof BMW.

'Why were you behaving like a bitch?' he shouted angrily. His pupils were dilated and his head buzzing with numerous shots of alcohol that he had downed through the evening. Roshni had been belligerent and created a ruckus, embarrassing him in front of everyone who mattered to him. He was furious. 'Say something now, bitch!' he snarled.

Roshni stared stonily at the footpath racing past her window.

'You are pissing me off; unless you are willing to talk, it is over and NOW.'

She turned and looked at him, her face showing a plain and simple 'Go to hell!'. Despite years of acrimony, she had never been so openly defiant. And her satisfaction at that shone through her eyes.

The chauffeur, Alok, watched the spectacle through the rear-view mirror, a show he had witnessed far too often.

'Stop the fucking car! Now... Alok!' yelled Atul, and the car came to a screeching halt.

Getting down outside the lobby of his opulent apartment building, Atul tripped on the pavement. Roshni got out the other side and stormed into the building. She refused to see if he was hurt, and a few seconds later, she had disappeared into the lift.

Alok helped him back on his feet, but Atul pushed him off and got back into the car. 'Drive,' he snarled. Alok stood there, rattled.

'Drive!!! Don't you understand the meaning? I said, drive!!'

Alok quickly got behind the wheel and started the car.

'Take me to the Taj.'

Alok did.

Once there, Atul almost tripped again as he got off at the lobby. Alok quickly dismounted and ran across to hold him just in time. Atul barely made it to the Harbour Bar without help. He took a table adjoining the glass facade that overlooked the Gateway of India. Boats anchored to the jetty waved back at him, jostling in the choppy waters. Atul called for a Black Label. The bartender would have refused anyone else in his state but not Atul Malhotra.

In the distance, he could still see the luxury three-storeyed yacht, the *Indian Princess*, where they had celebrated the tenth anniversary of his company with shareholders and well-wishers. With his Bond movie etiquette, razor-sharp reflexes, impeccable persona and outstanding achievements, it was clear that he had beaten everyone at the game. But he also exuded an aura that said his best was yet to come. Atul was just thirty-five.

By his side, welcoming guests as they reached the yacht in a flurry of speedboats, stood Roshni, resplendent in a bright blue Sabyasachi ensemble, flaunting a flawless diamond necklace and bosom.

The evening had started on a high note as he and Roshni welcomed their guests on the sun deck. The *Indian Princess* was anchored about a mile into the Arabian Sea, and the deck offered breathtaking views of the city of Mumbai and its sparkling lights as the night wore on. Looking seaward, one could spot ships blinking signals as they entered or left the harbour.

As the evening progressed, Atul found himself the centre of attention, drawing praise and applause as he mingled. He was elated at the recognition given to him for years of hard work and hard-won accomplishments.

After welcoming their guests, Roshni left his side and spent most of her time with her sister and father. Atul was left almost alone to play host. The last thing he wanted was to pick up another quarrel with Roshni, but as the evening wore on, her indifference was becoming rather obvious to everybody and he felt compelled to step in.

'I would appreciate it if you could play the host to everyone rather than just your beloved family,' he whispered softly, not wanting to make the issue more public than it had already become.

'Fuck off,' retorted Roshni, not bothering to whisper back, and more than a few heads turned.

'What's wrong with you?' he hissed, gripping her arm trying to pull her away from her father and sister and take her with him.

'Wrong?' she said in normal tones, 'Ask yourself that and let go off me, you are hurting me.' More heads turned and a hush began to filter through the gathering.

'Just what did I do?' asked Atul in anguish.

Roshni replied bluntly, without a care for the glances she drew. 'Does it even matter? Enjoy your party. Be thankful I am here and not someplace else; don't piss me off any more. And if you don't want me here, I'll be happy to take the next boat back.'

Anil Oberoi, Atul's college buddy, marketing head and a co-founder of TTL, decided to intervene before matters went completely out of hand. He uncorked champagne and poured it for some of the guests around, Atul and Roshni included. 'Ladies and Gentlemen,' he said, 'Let us all raise a toast to this dream.' He raised his glass and all the others followed suit. 'Cheers to the dream!' echoed through the crowd as glasses clinked. The party mood was restored.

Atul kept his distance from Roshni, making sure he didn't have to confront her again. The festivities continued, music blared without a rebound from the skies, mingling with the sea spray and the salty breeze. It felt like time stood still to make space for the occasion.

Atul recalled he had yet to make his address to the gathering and raised his glass, 'Friends! Welcome home,' he boomed to a standing ovation.

'We had no dream, you gave us one. We had no means, you gave us some. When confronted with challenges, we remembered you—you, who put your faith, hard-earned savings and prayers behind us. And how could we fail you? How could we let that trust die in vain? So each time, we rediscovered our way. We forged ahead, we progressed and how!' As applause thundered through the room again, he paused before continuing, 'Every crisis looks shallow in the prism of faith!'

Again he paused to take a moment to look around before saying more seriously, 'The challenges we face today are great, but the commitment even greater. Wait for another ten years and...' here, he choked up, his heart welling with gratitude. Truly indebted for what he had achieved, he surrendered and couldn't say more. His throat felt dry and his eyes moist.

Suddenly, he heard another voice shouting, 'We made us proud today. We made our efforts count. We proved them wrong. Love you bro...!' It was Prem Khatri, another co-founder of TTL, holding his arms wide open, waiting for Atul to hug him. Nostalgia, pride, gratitude and hope shone on almost every face.

'Hold on! Hold on! This calls for more, I've a couplet penned just for this day,' yelled Akram Qazi, standing in a corner at the bar wearing a white suit and now pulling a scrap of paper out of his pocket.

Heads turned to look. Qazi was fat and stout with thick eyebrows and a French beard. He was also the legal brain behind the business. Now he recited with a flourish:

Juda hoon main is jahan se,
Chaloon kaise is jahaan ke sang?

Auron ko jahaan manzil nazar aati hain,
Auron ko jahaan manzil nazar aati hain...
Wahan toh meri rahein shuru hoti hain!
Wahan toh meri rahein shuru hoti hain!!

Different I am from this world,
How may I walk apace with this world?
Whereon others destinations can perceive,
Whereon others destinations can perceive...
Therein my worlds do begin!
Therein my worlds do begin!!

'Kya baat haeh, Qazi sahib!' Atul joined the applause and rushed to embrace him. Despite his best effort, he couldn't get past Qazi sahib's ample paunch, but nonetheless, the spirit of the emotion conversed between them.

The party was now drawing to a close and many people had already thanked the hosts—Atul and the three other co-founders of TTL, Rakesh Mohanan, Prem Khatri and Anil Oberoi—and left. Atul took Qazi's hand and said warmly, 'Qazi sahib, please stay back for a while, I don't want this night to end, I want time to stop.'

'Time has no mind of its own, Atul! An old man's bones can handle no more. I wish Allah gives you abundant success and showers his benevolence upon you,' he said, hugging Atul for the last time that evening.

Atul and the other three co-founders were now the only people there, along with Atul, Rakesh and Prem's wives. Anil was single. The breeze was getting chillier, the waves noisier while Atul looked around for his coat.

Shrugging it on, he made himself comfortable on the thickly carpeted floor resting against a sofa, his hand propping his head up, lost in thought. He recalled his years as a management graduate, then as a business manager, then the launch of TTL as a consultancy, and finally, becoming a telecom service provider. The four of them had quit General Mobile to start their entrepreneurial journey ten years ago, this day. And what a journey it had been, he thought.

Prem Khatri was the eldest among them. Aged forty-seven, he was the money man with years of experience. The telecom business was capital intensive and all about infrastructure investments. They needed more money than they could ever have. As TTL's CFO, Prem efficiently juggled the bankers, investors, lenders and vendors to manage operations and expansions.

Rakesh Mohanan had run the technology arm for General Mobile. Now, while the competition was busy investing in advertising and marketing, Rakesh had stretched every penny to get the latest networking technologies on board. His foresight had made TTL one of the most sought after brands for its service quality. Each of the four excelled in their own areas of expertise. They made a dream team.

'So, what is next for us, amigos?' asked Atul.

'No one's taking tomorrow off,' said Anil firmly. 'We're going to work with twice as much energy, we're going to reach heights we can't even imagine.'

'But we can't go all in, all of the time and hope to stay lucky,' warned Rakesh. He was their 'sounding board', their voice of caution, along with Qazi. Atul hated this trait of his but couldn't ignore him, he had been bloody right far too many times. So he said, 'End it, Rakesh! Please spare us your gospels... not today!' as he laughed and put up a hand.

But Rakesh wasn't to be deterred. 'I don't say this out of caution. This is the reality and we must grow up to it. What was right yesterday will not necessarily be right tomorrow; speeding is no good without the ability to brake.'

But Atul's ego overrode any words of wisdom. 'I am your chairman. You've trusted me so far, you must trust me even more now,' he said authoritatively. After all, he was a jack-of-all-trades and even a master of some; the right catalyst needed to steer this engine. He owned more shares in the company than all the other co-founders put together, and was boss by default.

Now seated at the Harbour Bar, Atul's reminiscences brought a smile to his face. A smile of pride at building a company that gave the competition a run for its money. He remembered his years of courtship with Roshni, the love and the times together; and all the anguish and frustration that had brought the marriage to the altar of divorce today. It all ran through his mind like a film reel. But despite it all, he had a grin of acceptance for what life had offered to him. As a package, it was a bloody good deal!

Chapter 4

Roshni Sinha-Malhotra and Atul went back a long way, to the days when he had been a shy, just-out-of-college guy. She was 5'6", oozed confidence, had innocent blue eyes, amazing dimples and a French manicure, was always chirpy and bubbly, and hailed from an elite family.

They had met through common friends. Those had been Atul's days of struggle, but she judged him as ambitious and he had incredible ideas. He was full of life all the time, as he still was, but not for her, she thought.

They dated for two years before they tied the knot. The class gap was too big. She spent more on shoes and lipsticks than he earned each month. All that didn't matter to them, but it did to her father, Anand Sinha—an established kingpin in the cotton business who had eventually sold his business years ago, amassing a lot of wealth in the process. Roshni and Atul dated for two years before they tied the knot.

She had loved Atul dearly. He was a man with a huge heart and never hurt anybody. Roshni respected him and even without the financial security that her father presently provided her, she knew that Atul and she would build a happy life together. The eventful years of courtship had brought them very close. Their dates had always followed a ritual: lovemaking followed by endless talk about the dreams they had and the future that awaited them. Passionate lovebirds that they were, they treasured their time together and never missed an opportunity to express their yearning for the other. They were lusty, itching and eager to explore newer ways and places to make love. Several times, a cop or two had knocked on the windshield catching them making love in the back seat of Roshni's car.

The eventual run-up to the wedding was therefore pretty routine compared to all that led up to it. They were determined and nothing else mattered, though it wasn't easy to adjust in the new life. Within a year of getting married, Atul had founded TTL with financial help from Roshni's father; an amount that he paid off in time. TTL was his brainchild, but it took a lot of convincing on his part to get the other founders on board. He knew he needed each one of them.

Desires from destiny change with time, and so did Roshni's. She soon realized she had not only married Atul, she had married his dreams too; and one person's dreams can become another's baggage. Atul was a passionate man with dreams so large that nothing else seemed to fit in the canvas when he started to paint them. Life as a couple started to change. His success, money and growth led her to believe he was probably right after all. And wasn't his aspirational attitude exactly why she had fallen for him in the first place? Like a stream, life too finds a way to adjust and flow, and so did Roshni's life.

Nevertheless, for a long time, Roshni questioned whether she came second in her husband's life, since the first place seemed to be held by his ambitions for himself. And though she had lately begun to accept all of that as fate, there were a lot of things she was resentful about: Losing her husband to greed; not having an offspring in eleven years of marriage; not pursuing her career as a designer after all her education and experience. She always thought it was too late, and as is so often the case with such an approach, she never really took the initiative again.

The magic of their relationship had been passionate sex. Lust and desire had ruled their relationship for a long time after marriage.

But in the past few years, that had gone pale too. He had been full of life once, and still was; just no longer for her. As their relationship went downhill, their passionate interludes had receded and fast. Did this happen with all relationships, she wondered.

He was everything she had and she did everything to protect that. Unfortunately, the more she tried, the farther he went. She didn't know how to tread, nor did she know how to rekindle the magic—'life must go on' was something she had heard way too often. But this indecisiveness over 'how', over what to do and what not to do, gripped her, driving her insane at times.

But today, she was joyous, and hollered over the phone to her sister Jyoti, 'I'm so happy! I can't wait to share it with you!'

'Hey, hold your horses!! What's up, Roshni? Did Atul propose to you again?'

'No yaar…nothing of the sort, but I want you to come here right now. I cannot wait to break the news to you. How soon can you come?'

Jyoti hadn't seen Roshni so excited in a while. It had to be something momentous. She was a few years older than Roshni and had been married off at nineteen. Roshni, on the other hand, had not only gone on to study design after school but had also cajoled her father into allowing her a love marriage. Jyoti's had been an arranged marriage to Jignesh, a banker.

The marriage had provided her with an obedient husband; as a couple, they did not have a relationship of equals. He believed two aggressive people could not make a successful life together and accepted he had to be the one to compromise. He thought divorce was a messy affair.

In Jyoti's mind, there had never been any doubt since age nineteen that Roshni was the favoured child. Atul's fabulous success ensured that she remained envious of Roshni even today. Roshni, however, was utterly oblivious to this. She believed her sister always had her best interests at heart, was her best friend and so, she confided everything to her.

The latest fact that she wanted to confide was that she was finally pregnant after eleven years of marriage. As this could change the course of her life and her relationship with Atul, she had a renewed reason for being and was elated. She had yet to break the news to Atul. She wanted the celebration to be a passionate and unforgettable one.

'Girl! Oh Girl! Muaaah! I am so happy for you!' and Jyoti hugged Roshni kissing her on the forehead as soon as she reached. She knew what this meant for her. 'Please tell me you didn't tell Atul about this?'

'Nopes,' replied Roshni.

'We must celebrate. This is simply the most amazing news I have heard in a long time. When did you come to know?' asked Jyoti.

'Three days. But I reconfirmed it today. I so wasn't ready to believe it till I got the second confirmation. I cannot wait to break it to Atul. I've booked a table at our favourite restaurant; I want to see his expression when I tell him this.'

'Great, Roshni!! But you must take care, this is a gift way too precious.'

'Yeah, I know,' Roshni replied excitedly. 'I am going to decorate a new room; I want to do so many things. My mind is just all over the place. Okay, you are having lunch with me, let me tell Babu.' Babulal was the trusted cook who had worked with the Malhotra family for a decade now. She quickly disappeared to let him know.

★

Roshni called Atul's secretary later in the day, 'Hello, Radha, where is Atul?'

'Good afternoon, madam, he is busy in a presentation with Mr Anil and some guests. Should I tell him you called?'

'Okay, do me a favour, call me once he is out of the meeting. I need to speak to him.'

'Sure,' replied Radha.

A few minutes later, Atul and Anil walked out of the war room smiling.

Anil Oberoi headed PR and marketing at TTL and was the city's most eligible bachelor, or had been until it became common knowledge that he was single by choice. His growing years had been spent living through his parents' parting of ways, and his thoughts about marriage stemmed strictly from that period. Nevertheless, he always had a smile on his face and was a great friend to have around. A born prodigy at marketing, his heart was nevertheless filled with boundless charity—he wasn't one of those marketing geniuses who thought everything had a price.

Anil was also a team worker and knew the pulse of the buyer. His service packages always seemed like good bargains, but the truth was that TTL always profited from his disguised sales strategies. Now, he and Atul looked well pleased as they emerged from what all of TTL called the 'War Room'.

A soundproof conference room, it had been witness to the most important decisions at TTL. Inside was a massive semi-circular table with three large LED screens for video calls. Grey acoustic fabric panels lined the walls, a thick chequered carpet covered the floor, and the huge room had a door akin to that on a safe deposit vault.

Radha told Atul about Roshni's call and he excused himself politely, requesting Anil to go ahead with their guests, saying he would join them shortly.

'Roshni, you called?'

'Yes. How are you?' she asked.

'Well…good. Was busy with a few things, I am sorry couldn't call,' he replied.

Roshni, trying hard to hold her excitement, said, 'I've booked a table for us tonight at the Dome. You think we can go?'

It was one of the best rooftop restaurants in town and was Atul's favourite too.

'Sure,' replied Atul, 'but what's the occasion?' It had been a while since they had any impromptu dinners.

'It's definitely an occasion. A big one. You'll find out soon enough.' It wasn't easy to guess, she thought happily, even if she divulged a bit of excitement.

'Okay, but I'll join you straight from work. I have a few things lined up here that need my attention. I'll see you there at 8.30,' said Atul and hung up.

Chapter 5

Atul's intercom buzzed, it was Radha on the line. 'Sir, Mohammad Mir for you. What should I say?'

'Put him through,' said Atul.

Mir and Atul went back to the days when Atul was a business manager at General Mobile. Mir had been a Joint Secretary at the Telecom Ministry back then. He was Chief Secretary now, having recently been promoted. An ardent Muslim, he wore a long beard that had turned grey over the years. He was a practical man with a reputation of impeccable integrity. In reality, he was far from that. To him, corruption was a necessary evil that fired the engines of democratic politics. Corruption existed in political systems by design. He liked to believe that he did his dishonest work with a lot of ethics and accountability. That helped him deal with his guilt. He doled out favours to a very small and select group, which included Atul.

'Good afternoon, Mir sahib, how are you doing?'

'All good, Atul. How about a visit to Delhi?' said Mir.

'How can I refuse, when do you want me to come?' replied Atul.

'Hmm…how about next Monday… Does that work?'

'Very well, sir, done… Is there anything I must come prepared about?' Atul couldn't ask him more. He had good reason to believe the call concerned applications for the new spectrum being allotted by the central government. The government had invited bids for third-generation mobile airwaves. TTL had applied for all the thirteen circles being auctioned. It was a very aggressive move for a company that offered mobile services only in the city of Mumbai.

'It's informal, I'll see you at 4 p.m. You know the place,' Mir replied.

'Sure, sure, I'll see you on Monday,' said Atul, before disconnecting.

★

With plush white fabric seats and mint stone tables, the Dome was a rooftop lounge. It had its own infinity pool too, overlooking the Arabian Sea. Candlelight further warmed the already yellow ambient lighting. Soft slow music was perfect for two souls to find each other all over again. Atul loved the place and the Lebanese cuisine it served. He relished the time spent there with friends and family.

Roshni sat across in an opulent red saree and matching sleeveless blouse. Realizing she couldn't keep her composure for long, she blurted, 'Atul, I am pregnant.'

Stunned, Atul froze, his spoon halfway to his mouth, his eyes startled and fixed on Roshni. They had stopped IVF treatment years ago, giving up hope for that joy of life.

'Please tell me this is not a joke,' he said, to affirm he'd got it right.

'Atul, really, I am. I visited Dr Awasthi this morning. The blood reports confirmed it too,' she said, trying to keep her excitement in check.

Atul got up and walked around to Roshni, hugged her tight and kissed her. He was ecstatic. Somewhere deep in his heart, he had accepted it was a joy he would miss for the rest of his life. 'You must take care of yourself, sweetheart. You know what this means to us,' he said, holding her close. 'This calls for champagne, let's ask for it.'

'I've already done that, love,' she said softly, 'I am really glad you are happy.'

The champagne arrived and they raised a toast to the future.

For the rest of that memorable evening she had the undivided attention of her husband. Finally, they thought, the tide would turn and their life would set sail anew.

★

Atul and Roshni occupied the 37th and 38th floors of a lavish apartment block on the western sea-front of Mumbai. With white minimalistic interiors, the lower floor had the kitchen, Atul's working den, a guest room and a plush living-room with an independent dining area. It also had a media room with the best paraphernalia from across the world.

Near the entrance was a stairway to the master bedroom. The bedroom, which had a walk-in closet as big as the room itself, opened onto a large veranda with colourful cobblestone mosaic flooring and a glass railing overlooking the sea. There was also a tastefully decorated Japanese bamboo garden, while roses grew around a two-seater lounger and recliner that had a solid black granite table placed between them.

Mornings were usually a rushed affair in the Malhotra household. Atul left for the gym at 6 a.m., he was done before 7. A quick shower, a light breakfast, and he was at his desk before 8.30 most days.

'When is your next appointment?' he asked now, sipping his breakfast tea as he skimmed through the headlines.

'Next week... Will you come with me?' asked Roshni.

'Of course, darling. Just let Radha know the time, I'll be there,' he replied casually.

This was something Roshni didn't like. He was too practical, uncaring, but she liked to believe it meant nothing. That's the way he was and she must accept it.

'Okay, honey, I gotta rush. We have a board meeting today at noon, and you know how it is.' Atul sped past the breakfast table and was off. Alok was waiting for him in the lobby to take him to TTL's headquarters, a short drive from his home. TTL was housed in a gated complex at the city centre. Almost a third of its 2,500 employees operated from the three independent buildings of about five storeys each.

Atul hated board meetings. Those were the few occasions he wasn't the boss, plus he hated being accountable. Prem and he prepared for the meeting and mulled over the key items on the agenda to make sure they got the credit for all the hits and that there were convincing justifications for all the misses.

Atul respected Prem for his acumen, sharp wit and uncanny sixth sense. He sensed problems and, more importantly, in time. He had always known Prem was the right man to handle the financial experiments. Experiments they were, they walked a thin rope with little room for error. Sometimes, even they couldn't decipher the true complexity of the risks they took.

Prem had been Vice President Finance at General Mobile and was the oldest among the four co-founders. Atul had to work hard to convince him, and in fact, delayed kick-starting TTL until Prem came aboard.

Now, Prem asked, 'How do we sort the financing plan for the new spectrum applications? What do we suggest? We failed to reach a conclusion on the agenda at the last board meeting and deferred it for today. We are proposing that we apply for all the thirteen forthcoming licences. That's a bold move by us, we spent days before we decided to go for it. We will need Rs 12,000 crore for the expansion, even if we succeed in bagging six of them.'

'I am aware, Prem,' said Atul.

'500 crore for Earnest Money Deposits, 2,000 crore for licence costs for the first two years, 7,500 crore will be needed for the infrastructure over the next two years, and another 2,000 for supporting operations,' continued Prem, summarizing the details.

He continued, 'That's twice our turnover of Rs 6,000 crore, it is a huge leap. Since you insisted, I stretched the numbers and made it seem palpable, but the nominated directors are not dumb. They won't take long to figure that we are fishing in thin air.'

'I know what you are saying, Prem,' responded Atul. 'With our stretched debt/equity[1], bank loans are hard to come by in such volumes. We've always been short on cash, all growing companies are.'

'But this is suicide...' Prem intervened anxiously.

'Yes...but only if we don't pull it off. We must take the risk,' said Atul.

'Atul...'

'Opportunity knocks only once and we must make the most of it, Prem. This is our chance,' Atul intervened, trying to boost his morale. 'We need to stretch every rupee for what it's worth. We'll do a mix of bank debt, retracting working capitals to generate cash, and asking investors to pitch in with around 500 crore,' he said, trying to convince himself as well.

'That's exactly what I have put in these papers,' Prem snapped at him, 'but you know we cannot constrict working capital; as a matter of fact, we need to pump in more. And bank loans? They won't land in our lap from the heavens. I don't see anything more than 2,000 crore coming in from there. There is a gaping hole even if all of this does happen. We won't issue new shares to investors, we are already down to 81 per cent in promoter holdings, it doesn't make sense to get any lighter, at least not now.'

Atul saw no immediate solution and could only ask Prem to hang in there. 'You keep it that way for now, and we will see what to do,' he concluded.

---

[1]Debt Ratio; Also called 'Debt to Equity ratio'. It is the proportion of loans vis-à-vis owned funds in a business.

As expected, the external directors were sceptical of their plans. Rakesh was not in favour either, but at the meeting, he overwhelmingly supported the proposal. The six-member board included the four founders and two investor-nominated representatives. Being in a minority, the investors didn't carry enough weight to be counted as much.

Atul did not, however, disregard their concerns and assured them of a more meaningful proposition and concluded the meeting. As far as he was concerned, it was a successful meeting; he'd got them thinking in his direction, and he'd never expected to get any further than that today. He was more worried about Rakesh; he needed to be convinced because he did not concur with Atul's views either.

A chemical engineer by education, Rakesh Mohanan was a family man, a taskmaster, and a meticulous planner with a no-nonsense personality. He had to have a good reason for everything he did. He was clinical in his approach and left nothing to chance. He saw that speed and data would be the backbone of telecom much before the competition could even smell it.

Atul was in a good place today, and Roshni's news had only added to his sense of well-being. They stayed at home all weekend, talking, celebrating, and on Monday, Atul was more than ready to meet up with Mir in Delhi.

He always met the Cabinet Secretary at the Business Centre at Delhi's Taj Mansingh hotel. TTL had a reserved lounge and conference room at the hotel round the year. The company also had an office with a staff of 150 elsewhere in the city, mostly handling PR, lobbying, and some other subsidiary ventures that TTL had interests in, but Atul preferred the Taj.

After the initial greetings, Mir got down to business. 'You are aware, Atul, that we have been in power for the last six years and Shalikramji has been in charge of the Telecom Ministry for the last three. He has seen your work closely during this time. He has great regard for you and wants to invest in your company.'

Atul listened intently, but did not react.

'Anyone from the competition would jump at an offer like that. You know that!' said Mir.

Shalikram, the Union Telecom Minister, was a politician. Atul knew a few stories about him. He detested him. Now he spoke, 'I am not sure, Mir sahib. What are we talking about? I don't understand how this works. Wouldn't this be vested interest, a minister investing in a telecom company...while being the Telecom Minister?' He feigned innocence, though he knew exactly what the fuck the guy was talking about.

'Well, let me make this clear for you. Shalikramji has about 2,000 crore in cash. He is looking for a safe haven to park this fund. He wants to route this money into TTL. He will help you at the auctions. There is not much that he can do other than dumping a few competitor applicants on procedural grounds and guarantee you do the best,' said Mir, trying to sugar-coat the proposal as much as he could.

'And how does this money get routed? We are talking about cash here. How do we explain where it came from?' asked Atul.

'Please tell me you are smarter than that, Atul. I can only show you the well, you have to know how to draw water from it,' replied Mir smoothly.

'Mir Sahib, I have high regard for you....'

Before he could go any further, Mir snubbed him, 'You don't need to say that.'

Atul interrupted, carefully choosing his words, 'Well, I do. Just so I am sure you know that. But at the same time, this is a big decision. I am a simple and small man. I don't know how to respond to your generous offer. And without going into the costs and benefits... I can tell you, it is difficult to fly.'

Mir knew Atul well and had expected this response.

'Mir sahib, I have earned everything that I have with a lot of respect. I don't have masters, I love having the independence to take my own decisions… plus how do we channelize so much money? We neither have the experience or a business that size to accommodate this kind of cash. I am not too good at handling your minister. You and I both know that.' Atul had said everything, except the real thing—he didn't want dirty money to pollute TTL.

He didn't want to offend Mir and, more importantly, his minister. Mir heard Atul silently and then paused to order some coffee. It gave him time to make up his mind on how to take this forward. He quickly decided not to influence the agenda further and spoke persuasively. 'Atul, I want you to think about this, it is a game changer. I can tell you one thing about Shalikramji, he will not mess with your business and will help you with everything in his power. You get the money and with so much growth you need it for sure.'

The room went silent. Atul didn't have words for Mir anymore. The offer didn't make sense to him.

Breaking the silence, Mir continued, 'And lastly, he doesn't like to hear a "No", and you know that. I hope you do.' Mir finally made the veiled threat on instructions from his boss. Personally, he hated this end of the conversation.

'And Atul…I expect that you will think through this. This is what I take back to Shalikram as the conclusion of this meeting. This will help you to buy some time with the approaching bids.'

Atul quickly responded, 'I appreciate your support. I will think through this.'

The entire journey to Mumbai the only thing going through his head was how to find a plausible reason to refuse that bastard. Atul was both furious and fearful. Atul had rules. One of them was no connivance with politicians beyond suborning them to get his way through. In a country like India, that was not an option, and even that Atul did with all precaution.

He knew the minister was the murkiest insect crawling on earth. But he also headed the ministry, so Atul could not afford to rub him the wrong way. It was a catch-22 situation. He just couldn't figure out how to deal with the problem. But he had to, and at the earliest.

Chapter 6

Having sold his business interests for a remarkable profit before retiring, Anand Sinha now saw himself only as the father of two daughters. That was all that was left of him. Right now, the overjoyed man was paying a visit to his pregnant daughter Roshni.

Atul hurried through work to make it on time for dinner, but alas, he had to make the call. 'I am sorry, dad,' he said to Anand, 'I am boxed in with work that I cannot postpone, but I'll be there soon. You continue with the dinner and I will join you as quickly as I can.'

Anand responded in his somewhat high-pitched voice, 'No problem, son. I am already home, chatting with Roshni. And congratulations, I am really happy for you. Take your time, I am an old man with all the time in the world,' and he hung up.

'Did he say he was having dinner with us?' Roshni wanted to know.

'Not to me,' her father replied.

Atul arrived well after Roshni and her father had gone to bed. The next day, Atul woke up late, as he usually did on weekends. At breakfast, he met the old man and bent to take his blessings.

Having heard from Roshni that things were not so great between them, Roshni's father did not want to rub his son-in-law the wrong way but did not quite know how to strike the precise chord. So he spoke carefully choosing his words, 'Beta, I am really happy to learn about Roshni. You know, God finds a way to catalyze relationships. I heard a story somewhere that I would like to share with you. Would you like to hear it?'

'Of course, dad,' said Atul warmly, 'You have always meant a lot to me.'

'There were two friends,' the old man began. 'One of them was speaking of his quest for discovering the perfect woman, and said to the other, "You know, I met a beautiful woman, she was more beautiful than all others."'

'"So, did you marry her?" asked the other.'

'"No, I realized she was not intelligent. I passed her by and soon, I found another. She was both gorgeous and intelligent, just what I wanted."'

'The other friend quickly asked "Did you marry her then?"'

'"No" replied the friend again, "she was too juvenile."'

'"Then?" asked the other.'

'"Soon, I did find what I was looking for. She was young, intelligent, beautiful and perfect in every way," his friend said.'

'"I am glad you were able to find whom you wanted finally, and marry her," said the other.'

'"No, I didn't," came the surprising reply.'

'"But why?" asked the other.'

'"She was looking for the perfect man too... And I was not him!"'

Atul gazed fixedly at the old man. 'I think I understand what you want to say, I'll keep this in mind.'

They finished their breakfast without trading any more words, yet the silence seemed filled with furious conversation.

★

The dates for the auctions were closing in. Prem was struggling with the problem of financing. They had already paid close to Rs 500 crore in earnest money. They had to find a solution. It was a lifetime opportunity after all, they thought.

'Atul?' It was Prem on the line, sounding concerned, 'We need to meet and fix our final plan on this. We don't have much time now. I have Plan B but I need to talk to you about it. Do you think we can meet today?'

'Okay, 3 p.m. today; ask Rakesh and Anil to join us as well,' Atul replied.

'I've discussed it with them already, I really think we should do it one on one,' said Prem.

'Okay then. See you at 3 p.m. Your chamber.'

Atul quickly reviewed the math as he entered the chamber at 3.

Prem began, 'As discussed at the last meeting, for the first 6,000 crore we can apply for 2,000 crore in bank loans; 750 crore will come in from additional investments from private equity investors. We will temporarily retract 750 crore from the working capital. I spoke to Anil; he ran me though some workable plans for advance sale of airtime. I think they will work.'

Atul interjected, 'Yeah, I went over those too with Anil last week. I am sure they will work, we stand to lose some notional profit, but I wouldn't worry about it. There are also some interesting ideas he has about prepaid airtime sale to break into the markets. So basically what you are saying is we are still short of about 2,500 crore for the current year, and a full 6,000 crore for the next year.'

'Yeah, you are right, more or less,' replied Prem.

'What's Plan B then?' asked Atul.

'Well, we can stretch our bank loans to meet the entire requirement,' said Prem calmly.

'How is that possible?' snapped Atul, 'The bankers won't allow us that kind of leverage.'

'Yeah, but with 500 crore already invested, we stand to lose it all, that's our only choice; it won't seem so implausible—but we need to tweak our books,' said Prem, lowering his tone.

'Tweak our books? What do you mean by that!' Atul couldn't believe he'd heard him right.

'We over-report profits for the previous quarter. Fictional profit. That way, we can increase our projections for the coming year and become eligible for larger loans,' said Prem.

'Are you out of your fucking mind!' shouted Atul, 'Do you even know what you are saying? I hope you haven't talked about this to anyone else?' he asked, seriously alarmed.

'Rakesh. I spoke to him, and let's face it, Atul…It's now or never! The window of opportunity is small, and if we miss it now, it's gone,' Prem replied.

'And…What does Rakesh have to say? He can't agree to this!!'

Prem nodded, 'Well…he left the decision to you, he feels it is way too risky. We stretch the books, take more debt than the business can handle. Even after that, we have yet to figure where the remaining 6,000 crore will come from next year.'

'Look, I am least bothered about the next 6,000 crore,' said Atul, 'We'll dilute the stakes to raise that and with the licences in our bag, valuations will skyrocket. But,' he added, 'I am worried about the 2,500 crore for now. I don't think we ought to do this, Prem, not this way for sure. It's forgery. We could all go to jail.'

'Do you have a better way to deal with it?' demanded Prem. 'Besides, jail's a very remote possibility, though,' he added, 'I cannot rule it out.'

A perturbed Atul sat silent and unconvinced for a while, pondering the situation, and then asked, much to Prem's surprise, 'And how exactly do you propose to raise revenues in the last quarter?'

'We need to over-report revenues by 500 crore in the last quarter,' said Prem blandly.

'With our average revenue per user (ARPU) at Rs 1,500, we are looking at 30 lakh fake subscriber bills to raise 500 crore in revenue,' said Atul, quickly doing the math.

'Yeah, pretty much,' Prem nodded.

'That's a lot,' said Atul.

'500 crore in revenue will raise our ability to take on another 3,500 crore in loans, keeping our leverages in check,' said Prem.

'I need time over this, Prem. This isn't easy,' Atul replied.

'I understand your dilemma, Atul. Honestly, I wouldn't suggest this if there was another way,' said Prem, walking across to place a comforting hand on Atul's shoulder.

'There are other cascading effects, have you thought of them? The Telecom Regulatory Authority of India (TRAI), they track subscriber databases, they smell foul play and we are dealing with an entirely different animal. Plus, an 18 per cent jump in subscriber base in a single quarter!' said Atul, his head clogged with the dynamics of the whole proposition.

Just as Atul left his cabin, his cell buzzed showing 'Mohammad Mir calling...' He paused a moment before he took the call, 'Yes, Mir sahib, how are you doing today?'

'All good, Atul. I was wondering if you thought about what we spoke?'

'Can I call you back, Mir sahib?' asked Atul and disconnected the call, walking swiftly to his cabin and calling Mir on a secure line.

'Sir, well... I have given a lot of thought to this. I don't see how it can fly, Mir sahib. In fact, it won't even work for Shalikramji. Honestly, we are not the best in the business, you must drive home that point to him. You've got to help me on this one,' he pleaded.

'Well...,' paused Mir, 'is that your final decision, Atul?'

'Regretfully yes, Mir sahib... I don't see how a small company like ours can absorb so much money without the authorities sniffing it up. It could ground us all for good,' he said, trying to sound as convincing as he could.

'Let me talk to him and see what he has to say,' said Mir and disconnected.

Atul breathed a deep sigh of relief. Somewhere in his mind, the whole idea of cooking the books was a lesser evil than affiliating with Shalikram. At least the books were an in-house matter and it was a one-time thing, just a small financial delinquency. He was dead worried nonetheless; the auctions were their tickets to success. With so much riding on it, he had to make it happen. The bank loans were looking improbable and risks were rising fast.

And it was only 500 crore in fake revenue for one quarter. It didn't seem such a bad option, given the positives it had. He was choosing between two near equal evils; he had never been confronted with such a decision before—he realized that repudiating Shalikram could cause equal damage.

The fact was that TTL had already invested 500 crore in earnest money for applications. The loss of reputation in case they backed out could have a serious mid- to long-term impact and Atul was very worried about that too. He fervently hoped he could find a way to agree to Prem's suggestion so that they could move forward with the bank loans.

In time, his mind got around the immorality of cooking the books and turned to analyzing the legal risks involved; mulling over the problems that could spring up.

'Prem, Atul here. I thought about what we discussed. I think it is a go. Let's move ahead with it and make the applications. Can you run me through the definitive mechanics of how this will be done? Have you thought about it?' Having taken a week already to make up his mind, Atul did not want to drag it out any further.

'Yes, let's meet at 9 a.m. and I'll run you through the details,' replied Prem.

Just as he was about to call it a night, Roshni walked into the room and he decided to attempt a conversation. 'How is the new room coming along?' he asked.

'It will get done, but I don't know what colours to choose, since we don't know whether it is a boy or a girl. Do you think we should find out?' she asked.

'Well, I have no preferences,' he replied, 'we can keep it a surprise if you want, it's your choice really,' and he lay down and began scrolling through pages from work.

'How is it my choice, Atul? Shouldn't you have a say in this, how can you be so curt?' she said.

'Well... I didn't mean that, I meant I didn't want to know; it doesn't matter to me so much... I am happy either way,' he replied.

'Let's think about it,' she said, and then drew in a sharp breath, 'There's a little pain in my stomach.'

Must be natural in pregnancy, thought Atul; she was three months into her pregnancy now. 'You want to try some of the meds, a painkiller or something?' he asked.

'Yes please, it must be something I ate, it should help,' she answered.

Atul gave her an Ibuprofen thinking it might be a stiff muscle or indigestion, and it would subside. It didn't. Within about two hours, he decided to take her to the hospital.

Scans were run and Dr Awasthi came in at 4 a.m. She examined Roshni and went through the reports, and left the room beckoning Atul. Once outside, she spoke softly, 'The scans and other reports suggest it was possibly just indigestion. The reports are okay, Atul, they give me no reason for worry. She will be alright in a day or two... But there is something else I must tell you.'

Atul, thus far happy, was now worried. 'What is it, Doctor?'

'I ran a scan on the foetus. The development of the brain is at least four weeks behind the norm. It hasn't grown since the last scan.'

'What does that mean? Will everything be okay when the baby is born?' he asked anxiously.

'We cannot be certain, but risks in pregnancy increase with the age of the mother. We may be looking at a case of Down's syndrome. Usually, it can lead to undeveloped physical features, or it could be autism. Such problems are not rare in pregnancies above the age of thirty-five.'

Atul, keeping a storm of raging emotions in check, asked calmly, 'Can we keep this from Roshni, at least for the moment?'

'Absolutely. Besides, I want to run some more tests to be sure,' said Dr Awasthi. Then she smiled reassuringly at Atul, 'I didn't want to scare you, but it is my job to share what I find with you. I hope you understand. Things may not be so bad after all; let's wait for the results and see.'

Atul sighed, 'I hope so,' and spent the rest of the night by Roshni's side thinking through all his options.

Chapter 7

Akram Qazi, TTL's legal counsel, was already waiting with Prem Khatri for Atul's arrival. Prem used the time to debrief Qazi; nothing important ever happened at TTL without Qazi's consent. Dressed in a soft grey two-piece suit with silvery hair to match, he truly was a father figure to them all. A poet, musician and romanticist, he was a multifaceted personality and one of the sharpest legal minds around.

Now, Prem asked him, worry furrowing his brow, 'What do you think, Qazi sahib, how do we weigh our risks on this?'

'Of course... I'm assuming you know what you are doing,' replied Qazi, pausing before slowly saying, 'It really depends on who finds out first. Technically, we are only over-reporting revenue, so the taxmen won't be trouble. More revenue is more tax. And they are happy to see more tax coming their way. They won't give a second look towards how it came to be. The telecom authorities could be challenged in courts and dragged into long battles, and we may ruffle a few feathers with the unwanted publicity—Anil will have to manage that, just in case.'

'Hmm,' nodded Prem.

'As for the bankers, they won't bother once they have given the funds. Bankers make merry counting eggs, they care a damn who fathered the chickens,' he concluded, having deftly assessed all the issues at hand.

Atul, who had come in while they were talking, heard them through. He'd always relied on their knowledge and experience, blindly trusting their decisions. So even though his mind was still occupied with the events of the previous night, he now went through the actual process with them in detail.

'Prem, adding fictional subscribers could raise red flags, how about we play with existing subscribers and look at over-reporting existing customer bills. We can do that by rigging the software; we won't need an army to do this, so it's discreet too. We can simply program the software to increase the billing of random customers. By not creating fictional subscribers, we ensure the telecom authorities have nothing to snoop on. If we are exposed, we can blame it on the software, can't we?' said Atul.

Prem nodded but wanted to know, 'How do we get the cash in? How will we show the cash receipts from these fake invoices? You can have fictional income reported due to a software glitch, but where are you going to get fictional cash and a whopping 500 crore at that? Software doesn't print cash yet. It doesn't make sense. Also, nobody'll buy it—TTL got 500 crore from customers and stashed it in their office lockers? It's too far-fetched. There has to be a better way.'

After hours of mulling over various options, Qazi spoke up, 'Okay, let me ask something. I know it may be stupid but we have almost 1,000 locations where we receive cash from customers. What if we distribute the 500 crore over these 1,000 locations, each location getting approximately fifty lakh. Would that be too much cash-in-hand at every location?'

Prem excitedly pitched in, 'Well, it is, actually. But we can have about half of that, and it would still take care of half the problem. If we showed that we kept the other half in our cash deposit vaults at the head office, that would take care of the lot. Also, a lot of customers usually pay bills on the last day of the month, so it's pretty plausible.'

'Prem, you can work out the modalities, it looks safe to me,' and making a moral climbdown, Atul asked Qazi to put his years of legal experience to safeguard this loop.

'I guess it is fine,' responded Qazi, 'Just a couple of things—let's deposit the actual cash we have on the day to the last rupee in the bank. We can ask the bank to wait that day to close their cash, that way we don't have any more cash in hand except this 500 crore of fictional cash.' It sounded bloody convincing, at least to them.

'Prem, what is our average cash balance on the last day of the month?' Atul asked to dispel any doubts that remained.

'I am not really sure... should be around 150 crore,' replied Prem.

'I guess it's fine, it is a surge but shouldn't seem suspicious,' said Atul and turned to Prem. 'Who all are on your team on this? No one who is less than 100 per cent trustworthy will do,' he said warningly.

Prem had already thought along the same lines, 'Yeah. Shobha Rane, she is a manager in the IT department. I'll talk her into this. Also, we can use Prashant Nagarkar, Ramya Apte and Raman Babu for the accounting entries. I can trust all four.'

With the decision made, Atul did not waste time reconsidering it; all he did was execute it at breakneck speed. 'Well... I leave that to you. It's your kite, you fly it. Let's move the applications, it shouldn't take more than six weeks for the approvals. Keep me posted; I'll talk to the deputy MD at the bank to see them through.'

He then turned to the legal head, 'Are we good then, Qazi sahib?' he asked, just in case the latter had anything more to say. Qazi thought for a while and said with a sigh, *'Jab miya biwi razi, to kya karega qazi.'*

Between the devil and the deep sea, Atul chose to jump into the deep sea. It is always easy to gravitate into a jump. Effortless, even after you have leapt. Little did he know, a devil lives down deep in the seas too.

★

Atul no longer loved Roshni. Over the years, their constant bickering over trivia had begun to happen way too frequently; his patience shrank a little more each time they quarrelled. Lately, he'd often thought of ending the marriage, but wasn't sure how. She wasn't independent and he was concerned about her future if they separated. A part of him also repulsed the idea of being a father; it would complicate the situation further. The part of him that rejoiced simply thought that not loving someone and not being happy about it wasn't good enough reason to seek divorce. And rectification needed a chance too; he was far from being a maverick yet.

Quickly wrapping the rest of his work, he left office to attend to more important business. Roshni. Thinking about her had made her—if only for today—more than just an agenda in his diary. Until he decided about his life ahead with her, he would work at keeping the peace.

She was stable, he was told. Atul did not know how to break the news to her. He did not even know whether he ought to, in the first place. He decided to wait for a more appropriate moment.

'How are you now, Roshni, are you feeling better?' he asked gently.

'I am,' she replied, not looking at him.

He sat by the lounger silently while she continued gazing at the ceiling, the revolving fan periodically ticking like a clock. It sounded like a time bomb. A time bomb it was, and waiting for a fitting moment to explode, but in Roshni's mind.

The nurse came in a couple of times to administer some medication. Atul used the time to go through his emails, walking up to comfort her every now and then. A frail peace hovered between them. Until Roshni decided it was time the bomb exploded.

'You knew about it? You didn't tell me, Atul?'

Setting his laptop aside, he walked to her and asked apprehensively, 'What are you talking about, Roshni?'

'We are going to have a brainless child? The nurse told me everything.'

'Bullshit! She knows nothing!' he said, trying to calm her down, and himself too. 'I have spoken to Dr Awasthi, nobody knows anything yet, and they are still investigating. We will be fine, have faith, Roshni.'

'Nothing will be fine, I know it, you know it, and…,' and she started crying hysterically.

'Roshni, control yourself. Please.' Atul hated seeing people cry.

By now, the fireworks were out of control, 'You cursed my child, you never wanted it. I know. You don't even want me. You think I am blind? I can see it every day. Even God listens to you and not me,' she sobbed, before screaming, 'You have made me so desperate!'

'Roshni,' said Atul, panicking, 'please calm down, everything will be okay.'

But she was in no mood to calm down. She sobbed and blamed Atul bitterly for the state of the relationship, and for the way it had all led to this day. Atul couldn't bring the flood of tears or recriminations under control and eventually had to call the nurses in, who gave her something to put her to sleep. As soon as she was asleep, Atul walked swiftly to the nurses station on the floor and asked to see Dr Awasthi.

'Give me a moment, please,' said the nurse, making a call on the intercom. 'You can go to her chamber now.'

'Thank you, sister. Please take care of my wife till I return.' He wanted to talk to the doctor about the way forward. When he reached her room, she waited till he sat down and then came straight to the point. 'We went through the reports, and our fears have unfortunately been confirmed. The only thing we cannot confirm is the extent and scope of this damage.'

She paused, in case he had any questions. When he stayed silent, she continued, 'We really have only two options—abort the pregnancy, and it's not too late in this case. The other option is to go ahead and pray the baby develops well over the next few months, and deal with what we have in hand after the delivery. We haven't seen growth in the last four weeks, but that doesn't necessarily mean it won't occur in the next twenty-four weeks. Honestly, there is no way to predict. But, you have to be prepared as the situation could swing either way. Atul, it isn't easy to raise an autistic child.'

Atul had heard each word with rapt attention. His eyes had forgotten to blink and his breath held in until she finished. Now, all he could manage was, 'Let me talk to Roshni, doctor.'

He let himself out of her room and rushed to the washroom where he cried his heart out. Then, composing himself, he walked back to Roshni's room. His father-in-law and sister-in-law were standing outside. Atul bent to take Anand's blessings and then hugged him. Anand looked visibly disturbed. Atul spoke to him about Roshni's hysteria and ignored Jyoti, who turned and walked into the room. Anand assured him he would talk to Roshni and make her see sense. But before they could go any further, there was a loud shriek from the room; so loud it caught the attention of the whole floor. It was followed by her screaming, 'Tell him to go away, I don't want to have anything to do with him...'

They rushed in and the nurse asked all of them to vacate the room and injected another dose of Diazepam to calm Roshni down. Jyoti slipped back in, holding her sister's hand as she fell into an uneasy sleep. Once she was deeply asleep, Jyoti left the room.

'How is she now?' asked her father as she came out.

'Asleep,' she replied, coldly looking at Atul. 'It is better you don't see her now, Atul. We will take care of her tonight.'

Atul looked to his father-in-law, who nodded, patting him on the shoulder, telling him to take it easy and that he would do his bit to allay matters. With nothing to do there, Atul walked out of the hospital a disturbed man.

Atul could handle anything but indecisiveness, and the bad news about the baby, coupled with the dilemma about when and how to end the marriage, was proving hard on him.

That night, as he tossed and turned, it dawned on him that he was dragging the relationship out. He had been pained about it for a while; today, he had realized that she was pained too. But did that inevitably mean it was time to end it? The way Roshni had cried and screamed, it needed to end somewhere. The end was near now. But his mind still carried on... did he understand her? Did she understand him? Was there anything to understand at all? Why couldn't these things be simple?

Atul could handle anything but indecisiveness. Dragging this confusion around was hard on him, very hard.

The next day, he stayed away from the hospital. Jyoti told him over the phone that Roshni would be discharged that day. Atul also got another call from Mir.

'Yes, Mir sahib, how are you?' he said, trying to infuse some of the usual pep into his voice.

'Atul, things are not good. I am not calling you as the Telecom Secretary but as a friend. Shalikramji did not take your decision in the right spirit. He is likely to sabotage your applications. I just thought I'd give you a heads-up in case you want to do something about it.' Atul listened to what he had to say silently.

'And,' said Mir, concluding the call, 'I never made this call to you, we did not talk about this.'

'I get it, thank you for filling me in,' responded Atul politely, 'I appreciate the gesture,' and hung up the phone.

In a while, he called his secretary. 'Radha, Atul here. Please cancel all my appointments for the day. I will not be coming in. Is there anything important for me?'

'There is a meeting at 3 p.m. for the new campaign, and an induction address for the new finance recruits,' she replied.

'Okay. I'll fill in Anil and Prem on handling those,' he said and hung up.

That afternoon, Roshni walked in with Jyoti and her father and headed straight for the bedroom upstairs, while Atul was in his den downstairs going over a few documents.

'Bhabhi is home, sir,' Babulal informed him.

'Thanks. Please bring up some tea for me,' he said, shutting his laptop and walking up to their bedroom. Roshni was visibly calm. He knew they did not have time; he needed to take a decision with Roshni about the abortion. Dr Awasthi had called earlier and suggested they decide immediately.

'How is she now?' he asked his father-in-law, and then turned to Roshni, not really sure whether she was ready to talk yet.

'She is fine, much better now. Please take care of her, Atul.' His shoulders stooped with worry, Roshni's father beckoned to Jyoti and they walked out of the room and down the stairs. Atul sat on the edge of the bed hoping to start a conversation. Babulal came in with the tea, placed it on the bedside table and went out, shutting the door behind him.

Atul rested his hand on Roshni's forehead, kissed her cheeks and said softly, 'Everything will be fine, trust me.' Roshni caught his hand, drew him close and started to cry.

'We'll work this out, Roshni, it is God's will. These things are not in our hands, there's not much we can do. Sometimes, we have to simply accept our destiny. It'll work out, you'll see,' he said, but his eyes were moist. However, unlike Roshni, his greatest fear was that she would not abort the baby. Heartbreaking though it was, it was really the only choice that he could see. And so, he again appealed gently, 'We must let the baby go.'

But even as her tears fell faster, Roshni raised her voice and spoke firmly for the first time, 'Don't even think about it. I am not letting you do it. It is not your decision.'

Atul had known her for thirteen years. He understood the difference between her comma and full stop. This was a full stop. There was no point in pursuing it further.

'I want to sleep, Atul, can I be left alone?' she hissed, crying even as she completed the sentence. Atul took the cue, kissed her forehead, walked out of the room and called Dr Awasthi.

'Good evening, doctor, Atul here.'

'How is she now?' Dr Awasthi asked. 'I have given her some medicines to deal with the anxiety, that should calm her. Give her a while to recover.'

'I called to ask about the abortion, doctor,' replied Atul.

'She spoke to me about it. She wants the baby, Atul. I told her everything I could but her mind seems made up, she has her reasons.'

'What do we do then?' asked an anxious Atul.

'What can I say, Atul,' she said, 'it is for the two of you to decide.'

'What are the real chances of a normal baby, doctor?' he asked, wanting to draw from her long years of experience. He always tapped the expertise and experience of others in situations where he felt deadlocked.

'Well, medically, all cases are different. Most cases are aborted so any statistics on the subject are obviously biased.'

'Doctor, I still want you to give me a number. I insist.'

'If you insist, okay, I would say one out of three babies is born with manageable levels of autism. That is the best we can expect. A normal baby is almost out of the question, it would be a miracle from what we know today,' she said.

Now that he knew the odds, and coupled with Roshni's desire to have this baby, he knew he would organize everything as best as possible—the final outcome, of course, was in God's hands. And so he said, 'Doctor, we are going ahead with the baby. We'll do everything possible medically to get things right.'

'Are you sure, Atul?' Dr Awasthi asked.

'Yes, I am, doctor,' replied Atul, his voice ringing with conviction.

'Very well then, we will do what we can. I pray I am wrong. We'll hope for the best,' she said.

The next two months were uneventful; Atul decided to give his best shot to the relationship and avoided anything that would disturb the peace. Now that she was back home, there were no medical precautions to be taken, other than keeping her healthy and preventing any outside damage to the foetus, such as through falls, etc. But Roshni continued to be depressed and dejected, anxious about the future.

At work, it was business as usual. The applications for the bank loans were in their final stages. Atul and Prem did what they needed to do, and Shalikram did nothing to jeopardize the situation; Atul had good reason to believe he wouldn't do anything stupid, so he took his chances.

Chapter 8

It was Tuesday morning and Atul was to meet the twenty new campus recruits handpicked from the top management colleges by TTL during campus placements. Atul headed human resources personally and believed that grooming leaders was a quick ticket to growing businesses.

'Ladies and gentlemen,' he began, 'Good morning. I am Atul Malhotra, your CEO and chairman of the board of Transmech Telecommunications Limited. I welcome you to the family. I am thankful you chose TTL to start your career with, and we hope we can live up to your expectations.

'TTL is a 2,500-member family with revenues touching Rs 6,000 crore. Working with a billion-dollar company brings a lot of pride and carries a lot of responsibility. Over the next three years, you as management trainees will work with some of the best brains in the industry and I hope you can make yourself and your company proud.'

He paused for a sip of water before continuing, 'I have three rules for you and you have two choices. Either you follow those rules without question, or you convince me they are wrong and I will change them company-wide,' he said, as he moved towards the electronic white board, clicking his controller to change the slide on it.

'Rule No. 1: Honesty is not an option. It builds trust... You must guard that trust at all times, more than your grandmother would have her virginity,' he said with a smile. 'You lose that, you lose everything.

'Rule No. 2: Hard work. Most people here work for ten hours, I work for twelve, the additional two hours got me here. There is no alternative to hard work. The sooner you accept that the faster you will be on your way to glory.

'Rule No. 3: Believe in yourself. If you have done no wrong, you should feel no fear in standing up for yourself. And when in doubt, refer to Rules 1 and 2 and you will not make a wrong decision ever.

'That's it. I haven't told you anything you haven't heard before. Here, you will see it in practice, every day of your time with us.

'I wish you all the best and yes, I am always an email away for every member of TTL, 24/7. Approach without apprehension but after a lot of thought. The floor is now open for any questions.'

There were none, and the TTL senior team began mingling to learn more about the newcomers and to put them at their ease. The catering staff uncovered their heated containers and began to serve snacks and refreshments. Seeing him now, one would think that Atul had his life sorted. He was seen as not just a high achiever but also someone who was articulate, decisive, polished and, of course, adept in the use of soft skills, garnished with the right mix of humour.

'Hello, sir, I am Aarti Mathur,' said one of the recruits as she introduced herself to Atul.

'Hello, Aarti,' he said, shaking hands with her.

'Sir, I am from IIT Kanpur and completed my MBA from IIM Lucknow. I am working on the financial modelling for TTL's Vision 2015 program with the team.'

'That's awesome. There is a lot of exciting work out there. We will be seeing a lot of each other. I hope you are enjoying your work and Prem is not troubling you too much,' he said jovially, before moving on to meet all the other members of the group, exchanging pleasantries and making them comfortable. His phone buzzed. 'Atul, we have a problem.' It was Prem.

'What is it?' he asked, concerned. Prem never called in panic, it was not his way.

'I want to see you, and now!'

'Okay, my office, five minutes. I am just wrapping up an induction.' He hurriedly took leave of the group and headed back to his office. A minute later, Prem rushed in with a couple of other executives and placed a letter on his table. Atul's face paled as he read through it. It was a letter from the bank, rejecting their financing proposal, saying the project carried too much risk. The Deputy Managing Director, the same guy who had given Atul a personal assurance that the loan would be sanctioned, had signed it.

'Did you speak to him?' he asked Prem.

'Yes, he said the MD was against it, he thinks we are over-leveraged and too risky.'

'Bullshit!' said Atul, enraged. 'They issued us an in-principle approval, how can they do this now? We have a lot at stake, this is no child's play. We already made our expansions public, paid a fucking 500 crore as earnest money deposit. We can't go back, that is not a choice.'

He called in Anil and Rakesh, and they all pondered over the development for the rest of the day but found no solution. He even spoke to the Deputy MD and expressed his displeasure. He threatened to withdraw all TTL accounts from the bank, but there wasn't much the Deputy MD could do either, it was his MD's decision.

'Get me everything you can on this MD,' said Atul. 'Set up a meeting, I want to meet him; they cannot do this, not at this stage.'

A meeting was arranged and Atul went, with Prem in tow, to meet the MD of National Bank.

'Good morning, Mr Baijal,' he said, as they shook hands across the table. Baijal was an ageing man in his late fifties, dressed in a blue checked coat, had receding grey hair and wore thick black-framed soda bottle glasses.

Atul sized him up quickly as a sycophant working in the corridors of power—information he already had. After exchanging a few pleasantries, they came to the subject of the meeting.

'Look, Mr Malhotra, you know this is not about you, and I have nothing personally against you. I am a humble public servant with a small salary. We deal with public money; we have to guard the interests of the common man. You know if anything goes wrong, the government comes down on us hammer and tongs, there is very little we can do, we are only public servants.' Atul and Prem listened politely to his public interest bullshit.

'Sir, there has to be a way,' Prem pitched in with his bit. 'We have paid a huge EMD. We have gone public with this announcement; withdrawing it now will give us a lot of bad publicity. You must understand and help us, there must be a way?'

'I am sure you have a lot of friends out there who are more than willing to help you,' responded Baijal and turned to Atul. 'You are a big man, but I cannot risk public money on your venture.'

Like a bolt of lightning, insight struck Atul. That bastard Shalikram, he had used his muscle to do this. Without wasting a minute more, he wrapped up the meeting; he knew Baijal could and would do nothing to change anything.

Now, he decided to use his last card. He called a few people at the Finance Ministry and requested a meeting with the Minister of State for Finance; he didn't expect much, but he had to try. As expected, his efforts yielded nothing, but only confirmed that Shalikram had indeed put a spanner in the works to ensure TTL was denied the loan.

Atul was now in a serious fix and running out of choices. He mulled over his options—was approaching Shalikram the only alternative? After all that Atul had done to piss him off, and all that Shalikram had done to piss him right back, did any truck with him even make sense?

He had always known Shalikram would never jeopardize his applications; it would have made national headlines. He was too smart to do anything like that because Atul would have used the media to overturn that, but by scuttling the bank loans, Shalikram had got the better of Atul. Taken him by complete surprise. Now, making a call to Mir seemed the only option ahead of him.

Once he'd spoken to Mir, Atul set up a conference call with Prem, Rakesh, Anil and Qazi. He needed a consensus on the partnership with Shalikram. He opened the call saying, 'I suggest we borrow 2,000 crore and offer him a ten per cent stake in the company's profits. We will figure a way to repatriate the profits in cash. At the end of three years, we keep the rights to continue or return the money.'

'You think we can pull this off?' Anil wanted to know.

'I'm not sure what I can pull off, but I am meeting him tomorrow evening at his farmhouse in Chattarpur. I need a go, guys. We don't have a choice on this.'

'What do we tell the private equity guys?' Prem wanted to know.

'We tell them zilch, they don't need to know, the investment is in cash and off the books,' Atul responded.

Qazi finally spoke up and it was a voice of dissent. 'Friends, for whatever value my vote has, I vote against this decision. I think we ought to let the 500 crore go, invent a story for the markets and live with it. These guys are pimps. Once they are let in, they will make a whore out of TTL.'

There was a minute of stunned silence before Atul spoke, addressing the others, 'Anil, Rakesh what's your take?'

'Look, Atul,' said Rakesh, 'we cannot have him in unless you can control him. Can you?'

Anil followed, 'The real problem will be his interference, he is a businessman at heart. How does it matter who supplies the dough? We'll bake bread anyways. We must nail it into him that we will accept no intrusion from him.'

Having got everybody's opinions, Atul decided it was time to take a final call. So he said, 'It's not really the 500 crore or the bad publicity, the devil won't stop at that. Till he is a minister, he will continue to gut us if we refuse him. We need to see him off. The colour of the money is not the worry; it is the gutter it comes from. I agree with Qazi sahib, but what real options do we have? We will do it for the larger good of the 2,500 families whom we serve.'

The next morning, Atul flew to Delhi, checking into the Taj Mansingh hotel. That evening at 6 p.m., Atul, dressed in a casual yellow Hugo Boss T-shirt with beige chinos, got into his car and headed to the farmhouse in Chattarpur on the outskirts of Delhi.

The signage on the entrance read 'Mysore Bhawan'. Atul gathered it wasn't the minister's farmhouse, at least not officially. He stopped his car at the security window. 'I am here to see Shalikramji,' he said to the guard walking up to his car.

'May I know your name, sir?' asked the guard.

'Atul Malhotra. I have an appointment with him.'

The guard walked back to his cabin and made a call on the intercom.

The motorized gate opened and as he drove in, another guard, with the look of a bouncer, guided the car to the parking. Atul got out and looked around.

On the far end was a two-storey bungalow cladded with exposed red bricks. On the foreground, on either side of the concrete road that led him to the main bungalow, were hedges that bordered neatly trimmed lawns. Beyond the hedges stood tall false Ashoka trees, marking the end of the property just within the high boundary walls. There were three more vehicles parked there—a Honda Accord with a red beacon on it; the two others were white police jeeps, probably security vehicles.

Another guard dressed in a white safari suit escorted him to the ground floor of the bungalow. He was asked to sit in the waiting lounge. He hoped the man would come soon. He wanted to make this real quick. The environment repelled him. He tried to make himself feel at ease with the situation, though he knew he would have to see more of it, and often too.

In about five minutes, a young woman entered the room and walked up to him. She was in her early twenties, tall, gorgeous and fair, dressed in a low cut blouse liberally showing off a moderately large bosom, and a bright yellow saree tied low enough to show her belly button.

'Hello, Atulji, I am Kamini. Sir has asked me to escort you, you may follow me.' She offered her hand, which Atul ignored.

Trailing her, he took the stairs and followed her down a long corridor to reach a large chamber. Inside, across an oversized rosewood desk, sat a short man the size of a baby elephant. He was dark, dressed in a starched white kurta, and boasted a salt and pepper stubble.

He got up with difficulty from the extra-large leather armchair and leaned over the table extending both hands. His paunch rested on the table.

'Welcome, welcome, Atulji, welcome to my humble abode. I've been waiting for this day for months, doubting if it would ever come,' he said sarcastically.

'Please don't say that, you are embarrassing me, Shalikramji; it is my good fortune to be with you,' Atul replied smoothly.

'Forget whatever happened. Let's lay a new foundation, we are partners from today,' said Shalikram.

Kamini walked across the desk and stood by Shalikram's side, gawking at Atul. Atul glanced at her a couple of times, a tad embarrassed, expecting her to move out of the room so they could get on with business.

Realizing his predicament, Shalikram beamed at him, while running his hand up and down Kamini's exposed back before pulling her closer to him. 'Don't worry, Atul, you can talk. Kamini is family. She is now your family too, just give her a shout and she will make your day too. Right, Kamini?' he leered at her with a dirty smirk and kissed her bare midriff. She gave Atul a smile of acceptance.

'Please take Atulji to the anteroom, I will be there in a while.' Kamini moved across to Atul and extended her hand to escort him again. He got up to follow her without taking her hand.

The lounge was dimly lit. Two black leather sofas had been placed against adjacent walls and a bookcase stood in between, filled with books that seemed mostly irrelevant. A bar unit stood to one side filled with the choicest liquor from around the world. Atul took a seat at the far end and Kamini sat on the adjacent sofa.

Atul was visibly embarrassed, but it wasn't something he hadn't expected; he had, in fact, been prepared for worse.

Shalikram walked in a few minutes later and perched himself right beside Kamini. 'So tell me, Atul, how do you want to do this? I have about 2,000 crore in cash, I can place about 1,250 crore instantly at your disposal, and you can take that now. The rest will be with me within a week.'

Then, he got down to business, 'What will my share be?' And he flung one of his hands across Kamini's shoulders, guiding it down inside her blouse and rolled his fingers playing with her nipples shamelessly, in a wildly obscene manner. Pervert, thought Atul, but kept his mind on the business at hand, not trying to judge the fellow. There wasn't much to judge anyway.

'Sir, we will offer ten per cent of the profits of the company as per the balance sheet. We think an annual payment should be good. Also, whenever you want to withdraw your investment, we will give the principal back in cash.'

'Who the hell wants the money back, we are cronies for life. We will revel together,' said Shalikram, laughing crassly.

'Well, that is up to you, sir. I would look at it with a three-year horizon and then we can review the matter.'

Shalikram thought about it for a few seconds, then said, 'Here is the deal. I want twenty-five per cent every year on my investment. I don't care about your profits or losses. I withdraw when I want, place more if I want. You make sure I get 500 crore back every year.'

Atul quickly intervened, 'Sir, I cannot take more, my business is small, I cannot thrust so much cash into the system, it will look very suspicious.'

'Make it big then, that is why I am investing. Don't give me stupid reasons. With me around, you don't need to worry about suspicions or anyone creating a problem; make one call, it will be taken care of.'

Atul wasn't being given a choice. That was the problem in doing business in an unequal partnership, and this was an unequal partnership. 'Very well, sir,' he capitulated, extending his hand. Shalikram withdrew his hand from Kamini's bosom and shook Atul's hand before turning to Kamini, 'Kamini, get the best whiskey, let us celebrate.'

She walked up to the bar, picked up a bottle of Blue Label, poured a measure into three glasses already set out on a tray, and brought it to them.

'Cheers to our new partner,' said Shalikram, as he raised the glass and gulped it down faster than water. Atul was forced to make trivial conversation with him and Kamini until he could politely take his leave. Finally, just as he was leaving, Shalikram said, 'Let me give you a present. TTL will get seven of the thirteen new circles. I hope that makes you happy. I thought I must give you the good news to coincide with our new partnership.'

An astonished Atul thought, 'How the fuck does he know when the bids are still sealed!' He didn't want to sound like a fool by asking that, he would know it in time anyway. So he blandly replied, 'Thank you, sir, I am truly obliged. I will coordinate with Mir sahib on the transfers,' and walked out of that hall of shame and sack of shit.

The first results of the gravitation from the jump were unmistakably visible. Atul was about to befriend the devil he had repulsed for so long now. It was for a greater good, he believed, But alas!

Chapter 9

Roshni was now in the sixth month of her pregnancy. She looked pale, seldom spoke and remained an introvert most times. The only people she spoke to were her sister and, occasionally, her father. The discovery of the stunted growth of the baby's brain troubled her immensely. The brain did show growth in subsequent scans, but it was impossible to predict a positive outcome with certainty.

Jyoti visited frequently, usually in the afternoons. One particularly maudlin afternoon, Roshni was caught up in the anger that lay deep within her against Atul. 'All I ever craved was his affection and attention; I did everything to get it. I have a feeling that he gets physical gratification elsewhere.'

Jyoti promptly responded, 'If you know that, you cannot accept it! You must confront him, Roshni. Men are emotionally weak. You must know how to nail them. There must be something he must be afraid of. You must find out. Threaten to walk out on him and he'll come around. Look at Jignesh, he never does anything other than what I tell him to do. If I can do it, you can too. I am not saying you must absolutely control him, but he cannot take you for granted.'

'Jyoti, I am not you,' Roshni said in a muted voice. 'And he is not Jignesh.'

'I understand, honey,' replied Jyoti soothingly, 'but what choice do we have but to voice our rights?'

Roshni, her gaze fixed on the Italian marble floor, stayed silent, neither acknowledging nor desiring to confront her thoughts.

As for Atul, the week passed in a flash. He was happy about

the cheap deal he'd got from Shalikram. The news that sixty per cent of the licences could fall in their kitty was great, but caused a problem too—it would change their financing needs in the future. Atul knew he had limited his legal options because of the illicit money he was pumping in to secure TTL's future.

Today, a senior TTL team was at the ministry waiting for the spectrum bids to open. The media was tracking the developments live. Prem, Atul, Anil and Rakesh sat in the War Room glued to the screen and deliberating among themselves, while receiving feeds from the TTL team at the ministry. Mir was administering the processes from the government end.

Finally, of the thirteen circles allotted, TTL did win seven circles.

The team was euphoric. Life was about to change. TTL would start services in Delhi, Maharashtra, Goa, Kerala, Gujarat, Rajasthan and Tamil Nadu. Presently, it offered mobile services in Mumbai region alone. The company was looking at a 200 per cent jump in revenues within two years, and an almost four- to five-fold jump in the next three. A quick calculation revealed that they needed almost 8,500 crore in the current year and an identical amount the next year. With the licences in his bag, all other concomitant problems seemed like minnows to Atul.

The competition was stunned by the outcome. A syndicate, seventh in rank at that, had made a huge leap. This spring would put TTL at number three overnight. Their Vision 2015 plan needed to be written all over again.

A flurry of congratulatory calls started to pour in. They were ecstatic. 'This calls for a celebration, guys,' roared Atul, as he excitedly dialled Akram Qazi.

'Qazi sahib, where are you? You should be in the War Room with us, we need to celebrate today.' A dinner was quickly arranged and around twenty of TTL's top executives were invited.

They spent the rest of the day understanding the dynamics of the outcome. Atul called Shalikram and Mir and thanked them too. He still didn't know how Shalikram knew about the allotments when all the proposals were sealed and had been opened just this morning. It only told him the fellow was craftier than he had anticipated.

There were consultations on the core team set-ups in each of these circles, including choices of regional managing directors and key HR personnel to handle recruitments. Tie-ups and contracts to set up infrastructure—towers, offices, stores and equipment, et al.—were discussed with Rakesh Mohanan. They even lined up an itinerary to China and Europe for sourcing. Comprehensive numbers were drawn up for investment requirements and timing firmed up as to when they would be needed.

An Execution Team made up of three members for each circle, each headed by one of the four founders, were set up to oversee the timelines. Qazi put together a legal squad to handle the operationalizing of the licences. They even managed a quick meeting with the private equity investors, taking a cue on how much they were willing to pitch in for the new operations. All in a day!

They worked faster than the wind. That was the zing about this band; they never rested on their laurels. Soon, the sun set upon the horizon and Atul called Roshni to tell her the news. She was happy too; at least she said she was.

A table was booked at an elite lounge, each one of them certain to get wasted. The whole evening, they tapped to the music and downed any form of liquor they could get their hands on. The revelry continued for hours without an end in sight. It was another moment of collective ecstasy triggered by alcohol and led by Atul.

The next day, a meeting was set up at office to discuss the dynamics of injecting Shalikram's cash into their system.

'So this is it, Prem, Anil, are we ready?' asked Atul.

They were about to craft the most legit way to push in 2,000 crore of illicit money into TTL. It had to be done in an exceptionally discreet manner. Once again, there could be no risks.

'Thanks to the missed bank loan, we have 500 crore lying as fictional cash balance, so we have only 1,500 crore to look at now. A quarter of our job done even before we start looking for answers,' said Qazi jokingly.

Atul and Prem smiled at each other thinking of the endless hours they had spent mulling over the generation and cancellation of that fictional profit for the bank loan.

'How do we push the remaining 1,500 crore in? Any ideas?' Qazi wanted to know.

'There cannot be just one way to do it, we will have to do a lot of things, and assuming we are paying back the minister, there must be a way to withdraw it,' replied Prem.

Atul agreed, 'You're right, so let's list the options.' After hours of pondering, the final list looked like this:

1. 500 crore of the cash would be pushed in by precisely the same method used for the bank loan applications. As they already had a fictional cash balance of 500 crore, all they needed was to deposit the cash now available into a bank.

2. Another 500 crore would be sent out of the country through hawala channels and brought back in as Foreign Direct Investment (FDI) into TTL. Globally reputed banks would make this investment through legal banking routes. Since the title of these investments could be traced back to TTL (though that would need a lot of investigation), they would create a web of companies operating from different parts of the world to hide the real ownership.

3. Finally, the once dreaded proposal of creating fictional

subscribers was accepted. It would have a fixed monthly billing of Rs 50 per subscriber and there would be 10 lakhs of them. That would mean a five crore monthly income, but it would take ages to absorb the 1,000 crore that remained and also create a lot of taxable profit.

4. So, a new scheme would be launched for this fictional consumer group. The scheme would require each subscriber to put Rs 10,000 each as deposit to subscribe to the service. That would generate 1,000 crore as deposit. The high deposit would explain the low fixed billing and no one would doubt such a scheme.

5. They even thought of a way to deal with the Telecom Regulators if they knocked. When the money needed to go back to Shalikram, the subscribers would simply cancel the service so the 1,000 crore deposit would be returned back to them in cash. The FDI could also be reversed in a similar manner.

'That's done. Easy, peasy,' said Atul. 'The software glitch could handle items 1 and 2. Item 3 will need a real team.'

'I'll use the same team which did the fictional documentation for the bank loan,' replied Prem.

'You'll need to do this round the year, the team must be able to deal with stress in the face of any investigation. Are you sure they can handle it?' asked Atul.

'They haven't given me a reason to believe otherwise,' replied Prem.

And so, it was all settled. Anil would make the operative documents for the new scheme. Prem called in his core team to review the dynamics of implementation. A board meeting was also on the cards. They avoided all media requests; they were not a public company, so they didn't need to oblige them.

At the Vision 2015 meeting, Prem presented the vagaries in it, in light of the new developments. They all knew it would be mindboggling, as Prem started filling the promoters in on the dynamics.

'We are looking at revenues exceeding 30,000 crore in the next five years, with a profit after tax of about 2,500 crore. We will grow from 2,500 personnel at present, to about 17,000 personnel across the country. Our current net worth of about 3,250 crore will rise to almost 8,000 crore in the next five years—most of this will be from share premium, the profits will kick in later. The total capital expenditure budget for the next five years is 18,500 crore… and the crazy details continued to pour out, drawing them a really rosy picture.

'What challenges are we looking at?' asked Atul, wanting to show transparency and further increase investor confidence.

Aarti Mathur asked Prem's permission to take this question; Prem gladly agreed. She looked towards Atul and the promoters, and began, 'Sir, for one, we will have an enormously stretched debt-to-equity ratio. TTL does not have sufficient equity to justify the debt it needs to raise for the large capex.'

She paused for that to sink in, and continued, 'There is little room for any error; losses in two consequent quarters can undo us. The massive growth in personnel will need a robust appraisal system in place; the current structure does leave a lot to desire. We haven't thought of marketing either, we will be contending with established market leaders in all the circles. All our customers would be takeovers from the competition, so unless we come up with some blue ocean strategies, it will be an uphill job. I suggest we come up with incentivized prepaid airtime sales, while we strengthen our foothold on the post-paid mobile services market.' The pre-paid market is like quicksand the customers shift loyalties for pennies.

Once she finished, they contemplated the options at hand and concluded with a plan of pointers to address on another day, so that they could come up with probable solutions to the issues raised.

Later, Atul took Prem aside and said, 'Aarti is really brilliant, you must hone her skills, she can be a very valuable asset to your team.'

'Yeah, she really is a find; you must listen to her analysis on risk management, she is really good at understanding risk and, more so, addressing it.'

'Yeah, I could see that. Let's see. Keep her at what she is doing now, that's where our biggest gambles lie and need to be mitigated well. We need an efficient programme to address challenges. There should be no surprises on our way there. And how are we getting around the board meeting?' he asked, on his way out.

'Well, this should be our easiest one ever,' said Prem with a smile.

At the board meeting, while the external directors applauded the company on its exemplary performance at the auctions, they made an astounding proposal.

'Mr Chairman, your additional cash requirement of about 17,000 crore needs a lot of leverage. Anything above 2:1 debt: equity is dicey. Even with the current net worth of 3,250 crore, there is a lot of debt already. As investors, we have already indicated our interest in investing another 3,000 crore as equity. We can talk about the terms of those investments later; however, we think this should be done simultaneously with an Initial Public Offering (IPO). The investors feel that will give them an option to exit from time to time, while the equity will ensure that the leverage is within the mark. We would not like to invest so much money in a company without the option to exit or adequate price discovery. Without public listing, that option seems far-fetched to us. What do you think?'

Atul replied calmly, 'Well, gentlemen, we do not think the

need for that may arise. We are already aware of these concerns and are working on our options; unfortunately, those options do not include an IPO at this point. We, however, appreciate your views. Let us put this up for discussion at the next board meeting, when we would be better prepared to deal with this presently out-of-agenda question.' Having neatly ducked the question, Atul called the meeting to a close.

'What was the problem?' Rakesh Mohanan asked Atul after the meeting. 'Their proposal wasn't so outrageous after all, we always wanted an IPO, right? And what better time to get the best valuation than now?'

Atul looked at Rakesh with surprise, 'Are you out of your mind? With all the proscribed money we've pumped in, we cannot be the object of public scrutiny. An IPO will mean several public disclosures, it just limits our flexibility. Please get it out of your mind, not till we have Shalikram off our backs. And why do you think Shalikram wanted only us? We are the only unlisted company in the business today. How could you not get that?' Rakesh nodded, getting it.

★

At home, Atul was still grappling with relationship issues, and all the action at work had only made things worse. He knew that. They'd had continuous love-hate periods over the last few months. He did not know how to deal with her imaginary fears, but keeping the peace was still on his agenda.

As he was getting ready to retire for the night, he asked, 'How did your appointment go today? I spoke to Dr Awasthi and she tells me the growth has been very good over the past month. She is quite optimistic now.'

'Yes, she told me that too, but I don't know. I am scared, Atul. I am not sure we did the right thing. But I didn't want to let go of the only joy I had in hand.'

Atul replied gently, 'I am only hoping our greed for joy does not bring us more sorrow,' and realized instantly he'd said something he shouldn't have.

Quickly, to divert her, he said, 'Rakesh and I are going to China to look at some new equipment we need for the expansions. I have booked us an extended weekend at Sanya. It is a small beach town in China, it should be a perfect getaway. We can also meet Aditya on the way back at Bangkok. I thought it would be a much-needed holiday for you too.'

'When are we going?' asked Roshni, surprising Atul.

'Next weekend. I have already asked Radha to make the arrangements. Dr Awasthi okayed it too.' And even as Roshni was thinking how Atul had again taken her for granted, he kissed her forehead and, turning his back to her, slept.

Chapter 10

'Good morning, Atulji, how is it going?'

Answering on his secure line, Atul responded to Shalikram Bahujan. 'All good, sir, how are you? Everything is falling into place, thanks to your support.'

'This is the trailer, Atulji, wait for the full movie, we will be a super hit jodi,' replied Shalikram jovially. Before Atul could reply, he continued, 'Atulji, I have a small request for you. My brother-in-law owns a small pesticides business, Bharat Pesticides, which has been making losses since the beginning. The scoundrel does not know how to run it. I have about three crore invested there. I want TTL to buy it. I want you to run the finances so it makes some profit.'

Atul was surprised Shalikram would personally call to get TTL to invest a mere three crore. Anyone could do it, why would Shalikram need a telecom operator to do pesticides, he wondered. Aloud, he merely said, 'Of course, sir, but we know nothing about pesticides.'

'Ya, Ya. Bacchu, my brother-in-law knows all about that. Just that if I keep the finances with him, he will just blow it up on women and wine. You know how it is. Today's generation is totally wasted.'

An amused Atul nodded over the phone with a sly smile. 'Not a problem, sir, we will have it arranged. Please ask him to get in touch with Radha at my office, she will arrange the paperwork.' But he put down the phone with a sense of unease. Something wasn't right here, he thought. He quickly made another call to Mir.

'Mir sahib, Atul here.'

'Oh! Good morning, Atul,' replied Mir, plainly surprised.

Atul came straight to the point. 'Mir sahib, what is the story behind Bharat Pesticides. The minister called and wants us to acquire it.'

After a pause, Mir replied cautiously, 'I don't know much about it, but I believe his brother-in-law runs it.'

'Hmm…then why doesn't he shut it down and write off the paltry investment, why do you think he wants us to buy it?' Atul asked.

'He probably wants to keep his brother-in-law employed. Unemployed, he is a bigger cost to the minister,' said Mir, laughing at his own joke.

'Very well then, okay, one more thing—how do you think Shalikram would react if we proposed a listing or public issue for TTL?' Atul asked Mir.

'He won't be happy is my guess, for obvious reasons, but you can take your chances,' replied Mir.

'I thought so too,' Atul concurred, and added, 'Mir sahib, we are dry all over again. You must find us another well, we need some fresh water… They both laughed at the joke before disconnecting.

★

Rakesh Mohanan and Atul were given royal treatment by the Chinese manufacturers; after all, they had a budget of 10,000 crore for equipment alone. Finishing there, Atul flew on to join Roshni at Sanya, who was flying in from Mumbai.

'Hope you had a good flight?' he asked, hugging Roshni before escorting her out of the airport. She looked huge with a six-month belly. Dr Awasthi had taken a risk by allowing her this holiday. Flaunting a green gown, she walked slowly towards the waiting BMW.

Checking into the suite at Mandarin Oriental, Atul and Roshni spent the day in the room. Atul browsing books, Roshni flipping through magazines and TV channels. Towards the end of the day, they stepped out to the beach adjoining the hotel for a stroll. The sea seemed lazy, the waves submissively hitting the shore before hissing their way back, as Atul and Roshni conversed. Atul made sure they did not touch upon any controversial issues.

'Can we have our old days back, Atul?' said Roshni hesitantly.

'Roshni, nothing is wrong with us, you need to be a bit more understanding and to give us space.'

Roshni interjected, '*I* need to be more understanding to give *us* space? How does that work, Atul?'

Without correcting himself, instead tweaking it a bit, he said, in very dramatic non-Atul accents, 'It is more like you breathe, I breathe, we breathe. It's not either-or.'

But Roshni wasn't to be mollified. 'I always feel you are never there for me. Even when you are, you are there because of your responsibility towards me and not because of me.' She had hit the nail on the head and Atul knew it. Trying to be as logical as he could, he said, 'It is never like that, honey, you know, balancing work and home. Sometimes, I do have to give a larger share of my time to work, given all the expansions. You know all about it.'

'...And sex, where does the larger share of that go, Atul? Because I don't get much of that either,' she said, looking at Atul straight in the eye, waiting for a reaction.

'I don't know what you are getting at, Roshni. What are you implying? Are you accusing me of cheating?' he asked right back.

'You tell me, I asked you the question,' Roshni said, hitting back at him.

'What has come upon you? Where are you getting these thoughts from?' said Atul, alarmed at the dangerous direction this conversation was taking, and all for nothing.

'Why else would you avoid sex all the time, Atul, don't I know you? We have been together for years, it never was like this.'

'Roshni, please tell me you are smarter than this. Is this the basis of your horrendous accusation? How can you even use that to infer that I am having an affair? There are several reasons, if you want to know. Stress, your own health, pregnancy, time, everything but an extramarital affair! You should have been more careful before you allowed that to escape your lips.'

'Jyoti was telling me...

'That bitch sister of yours, I knew it,' said Atul furiously.

'Language, Atul, she is my sister.'

'So what! Does that give her the licence to make my life hell? She already has done that with Jignesh. Look, Roshni, I do not want to be blamed for your poor health, you are my responsibility. But I cannot sit here seeking forgiveness for sins I haven't committed yet,' and so saying, he stalked off towards the hotel. Jyoti got a sadistic joy out of ruining relationships. She had even tried to hit on Atul. He'd never told Roshni because she would never believe him. Several years ago, at a family occasion, Jyoti had tried to hold Atul's hand telling him she was not happy with Jignesh and longed for someone. He sized her up that night. She was a bitch capable of gulping homes before they could be built.

Back in the room, Roshni started again, 'Are you not happy with me, Atul?'

'Please! Roshni, stop it!' Atul shouted, unable to keep his cool under Roshni's consistent interrogation. 'I refuse to get drawn into this conversation. You are sure. Right? So prove it. And unless you can do that, I will not take this bullshit.'

'Can't we even have a simple conversation, Atul?'

'Roshni, we are done discussing this. And unless you have anything else to talk about, I am going to bed, and without any sex. And not because I just fucked someone else like you'd like to think, but I still got fucked and I am presuming neither party got any pleasure out of it either. That probably also answers why we're not having enough sex.'

And yet, the rest of the trip managed to pass off peacefully.

At Suvarnabhumi International Airport, Atul rushed to hug Aditya. An embrace, tight as ever, lasted long, each waiting for the other to release him.

'How are you, brother? It's been such a while... Atul fired a barrage of questions as he picked up the bags. Trudging behind, Roshni tried to catch up with them, 'How are you, Aditya, where is Sapna?'

'No, bhabhi, I came straight from the university. She is waiting for us at home.'

Tall, at 6'1", Aditya was bald by choice. A reader at Chulalongkorn University, he was a qualified macroeconomist. A childhood friend of Atul's, they'd pooled everything, even girlfriends, at college. With time, their paths diverged; Atul went on to do his masters in business management, whereas Aditya did his in Economics.

'Darling, how have you been?' said Sapna, hugging Roshni as soon as she saw her at the door. Over the years, they had built a good rapport. All they had was a few hours before getting back on a flight home. With Atul's busy schedule, that was all he could manage.

Sapna and Aditya lived on a busy street in Maharong village, not far from the university, in a two-bedroom apartment with nothing but the essentials. Aditya cycled to university and Sapna worked for an accounting firm. They made a decent living, enough for all the requisites, but sans any luxuries.

In a while, Atul and Aditya took the elevator for a round of drinks, while Sapna chose to sit back with Roshni and do some catching up in the comfort of her home.

Atul and Aditya made their way to a bar in Sukumvit district. There were just a few customers at that hour. Towards the night, the place would be bustling with go-go dancers.

'So, Aditya, what else is happening in life? Give me some juicy story.'

'Wow! You want gossip. You know that guy Suresh, we called him Monty…?'

'Yeah, yeah, I know, that stout fellow, he is in Bangkok, right? What about him?'

'Yeah, he got arrested recently; he beat up his wife, she got him behind bars,' said Aditya.

'Really, he was such a meek fellow, didn't know he had teeth to do something like that,' said Atul, cheekily, and continued, 'Where is he now?'

'We paid a bomb to get him out, and put him on a flight to India straight from jail. His woman divorced him too,' Aditya replied.

'Hmm,' nodded Atul, relishing his beer. 'What else? How is life with Sapna? How is the marriage coming along? It is what, three years, right?' Atul asked, glancing at some scantily clad dancers as they passed by. On the horizon, the sun was disappearing fast, cooling the warm day, perfect for a winter evening in Bangkok.

'Yeah, time flies. Sapna is a dream really. Our tiny world is enough of a stage with ample time for all the love and trivia,' said Aditya.

'I always feel envious of you. You find happiness all the time and in any situation. Not to mention still being chased by all the lovely girls. And the more you age and they don't, they simply get replaced by a fresh lot every year… what luck… Let's switch, buddy.'

They laughed, and Aditya said, 'Don't start again, Atul. Life is what you make of it. If you want to feel happy about it, you will find enough motivation; you won't have to look hard. So how are things at your end, how is life with Roshni? I keep reading about TTL, it really makes me proud, bro.'

'Well...you know all about Roshni. Nothing's changed there. And TTL, don't believe the media. They know stories about us that even we don't. Just last week they reported we would open 300 retail stores this year. It was news even to us!' They both laughed. 'Still, there is a lot of action in my life. Action is good.'

'I'm sorry to hear about the baby, yaar, I hope it all turns out well. I mustn't say that now, but you should have aborted, really,' said Aditya.

'You know all about that too, Aditya, I told you everything,' Atul said in resigned tones.

'No, Atul, I don't subscribe to your view. You should have persisted with Roshni; it's not worth the risk.'

Atul recalled Dr Awasthi's words and said, 'Her doctor and I both agreed on this. In fact, I didn't even want this baby. The whole thing was an accident. I don't know how I fell for Roshni's trap, I usually don't.' Then he paused and said, 'I have made up my mind, Aditya, I am going to discuss divorce with Roshni soon after the delivery. I'm hoping it won't be so bad then.'

But Aditya immediately said, 'Don't even think about it, Atul. It is not half as easy as you think, there's a huge price to pay. And by the end of it, you'll feel you would have been better off not going down that road to begin with at all.'

'Don't you see why divorce is so fucking expensive? Anything that good can't be cheap!' replied Atul, laughing; he did not want to be lectured on the subject. He always liked to talk about separation, at least till he could do nothing about it. It was as if the thought itself gave him part of the pleasure of getting there. The conversation did not stop till Atul had to be pushed out of the bar so he could make it to his flight back to Mumbai.

★

Back home, the board meeting was closing in again. Atul had tactfully ducked the question of an IPO the last time, but he had to be ready with answers now. Prem walked in with Aarti into Atul's cabin.

'Come in, Prem,' said Atul, and greeted Aarti, 'How are you?'

'Good, sir. How are you?' Aarti replied politely.

'Very well, thanks,' replied Atul. 'So, what are we looking at? How do we pull this off?'

'Well,' said Prem, 'there's a hiccup for sure. We are short of 1,250 crore in equity, and once that is done, we need to arrange another 8,250 crore of debt.'

'Any ideas on how we can mitigate matters? At least for the meeting. Aarti, can you think of something?' asked Atul, and for the first time, observed her. The way she used her hands and eyes to express her attractive confidence. Petite and naturally beautiful, she sported an elegant beige suit adorning the outlines of her moderate bosom, and contrasting her wheatish complexion. There was something alluring about her eyes. They seemed to glow with ambition and lust at the same time. He quickly dispensed with his thoughts and got back to business at hand.

'I have already spoken to Prem Sir. He tends to agree that is a possible solution. We could raise the entire 1,250 crore from fully convertible bonds, which may be converted to equity at the predetermined strike price after three years,' she replied.

'But we don't want any kind of public offer,' Atul snapped.

'No, this isn't public, it is private placement, a single buyer, at best two. At least, we can propose it, we will see how it flies thereon. Since we want to avoid an IPO, we will get an almost similar idea to sail eventually,' she concluded.

'Well, the idea will work for a board meeting, but won't fly higher than that. Anyways, get it up and running, come up with some interest letters from investors so we can back up our claims. Talk to our treasury managers, they will be able to arrange some credible ones,' Atul said, closing the meeting.

The proposal did fly at the board meeting, but another proposal took to the air as well, tabled by an investor-nominated director. 'Okay, Mr Chairman,' he said, 'assuming your proposals are indeed workable, we still do not have our exit option. If TTL does not want an IPO, as investors, we intend to bring in a Public Offer[2], that way, we can get the listing objective fulfilled too. It's a win-win for all.'

Atul knew he needed to sort out this one quickly. What the director had proposed was his right—as investors, the directors did not need any permission to sell shares they already owned. But such a sale would still require TTL to comply with disclosure norms post the listing and, hence, would not work. Forget raising an additional 1,250 crore as equity, Atul knew he could be looking at raising the entire non-promoter stake from elsewhere if this ended up in a deadlock.

In the remote chance that Shalikram was convinced and they actually did go in for an IPO, they would still need to significantly strengthen their shadow machinery to deal with the new disclosures. And so, Atul carefully crafted a response, 'Sir, the Public Offer is already in the share sale agreement with the investors, how could we have a problem with that? But that will require offloading a minimum ten per cent of your holdings. It is legally binding. With your eighteen per cent holding, you will be left with a mere eight per cent after the offer. Wouldn't that be a lot of sale? especially

---

[2]Public Offer = Non-promoters stock of a company sold through a public offer and listed on the stock exchange. The promoters or the company do not participate in such offer.

at a time when the company is just taking off. I am not sure you are looking at reducing your stake by more than half.'

Having successfully planted a seed of doubt in the mind of the nominee director, Atul left it at that, but he knew this was a problem that could have a domino effect.

Chapter 11

'Atul, we had a small problem, and even though it's been taken care of, I just thought I should run it by you,' said Prem softly at the end of a weekly financial review meeting held in Atul's office. He wanted the matter to be kept between them, even though the last of the team was leaving the room and pulling the door shut behind them.

'You remember Prashant Nagarkar, member of our laundry?' They had long since dubbed their money-laundering team and the area of the office they occupied as the 'laundry'.

Now Atul said, 'Yeah, yeah, I know him, you introduced him to me. What about him?'

'He comes from a very modest background, had a history of psychological disorders we didn't know about, but has been with TTL for about seven years. He was a bold and...'

'Cut the crap, Prem!' interjected Atul impatiently, 'Come to the point. What the hell happened?' He sensed this wasn't pleasant and Prem was trying to sugar-coat the story.

'Well,' said Prem, 'For a couple of months, Nagarkar was showing clear signs of depression, fear and guilt. He worked in extreme fear, he used to perspire despite the AC, and tell colleagues that he couldn't handle the work because of all the illegality and illegitimacy around it.'

'Come to the point, Prem,' said Atul, now seriously worried.

'We gave him a time-out, but once back, his symptoms amplified. He threatened to inform the authorities and felt burdened about it. He even hallucinated about being jailed. We got him admitted to the hospital at our expense to be checked for any mental disorders. We have a couple of guys on guard to ensure he is contained.'

Atul heard each word without batting an eyelid, then erupted, 'This is what you call "taken care of"? What happens when he is discharged from hospital?'

'Well, Atul, we'll talk to him.'

'Talk to him?' Atul shouted. 'I thought you did the due diligence? You couldn't find four guys with balls of steel within the 2,500 staff here? You go and appoint a psychopath who now wants to trumpet our business secrets around the world. One mad man will bring this company down! Is that it?'

It was a rare day when Atul lost his cool so badly. Today was one such. He took a couple of deep breaths to calm down, and apologized. 'I am sorry, Prem, but this is a massive issue. What is his family like?' he enquired, composing himself.

'His wife died delivering a daughter. That really triggered his depression. The daughter is just about five years old now. There is no one else we know of.'

'So he doesn't have any rudders to direct him? How do we get a hold on him then? We can't influence a five-year-old to put any sense into him. In fact, she is an additional drag. We can't take chances; he can bring us down. How could *you* make a blunder like this, Prem?' Atul sounded absolutely distressed. How could Prem be such a dud at handling this? Atul felt at a complete loss over how to resolve the matter. 'How long can we keep him there, I mean at the asylum?' he asked Prem finally.

'I didn't get directly involved, but it seems he is good to go, he has no apparent symptoms, the doctors are...'

'How long? Prem! It is a straight question!' snapped Atul.

'Five days, max ten.' Prem quickly replied.

'Give me a day or two,' said Atul. 'Keep him under surveillance

24/7. It's good you are not directly involved, keep it that way. Shift the girl to one of our guesthouses, take good care of her, that may calm him down and secure us too. I am going to Delhi in the evening. I will meet Mir tomorrow, he may have some ideas, they have some experience in these situations.'

Later that evening, Atul landed in Delhi and headed straight to the hotel. He was restless about this whole Nagarkar story. He was to meet Shalikram at 8 a.m., followed by Mir at 10 a.m. the next day. He went down to the lounge bar for a few drinks to slow down his thinking processes. He could hold his mind in the face of any crisis, but this was unprecedented.

The lounge bar was dimly lit, had red velvet interiors with fancy fixtures, a suspended glass bar, and was stocked with a distinguished variety of alcohol and liqueurs. Atul sat at one of the tables and ordered his usual Black Label, but his mind wouldn't stop loitering.

Suddenly, out of the blue, he saw Aarti Mathur dressed casually in a white Lacoste T-shirt and jeans, and she spotted him too. Coming to where he was sitting, she said, 'Hello, sir, what a surprise, how come you are here?' extending the warmest smile she could.

'I could ask you the same, Aarti,' he replied, standing up to shake her hand.

'Well, I just arrived. I am catching up with a few friends up in Shimla. I've taken a couple of weeks off. I have a flight in the morning.'

'I have a similar tale, but neither the places nor people are as interesting as yours. Mine suck.' They both laughed.

'So, have a seat, wanna catch a drink?'

'Sure, sure,' said Aarti. 'Can I quickly freshen up, if you don't mind? I'll be back in ten minutes.'

'Oh, by all means. Let's have dinner together if you are up for it, unless of course you have other plans,' said Atul, trying not to sound too eager.

'Why not, it would be my pleasure,' she replied, as she took his leave and headed for the elevator.

Atul had finished his Black Label by the time she returned. He was admittedly a little excited at the prospect of having dinner with her. He admired her beauty and intelligence anew each time his eyes fell upon her. His mind cheered at the welcome relief.

Aarti returned in a sky blue sleeveless top and a white mini skirt, her hair tied back in a bun. She looked elegant and poised. He noted she'd put on a bright red lipstick; she was looking as luscious as could be.

'Have a seat,' invited Atul.

'Thank you, sir,' she said politely, as she sat gracefully.

'So what's your poison for the night?' asked Atul, seeing the bearer arriving with the menu.

'I'll take a Chardonnay,' she said.

'I'll continue with Black Label,' said Atul.

'Would you like some starters on the side?' the bearer enquired.

'Yeah,' said Aarti, 'I don't mind some grilled fish. Can you get some if you have it?'

'That's a good choice,' the bearer replied with a smile, 'I'll be right back. Enjoy the evening.'

'So, tell me your story,' said Atul, turning to her.

'Wow! My story. It is not a tenth as exciting as yours. You are an achiever, sir. I've just started, you are my idol,' said Aarti, stars in her eyes.

'Oh my God!' said Atul, 'I'm flattered, where did you get that from? And why me?'

'You are being humble, sir, I really mean it. In fact, that's why I joined TTL. A start-up. Reaching the billion-dollar club in ten years, that's not usual. And look at where we are headed!'

'So are you happy with TTL?' Atul asked.

'Oh, unquestionably, sir,' she replied with a smile, 'it is an incredible place, works for me!'

'Hmm... I am pleased you think that way,' smiled Atul, sipping his whiskey. 'And can we drop the "sir" bit? We are not at work. I've never liked people calling me sir, I used to stop them, but over time, I've given up. I guess it is one British legacy that's hard to let go.'

Aarti smiled in response.

Atul's admiration for her was growing and he hoped it wasn't showing too openly; he would be embarrassed if she guessed. 'So what is your story?' he pressed, diverting her, 'You still haven't answered the question.'

'Well. My father was in the army, so I spent my childhood at various places—Pune, Shimla, Chandigarh, Amritsar. I did most of my schooling from Mayo College as a boarder. Got into IIT, did my electrical engineering. After that, I worked a couple of years before I did an MBA from IIM Lucknow and landed in the arms of TTL.'

With her usual flair Aarti had narrated her life's account succinctly and without any embellishments. She was an achiever, of that there was no doubt.

'Pretty impressive,' said Atul raising his glass, 'Cheers to that!'

'Cheers!' replied Aarti, raising her own. 'And what about you, sir? Oops, Atul... God, this isn't easy,' she muttered.

'You'll get used to it,' smiled Atul. 'The quicker you consider me a friend, the easier it will be.'

Aarti nodded.

'I didn't have a father who could afford all the schools you went to,' said Atul. 'My father was a clerk at the Mumbai Municipal Corporation. I grew up in a chawl near Virar. My mom suffered from tuberculosis, I was around ten. Our income could barely pay for two square meals. He couldn't save her. She suffered a painful death and it pained my father even more. He never really recovered from that.'

Aarti, who had been listening to him earnestly, gasped, 'I am so sorry to hear that, Atul.'

He continued, 'I decided then I would learn and earn so much that money would never again be a worry. Unfortunately, before I could get there, my father suffered a stroke too. I was eighteen then. The stress of raising a single child and an 18-hour workday did him in. A lot of my lessons were learnt on the streets of Virar.' It was evident his memories still brought him pain.

'I have never come across a story as sad as yours, Atul, it must have been very hard on you,' said Aarti.

'Anyway,' he continued, 'I got my share of government schools, did odd jobs to pay for my engineering from COEP, Pune, did my MBA—I did it from IMT Ghaziabad, I wasn't so bright after all,' he added, smiling. Aarti smiled back in appreciation, now on her third glass of wine.

Atul continued, 'I got into General Mobile, spent three years there, didn't like how things were done. The place sucked, the processes were sluggish, it didn't enlighten me. We decided to rewrite the rules and we launched TTL from there. That was about eleven years ago.'

'Wow!' said Aarti.

'And I have a wife and will be a father by the end of the month,' he concluded.

'Really?!' exclaimed Aarti. 'That's amazing. Congratulations!'

'So what about you?' asked Atul, 'any husbands, boyfriends?'

Aarti laughed out loud. 'Are you teasing me, Atul? No husband, for sure. Boyfriend…hmm… let me think…' Aarti muttered, her expression somewhat childlike as she thought.

'Look at you. You are so amazing. You are actually thinking about it, if you have one…

She laughed, 'It's not that, Atul. He is on his way out of my life. I mean, maybe…Deciding if I must pronounce him ex. Yet.'

'Hmm. So what have you decided?' he asked, suddenly impatient about her response.

'Okay, I guess. I'll keep him for now,' she replied, laughing out loud.

'Hmm, I'll leave you with that, tell me when he becomes ex. I have someone in mind who may be interested in you!' Atul said naughtily, taking his chances.

'Really, that's exciting and who's that!' Aarti asked, even more excited at this prospect.

'We will see about that, first you let me know when that happens,' replied Atul.

They couldn't get done talking. She finished two pints of wine in as many hours, and Atul was down so many drinks, he didn't remember the count, but he didn't want to get wasted and kept a check on himself. He was thoroughly enjoying himself and Aarti was clearly enjoying his company.

'Want to take to the floor?' she asked Atul.

Taken aback, he replied, 'I'm not a great dancer, a pretty bad one actually. You gotta save your feet.'

'I'm always up for chances. We'll see about that, let's go,' she said, laughing.

Atul left his coat on the sofa before taking Aarti's hand and heading for the dance floor that had some shimmering lights above. There were already a few people swaying to the latest tunes.

Alcohol had lowered their inhibitions and the dance slowly started to turn intimate. Atul's hands softly held on to Aarti's waist. As time moved on, they moved closer; the music slowed down, as though taking a cue. Aarti's hand lay on Atul's shoulder and the other at his waist. Pretty soon her head rested on his shoulder too, and her breasts brushed his chest every so often.

After a while, she didn't care and they began to cherish

the intimacy. Atul was horny too, he realized. It was a natural progression. He tried hard to hide it, but given such proximity, it wasn't easy. He was sure Aarti had guessed that by now.

'Atul, I guess we must call it a night I have a flight at 7 a.m.,' Aarti said, standing on her toes to speak into his ear. Her touch titillated him.

'I have a meeting at 8 with a monster,' he replied.

'…Which monster?'

'A beast called Shalikram,' said Atul, immediately realizing he shouldn't have brought him up. More to divert her, but also to delay their moment of parting, he said, 'I can manage, can you?'

'Well, I guess yes,' replied Aarti.

'Yeah, and if you miss it, you can take the next flight, though I don't have that option,' laughed Atul.

Back at the table, they sat on the same side, caught completely off guard by the sudden build-up of intimacy. Atul even forgot he was in a public place after a while. Carried away by this new-found euphoria, he forgot he was a national celebrity with a reputation to uphold; at this point, he cared little about that. 'Can I hold your hand?' he asked Aarti.

'How will that help? I mean, what will it do?' Aarti replied, apparently having regained some of her dissolved senses.

'I don't know, maybe nothing. And if it is nothing, there shouldn't be much of a fuss,' said Atul, trying his best to get her to agree. She did, in a while.

Atul felt exhilarated, feeling her palm, every finger, and exchanging warmth. He was ecstatic. Her mere touch made him tremendously horny. For a couple of moments, he did wonder what if she sued him for molestation, but shrugged it off in a manner that was most unlike him.

'You are a married man, Atul, I hope you know what you are doing,' Aarti said soberly, sceptical of his gestures and actions.

'Married to whom, that bitching wife of mine, who has made my life a living hell? You call that marriage?' said Atul scathingly. Aarti didn't make too much of it, knowing how wasted both of them were.

Finally, in the early hours, they did decide to retire. Nothing interesting was happening, as far as Atul was concerned. He did not want to push his luck and destroy the prospect of moving ahead. He knew what he wanted and was sure of what he was up to. He had forgotten all his worries that night. He had experienced a different high, something he hadn't in a very long time. He discovered a pleasure in living, something he had been missing for so long he'd almost forgotten it existed for him. Today had rekindled all that.

He was anxious about who this boyfriend of hers was. Up in his room, he put on his laptop and then invited her on Facebook, as a first step to finding out more. Then he finally called it a night.

The next morning, he made calls to enquire about Shalikram since Shalikram was no stickler for time. Atul was, and it irritated him like hell if someone canned a scheduled appointment without warning. Shalikram missed most of his. He cared little for time and even less for people. Missing appointments and keeping people waiting was a privilege the minister took pride in abusing.

Today's meeting looked like a washout too. Shalikram wasn't traceable, and Atul soon got a message that the minister wouldn't be available. The beast must be sleeping in some gutter with his face buried in the groin of some filthy whore, thought Atul.

With the meeting canned, he wasn't so upset because it gave him a couple of much-needed hours to recoup before he met Mir later in the morning. That meeting thankfully took place.

The niceties taken care of, Atul cautiously decided to test the waters, 'We haven't met in a while, Mir sahib, how are things at the ministry?'

'Nothing worth talking about,' replied Mir wryly, 'You know

how a government job is. Nowhere close to your corporate excitement. By the way, how serious were you when you asked me about a new well?'

'Pretty serious,' replied Atul immediately. 'But you need to look at the quality of water too. I don't mean to give offence, but what I get today stinks way too much for me to bear.'

'Let me see if I can find another,' said Mir, acknowledging his point.

'I have another issue I wanted to discuss with you,' said Atul, bringing up Prashant Nagarkar. He narrated all that Prem had told him.

Mir agreed with him, 'This is a matter of grave concern,' he said. 'As I see it, the only way out seems to be liquidating him. Just finish him.'

'What do you think we do here?' said Atul, appalled, 'I don't want blood. I am a businessman; blood cannot be my way, no way.'

'It's either kill or get killed, Atul,' said Mir grimly, 'the choices are limited, what are you thinking?'

'But, Mir sahib, I know the guy, a few threats and he won't be a bother, plus he is the only guardian to his daughter,' argued Atul, even as he knew Mir was dead right.

Mir thought for a while and said, 'Listen, Atul, you are being emotional. This is business, and as you say, there is no place for emotion in business. You and I both know this well. But if you want to take it another way, that's up to you. The best I can do is to put you in touch with Salman, he is a contract killer. He will take care of it the way you want, but there are no guarantees. You can still take your chances, assuming you are right about the guy in the first place.'

Averting his eyes, Mir looked down at the files on his desk and continued, 'Shalikram uses him too. I could talk to him, but he won't stop short of killing the fellow. He doesn't take stupid risks, and honestly, I don't suggest you take any either. That's all I can say.'

Atul was desperate to find a way out, one without violence, but he needed more answers just in case things did go wrong.

'I'm sure Nagarkar will come around with some intimidation. But what if he does not, Mir sahib? After all, he is demented,' said Atul apprehensively, trying to map the options ahead.

'From what you say about the guy, that shouldn't happen,' said Mir. 'Assume it does, we will look at it then. Up here we don't plan funerals till the body is dead.' Atul understood his point quickly.

'Okay,' said Mir, 'Shalikramji had a small request. You should be able to get this done without moving a muscle,' Mir said, handing him a list of cell numbers.

'He wants surveillance and tapping on these numbers.'

'Not a problem. We cannot share transcripts though, that can cause big trouble. You can send someone in and I will give access to the recorded data,' Atul assured Mir. 'Who are these people, if I may ask?'

'Well, they are all coveted lawmakers, nothing that should worry you,' replied Mir, smiling at Atul.

★

Back in Mumbai, Atul waited for action from Mir; it didn't take long.

'Who can give Salman coordinates for this Nagarkar?' Mir asked over the phone.

'I can have someone call him. Where should he call?' Atul asked.

'Whoever calls must tell him it is regarding Prashant Nagarkar, he will know the rest,' said Mir, and read out a number which Atul scribbled on a pad on his desk.

'Very well. Thank you, Mir sahib,' said Atul before he hung up. Next, he called Prem and said, 'I am sending you Salman's coordinates,' and also told him to maintain absolute secrecy and keep any TTL employee out of it. Then, he passed on the other list of numbers Mir had handed him in Delhi to Radha, and asked her to instruct the Quality Assurance Cell (QAC) to start monitoring them. The QAC did the illegal work of tapping calls under the garb of quality checks.

Prashant Nagarkar was discharged from the psychiatric ward on Sunday morning, just as Salman wanted it. Two of Salman's cronies followed him and would continue to do so until Salman took them off the case. At TTL, the QAC had been tapping Prashant's phone.

Prashant headed to the TTL HQ from the hospital. He had a valid ID, so that wasn't a problem, and Salman's men gained open access through Prem. Prashant entered his office and started collecting some prints.

'What do you think you are doing?' one of Salman's men dressed in a Pathani suit asked Prashant.

'Who are you to ask?' Prashant bristled, 'I work here, why should you have a problem?'

The second man stepped in, 'We are the ones asking the questions and you are the one replying, we'll keep it that way for now. So, if I may repeat the question, what are you trying to do?' and he turned sideways displaying a pistol slung on his belt.

'Who do you think you are intimidating here? You've got the wrong guy,' a scared Prashant said. Then, realizing what was going on, he got angry and shouted, 'All these years I thought I worked for honourable people, little did I know they were also the biggest rogues.'

'Take the name of your lord and straighten up, brother, else I'll cut your sweet daughter into pieces so small, you won't be able to count them. And I won't twitch a bit, I can assure you,' the man retorted, pulling out a short, sharp knife. Sharp enough to inflict wounds, not deep enough to kill. He had been instructed to wound, but his experience told him that Prashant Nagarkar wasn't going to crack.

Prashant replied, 'I believe in my lord, I've done enough disservice to him. No more. You can kill me and my daughter, but neither will save you, it's too late now.'

Angered by this show of belligerence, the first man stabbed Prashant, striking deep into his right shoulder. His accomplice pulled back and punched Prashant, knocking out his lower jaw. Bleeding profusely from his stab wound, Prashant screamed, holding his jaw in pain. 'You cannot stop me, kill me if you must, else you are done, you are all dead ducks.' He sprinted out as best as he could with some pages, some kind of a list, and ran towards the exit. Except for some guards at the main gate, there wasn't a soul around.

The men closed on him in hot pursuit and one of them managed to give his back a hard push. The blow knocked him off balance and Prashant banged his head against a sharp sidebar. The impact broke open his skull and he fell unconscious, lying in a pool of blood. He was out cold but still breathing.

The two thugs looked around and spotting a utility room nearby, dragged Prashant's unconscious body there before anybody could see it. Then, one of them ran out to the parking lot, pulled off the cover of one of the parked company cars and ran back and concealed the bloodstained floor with it. The other man nervously called Salman, 'Boss, he is severely injured, it was accidental, what should we do?'

'Finish it. Kill him and vanish from the scene,' Salman instructed.

'We are inside the TTL compound, but...' the man said, as Salman interrupted him, 'Let me send you some help. Hang in there, cover it up if you can,' and he disconnected.

Prem called Atul; at this point all he knew was that Prashant had entered the office building. Without getting into the details, Atul said, 'I am on the way, you meet me in my office. I will take about fifteen minutes.' He wanted to talk to Prashant and put some sense into him.

Meanwhile, Salman called Prem with the latest news and Prem called Atul again. Atul's heart sank as Prem narrated the developments. He was lost for words. He said absolutely nothing. His mind felt numb; he was out of options.

'Atul, you there... Atul? Atul?' Prem asked, petrified.

'Don't go to office, Prem,' he said quickly, 'Come to the guesthouse next door, I'll see you there.'

In the background, his phone was buzzing; it read 'Babulal calling... He didn't take the call, it kept buzzing and disconnecting several times.

On his arrival at the guesthouse, they got the news that Prashant was dead.

Atul called Mir, there was no time to mourn or ruminate. 'We have to arrange the funeral, Mir sahib, the body is dead,' he said, repeating the phrases Mir had used at his office.

'Atul, don't get emotional about this, get up and do what needs to be done. I told you the risks,' and Mir disconnected the phone.

One jumps into the deep sea, leaving the devil behind. Deeper in the sea, he meets the devil again, another one, an unknown one. Seemingly with no place else to go, he befriends him. The devil becomes the friend. As an accomplice of the devil, you must do what the devil does. Sin. The long forgotten jump was voluntary though.

'Babulal calling... Atul saw his phone ring again.

'Babulal what is the matter? Can't you understand if I am not picking up, I must be busy,' barked Atul.

His cook replied, 'Sahib, I got bhabhi to the hospital. I didn't know what to do, I kept calling you, you didn't answer. They took her to the operation theatre.'

'What! Is there any hospital staff around? Give them the phone,' Atul reacted in absolute disbelief.

Babulal handed the phone to somebody, and Atul spoke, 'Hello, this is Atul Malhotra. I believe my wife is in labour, right? Do you have any news? I am on my way, I hope everything is all right, Is Dr Awasthi there?'

The person on the other end identified herself as a nurse and said, 'Dr Awasthi is in the OT, your wife just delivered a baby girl. I don't have more information, you may call the doctor directly.' She seemed to be in a big hurry, as she disconnected.

Atul called Dr Awasthi, 'Congratulations, Atul,' she said, 'you are a father. The mother and baby are fine...'

'Doctor... how is the baby, is everything all right? I need to know, doctor. Oh god, I should have been there. Doctor, I am really in a mess, it will take a while, just be there with her... Please tell me about the baby.' He knew he was blabbering, but the events of the day would have possibly felled even a hardened criminal.

Atul's mind was still racing, divided between the conversation on the phone and wondering how Prem was handling the crisis and coordinating the disposal of the body. Salman had arranged for a pick-up wagon and some helpers, so that the body could be moved out discreetly.

Dr Awasthi, speaking to Atul, muttered a few sentences that he did not catch but towards the end, she said, '...physically, she looks fine. That's all we can tell now, the level of mental development will take a while to know.'

'Can I speak to Roshni, Dr Awasthi?'

She handed the phone over to Roshni. 'I am sorry, darling,' said Atul, 'I'm caught up in something I couldn't avoid...I am on my way. Congratulations. I am so happy for us...' he trailed off, his voice still somewhat preoccupied.

Roshni's reaction was immediate, 'Atul, today is a Sunday and you are not a fireman! What am I to make of this?' She was very angry but didn't really have enough energy to yell at him, also she had a lovely little baby now; someone that was her own to love, and so, Atul got away.

'I'll be there,' Atul was busy promising on the other end of the line, 'Congratulations, baby, just give me a while.'

Back on the TTL premises, Salman had moved the body out for disposal, neither Atul nor Prem knew where for now, but they would soon. The helpers who came with the truck stayed back after loading the body. They were proficient in destroying evidence. Now, they set to cleaning the stained floors, fingerprints, weapons, and even cleaned up the CCTV and other electronic surveillance footage, then looked for any other evidence that needed to be dealt with. They worked with clinical efficiency and were done in thirty minutes flat. The place looked like a virgin's honeypot all over again.

Atul rushed to the hospital. Enveloped in white cotton, lighter than air, he saw two splendid eyes, a nose as sharp as his; frothy tongue twisting those tiny lips, moistening them on the way in and out, he saw his life shining in his arms. He needed a bit of tuition before he could hold his bundle of joy. He looked for signs of anything amiss, but couldn't find any. She was too little to let them out.

Vigilantly handing the baby back to the nurse, he clasped Roshni, 'I am so happy for us, sweetheart.' Then he thanked Babulal for his presence of mind, and fishing through his pockets, handed over as many notes as he found to Babulal as reward.

Chapter 12

Though Atul felt badly about Prashant's ending up as collateral damage, he had convinced himself that it was an accident, maybe a necessary accident. He never really found the time to repent or let the guilt consume him, though the incident did agonize him immensely for a while—his mind lingered on the happenings of the day, but he could not afford to grieve for long.

In time, it was business as usual. He never enquired as to how they had disposed off the body, or what happened to the daughter. Atul needed to forget everything about 'the accident' as quickly as possible. Shalikram's unique brand of poison and his dirty wealth had penetrated deep into TTL, and any retreat seemed far from possible.

A distressed Rakesh had a heated argument with Atul and Anil soon after the murder. He felt personally responsible, and for the first time regretted—utterly and bitterly—being a part of TTL. He was completely against what all was going on, he wanted to stall the poison from making further inroads into TTL's veins and arteries; to find an antidote, if possible, or to simply walk away from everything. Though all or any of that seemed like a distant possibility to him.

Finally, he took it upon himself to contain the poison and decided to begin by visiting the pesticides factory. He had never been able to fathom why Shalikram would want to dump a worthless pesticides factory on TTL. The story of the useless brother-in-law's mismanagement had never quite rung true with him.

So he quietly flew to Lucknow and from there went on by road towards the southwest of Etawah district, down state highway 92, before taking a detour and leaving the highway on the left, after crossing the Yamuna. Driving a further six kilometres, picturesque rice fields lining either side of the single lane road, with the Yamuna on the far side, Rakesh reached the village of Mahua. Scarcely populated, this was the village where the factory was located.

Rakesh told the driver to stop as soon as he spotted a small roadside eatery. It was depleted but still in business. There, he asked for directions to Bharat Pesticides. A dark man, looking like the twig of a tree covered in thin skin, gazed the luxury sedan and pointed the way. It seemed pretty close, he even pointed out the shed.

About 300 metres of muddy pathway connected to the single lane road that led to the factory, with nothing lying beyond it, as far as the eye could see, other than a shed, roughly 10,000 square feet in size, with hardly any civilization around. A few electrical cables and a telephone cable travelled over the twelve-foot high wall into the compound. He couldn't see clearly but there seemed to be two thatch-roofed structures inside—a large unit adjoining a smaller one, resembling a garage or an outhouse, with two large chimneys smoking out some hazy chemical waste.

Getting out of the car, he gazed at the signage. A mandatory board on the side of the security gate read 'Bharat Pesticides' and in brackets below was written '100% Subsidiary of Transmech Telecommunications Limited'. It also mentioned TTL's address as its Registered Office.

A tall, beefy security guard in a sleeveless vest and dhoti, sporting a thick handlebar moustache and brandishing a double-barrelled gun, emerged from a smaller gate within the large metal gate and stood patiently, waiting to hear what the unannounced visitors wanted.

'I am Rakesh Mohanan, director of TTL. I am here to meet Bacchu,' he said to the guard, handing over his business card as if to confirm his identity. The guard took the card with one hand, settling the gun on his shoulder with the other; it almost looked like a part of his uniform. By the manner he held on to it, he must have been sleeping with it in his bed, thought Rakesh. In one word, the guard was intimidating.

A frail teen, smoking a bidi, observed the proceedings from the security cabin window. While the guard refused to admit Rakesh, he muttered something in Bhojpuri. The young boy, about fourteen, sprinted out of sight having received instructions. The guard continued to keep a tight vigil.

Rakesh was by now riled and frightened, but all this only bolstered his doubts about the place. In a while, a stupefied Bacchu came out hurriedly and loped towards Rakesh, 'Sir, sir, welcome. You should have called, I would have come to pick you up. Why did you take the trouble to come so far?' The gate quickly opened, allowing the car in.

'No, no! It is absolutely okay, Bacchu. We are looking for some land for one of our ancillary units. I realized we were nearby and I had some time on hand, I thought I'd pay a visit on the way back to the airport,' said Rakesh glibly, even as he took note of the huge black barrels of chemicals lined along the compound wall as they walked into the shed.

Bacchu was a short quirky fellow, restless like a squirrel; he couldn't hold himself steady even for a second as they walked on.

A bunch of weird looking guys sat smoking chillums, they looked like goons and they were that. Bacchu's cabin was grungy and full of litter. Worn out furniture and peeling walls, even the cement within the putty now seemed to be coming off, one could see the coarse aggregate falling off at places.

The place reeked with the pungent odour of chemicals. A few empty glasses lay scattered with dried stains of whatever drink remained in them. Bacchu asked one of his guys to arrange tea for all the guests, and Rakesh quickly said, 'Can we take a quick look around? Need to rush to the airport as well.'

Replying in his Bhojpuri-English accent, Bacchu replied, 'What is the haste, sir? Tell me your flight number, I will call the airport, it will wait.' He sounded so convincing, anybody would have fallen for it. Rakesh did not.

'They are washing up the workshop, enjoy the tea and I will escort you around,' Bacchu continued. But he was twitchy, repetitively glancing through the cabin glass, as he sipped the tea and kept the guests engaged. It bought him the five minutes he needed, he needed to hide a few things. He hadn't been expecting a high profile guest.

Nevertheless, as soon as it could be safely managed, Bacchu took him around. Rakesh saw a seemingly fully-equipped pesticide factory with machinery for synthesizing and formulating the chemicals and the agents to dilute them to be used as pesticides. As a chemical engineer, Rakesh knew it had to have a test laboratory too. He did not find any around.

'How is it that there is no laboratory for examination?' he asked.

Bacchu, laughing at the question, replied, 'You are joking, sir. Here, people buy what we sell; testing can't produce mangoes on apple trees, they will still yield apples.'

An unimpressed Rakesh let him be for now. As they moved around the backyard, his eyes fell on a pick-up truck with a Mumbai registration plate. He had never set eyes on the truck that had removed Prashant's body, but he had a feeling this was the same truck.

'This is where we carton the pesticides in batches before they are despatched in pick-up vans,' Bacchu concluded, as he ran Rakesh through the final phases of the process.

Rakesh's eye had been looking for clues right from the gate, and he did find quite a few. He had noted how the exhausts had something weird about them. They obviously connected all the ovens and cooking trays, but a branch also went into the small garage at the rear. There must be something there. He had seen canisters of chlorine, hydrogen peroxide and a few other chemicals that had no business in the pesticide manufacturing process.

The factory had atomizers installed—high-tech industrial air-cleaning equipment meant for very advanced facilities; this was far from that. The Mumbai pick-up truck also bothered him. The whole factory had virtually stopped working, and the workmen gawked at the three gentlemen as if they were aliens from another planet.

'You won't show the other unit? What do you manufacture there?' Rakesh asked Bacchu, pointing to the rear shed.

'Oh, that,' Bacchu said dismissively, 'it is just a storage area where we stock finished goods, there is nothing to see there,' and turned to walk back to his cabin.

'No! Let's have a look, I insist!' said Rakesh firmly. Bacchu sighed and gestured toward his cabin, he wanted to tell his high-flying visitor a few things. Rakesh followed him, as did Bachhu's little entourage.

Having made him comfortable, Bachhu spoke, 'You should not have come, sir. You know politics, oratory skills don't always work, sometimes we use that garage to lock up unruly elements when we need to explain a few things. I don't want you to see it, and there is nothing there—you can take my word for it.'

A horrified Rakesh listened impassively, but knew something was very wrong. Bacchu was still trying to hoodwink him, he knew that too. He considered walking out of the place, but he already knew too much. Bacchu knew he knew too much too.

'Can we just have one look inside and I will be gone.'

'Okay, let's go,' said Bacchu, and he and Rakesh walked out, while Bacchu motioned to the entourage to stay put.

The front was like a typical garage with six wooden doors

hinged to one another; one could open one or all six together, depending upon how much space was needed for the movement of goods or vehicles. Bacchu opened one door just enough for the two to enter.

Inside, Rakesh saw a dingy room with tattered clothes and spent canisters of chlorine and hydrogen peroxide stashed in a corner. The place had a pungent stink—piss, puke, body odour, chlorine, even with the atomizer trying to put in fresh air and take the stench out. The exhaust pipe leading to the chimney passed right through the garage into the ground. There was a basement. Rakesh looked at the exhaust leading down. Bacchu knew what he was looking at. He stood exposed.

'What is down here?' he asked.

'There is an oven below. We dispose the bodies we bring in here, or the people we kill in this room. That is our business, we charge for the exterminations,' said Bacchu in flat, stone-cold tones. Rakesh was flabbergasted, speechless. This was way worse than anything he had imagined.

'I suggest you keep this to yourself. You are more culpable than I am. I am the manager but you are the owner. I am sure you know that,' said Bacchu quietly, now dropping all pretence of servility.

'Did you bring Prashant Nagarkar in here?' Rakesh asked.

'Prashant who?' a confused Bacchu asked.

'The one who was brought here in that pick-up parked up there,' Rakesh replied.

'Oh, that, Salman's consignment. How would I know his name was Prashant? He was brought in here last week; we did the job in five minutes. He didn't make a sound,' Bacchu replied.

Rakesh had somehow always known that the body was headed for the factory Shalikram had sold to them at Etawah. He had actually connected the dots even before getting here.

He walked out of the place, a little shaky at first, before sprinting to his car and telling the driver to get a move on. The car had gone only about 200 metres before Rakesh had to ask the driver to stop. He got out and puked. The stink, which now reminded him only of blood, clogged his mind and body. The driver helped him pull himself together and put him back into the car and headed out of the graveyard that was Bharat Pesticides.

Thoughts seared his conscience without a pause. He called Anil, 'Where are you?'

'I'm in office, what's the matter?' Anil asked.

'I will land around 10 p.m., meet me at the airport, don't bring a driver,' he said brusquely.

'Not a problem. Is all well, Rakesh?' Anil asked cautiously.

'We will talk, but the time has come,' he said, and disconnected the call.

On the flight home, he wrote out his resignation from all positions with the company. He kept away from any reasoning and wrote a one-line email citing ill-health and put it in his outbox. He could live with financial irregularities, but this had gone too far.

After landing, he got into the SUV with Anil and drove out of the airport, composing his thoughts for a while, as a restless Anil waited for him to say something. And then he finally spoke, 'I have resigned from TTL.'

Anil brought the SUV to a screeching halt, and turned to look at him in complete astonishment. Then he turned on the hazard lights and drove a little distance to park the SUV out of harm's way on a sidewalk. Then, he again turned to Rakesh, who began narrating all that he knew and all that had happened.

There was no time to break the conversation. Anil wanted to hear it all and now.

'But how will your resignation benefit matters, Rakesh? Whom do you think you will punish by putting in your papers? Atul never did any of this for himself. He conferred with us at each step and we approved every move he made. It is too late to think about that now, and Bacchu is right, we are all equally culpable.'

There was a moment of silence as he paused. Then he spoke again as another thought struck him, 'Rakesh, if you are a victim, then Atul, Prem, Qazi and me are equal victims, Atul probably more than any of us. Remember, he implements the dirty work, out of compulsion for the choices we jointly made, and we can't even bear the stench of it? How does this make sense?' he asked passionately.

'If anything needs to be rectified,' he continued forcefully, 'it must be done, and jointly. We cannot empty a sack of shit on Atul and walk away. We just cannot.'

He looked at Rakesh in the eye and continued, 'Atul and I go back a long way, longer than any of you. I can see he is pained, you think he likes to deal with filth like Shalikram? He does not even let us see his pain. Deep inside, I know he wants it clean again.'

Rakesh appeared deep in thought as he considered what Anil said. Then, Anil spoke again, 'We have come too far. We cannot jump off this train without killing ourselves, we cannot slow down, and we have already deactivated the brakes to gain more speed. I remember your words at the anniversary party. "What good is speed without the ability to brake?" They seem like a gospel today. Yet, we cannot leave Atul alone. Can we?'

Anil had brought home a lot of truths to Rakesh, who was now emotional but mellow and calm as he replied, 'The path ahead will take us further down, it is an abyss. We all know where this road will lead, we cannot raise money, we cannot do an IPO, so there is only one source left for raising that kind of money.'

He turned to Anil, 'Why do you think the banks didn't lend and we resorted to these dirty means of funding? Because the leverage is too high, their money is at risk. And we do the same thing from the back door! Anil, we are way smarter than our bankers. We bloody well know what they say is right, and yet, we do the same thing, what happens if we actually don't pull it off?'

As Anil stayed quiet, Rakesh carried through with his argument, 'The bankers will auction our homes to get their money back, these politicians will auction our wives and daughters to get their back.'

Drawing his argument to a close, he said, 'I don't see any sense, we must retreat. Nothing is lost; we withdraw from all the circles, pay Shalikram back, take a 2,000 crore hit and move on. Either it's that, or I am out. No ambition that feeds on blood can be worthy. This is business, not war.'

Anil lost patience, 'Snap out of it, Rakesh! Think it through in your head. We signed up for it, severally and jointly. You and I both know neither of us have an option. You want to have this discussion, let's have it. But all of us, if we have to, we got into this together, we get out together, let all of us resign from the company, or simply sell it or do whatever, there are numerous ways really, but running away is not one of them. I'll drop you home, Atul will be back in a couple of days; let's sit down and think this through and don't do anything stupid, worse still, don't do anything that arouses suspicion,' and Anil dropped off Rakesh and drove home too.

Chapter 13

Atul had crucial engagements in Delhi associated with implementing the licences. Qazi accompanied him.

He had also begun thinking about Aarti far too often and was well towards being infatuated with her. Memories of the evening they had spent together continued to bring a smile to his face, just as though he were a college kid. Being a taskmaster and a prudent administrator was just one side of him. There was a complete other romantic side to him that had too long lain almost dormant, and which now happened to desire a lot out of him.

He messaged Aarti that morning, 'When are you back? I am back in Delhi.'

She didn't reply the whole day, but late in the evening, when he was heading back to the hotel with Qazi, his cell buzzed, it read, 'Tomorrow evening, will you still be there?' Atul was scheduled to leave the next day. He replied, 'If you are having another dinner with me, yes ☺.'

He did not mince words. It was not his style. He also planned on speaking with Qazi about her. There was no reply from her after he made the offer. It did bother him, but not too much yet.

When Qazi invited Atul to his room to have dinner, as expected, Atul replied, 'Why don't you come to my room for a change, we can order some food, maybe have a couple of drinks as well.'

'Fine, Atul, I'll join you in a while,' he said.

About half-an-hour later, the bell to his suite buzzed and Atul opened the door to welcome Qazi in. They sat in the suite's elegant drawing-room and chatted. Qazi enquired about Roshni and the baby, adding, 'I must come to visit them, have you thought of a name yet?'

Atul smiled, 'She was discharged yesterday. The baby is doing fine, had a fever, but I guess that is normal and she's now okay.'

'Haven't thought of any name yet?'

'I have left that to Roshni, she was thinking of calling her Ananya.'

'It's a nice name,' Qazi nodded. 'And how are things with Roshni? Newborns bring a lot of joy and responsibility with them, they renew the bonds between a man and woman, and its God's way of showing us the magic again, the magic that vanishes in relationships with time.'

'Qazi sahib,' said Atul, 'it's been eleven years now, I have seen enough highs and lows. I never understood a few things, but I reasoned with myself and felt content when my mind questioned me about what I was doing in the relationship.'

The mood in the room was mellow and Atul spoke on philosophically, 'In time, I trained my mind to stop the questions and stopped my conscience from giving answers too; with the questions killed, no answers were necessary. And soon, I forgot there had been any questions at all.'

He took a deep breath and continued, 'I've been trying to fulfil that missing sense of purpose elsewhere—at work, among friends, doing things that ensure I will have a peaceful life. So much so that I believed that living that way was the only way to live. Indeed, a time came when I forgot there was any other way...'

Qazi heard his pain, trying to understand what he was saying. As Atul continued, Qazi chose not to interrupt. 'The love was long lost, Qazi sahib, I am only serving my responsibility now. I am concerned for her, I care for her, but however hard I think, I do not see love for her. Not any more.' Atul sipped his whiskey as he spoke, full of sorrow, a sorrow he did not have any answers for, but in his heart, burning to find answers. He was beginning to find them in Aarti, but wanted someone to second it. He was hoping his friend would do that for him.

'Qazi sahib, I feel that now I have sacrificed enough. I must live for what I seek, I cannot be doing this to myself, I have only one life, I want to live it too.'

'Are you in love, Atul?' Qazi asked Atul bluntly, without a doubt in his mind.

'Is it a crime to be in love?' Atul asked right back.

Qazi paused as though gathering his thoughts before addressing Atul. Then he spoke, choosing his words carefully, 'You know best what's on your mind, Atul,' he began. 'Either you can continue on your quest to mend things with Roshni, and by that I mean either changing her, or conditioning your mind, as you say. The path is difficult but possible all the same.'

He sighed and continued, 'You also have the discretion to denounce her and seek your path all over again. That is surely an option. I promise you it won't be a bed of roses either.'

He continued, 'All suffering is a consequence of a constant quest. A quest to follow a mirage, the mirage that is the creation of our mind, the illusion of happiness, the illusion of being loved. That is what it is. Love itself is an illusion. We misuse the word so much we forget what it means. It means nothing, because it simply does not exist. It is the destiny of the mind to seek. When it does not discover what it seeks, it gives birth to hopelessness. And given our undying spirit, from that hopelessness rises hope itself. This hope takes us to the quest all over again, churning us in an endless cycle of suffering. This cycle is called life. Suffer you will, one way or the other...' and he looked up at Atul with kind eyes filled with a detached wisdom.

He knew what Atul wanted, but he wanted to really show him the mirror, a mirror he already had within him but refused to use, frightened that he might have to concede and confront a truth he already knew.

Atul realized Qazi wasn't helping him get to where he wanted to go with this. His heart had already decided for his intellect, he just wanted someone to reason like him and come to the same conclusion. The atmosphere remained mellow and amicable—a comfort born of trust and long association. They finished their meal still mulling over options, and then Atul saw him off.

Just as Atul was getting ready to retire, his phone buzzed again. He smiled as he read 'OK'.

Two letters on his phone and his mind shut all questions down. He simply surrendered to renewed hope, his being fluttering like a butterfly with a million colourful thoughts. He had fallen for Aarti and the mere thought of her elated him. His life was beautiful all over again.

Atul spent the next day in a heightened state of exhilaration and anticipation, even some anxiety—after all, his passions were only one side of the story, and there was a whole other side he did not know.

He went down and spoke with the chef, and selected a menu featuring opulent Mughlai cuisine and Dom Perignon champagne after much deliberation. Seeing Atul's interest, the chef knew this had to be special.

Then, he called Aarti in the afternoon to find out her schedule, happy to just hear her voice. 'I am stuck, Atul,' she said, 'my flight is delayed, I don't know when it will take off, but I should be there before 8.'

Atul was so fervid, he thought of getting a chartered flight to have her airlifted from Shimla. He didn't do that, of course; instead, he prayed things wouldn't go downhill from here. 'I'll pick you up at the airport,' he said, 'just message me the flight details and I'll be there. I've made the reservations already.'

'Thanks, Atul, but that won't be necessary, just tell me the place and I'll take a taxi from the airport. I don't want to drag you out, you must be busy too,' said Aarti.

'It'll be my pleasure, let me do this,' countered Atul.

The flight arrived. Atul spotted a casually dressed Aarti and escorted her to the chauffeur-driven SUV, held the door open for her and then climbed in himself.

'Is it okay if I change before we proceed?' she asked, 'Where are we going for dinner?

'It's the same place. Taj Mansingh. I believe you are staying there again,' replied Atul.

'Well, yes, so that is good, I can freshen up and join you,' said Aarti.

They soon reached the hotel. Atul found it difficult to hold his enthusiasm in but Aarti showed no emotion, at least not enough for Atul to make any guesses. He was not sure if Aarti saw his excitement, but he had let out enough to tell her that he was entranced by her.

Aarti met Atul in the lobby. She looked like a princess in a flawless white, sleeveless gown, showing her shoulders and cleavage, nothing sleazy, but enough to drive Atul crazy. Clasping a studded clutch, she walked with style and an attitude that didn't care about anything. Atul had changed into a suit and bow tie, in hopes of impressing her. They quietly took the elevator to the rooftop restaurant, where the chef was waiting to welcome them.

In a far corner of the restaurant, a bonfire heated up the cool evening. The shamiana was made from glossy white fabric with purple shimmers, and the antique lighting was just bright enough to reveal the texture of the fabric. The only other light came from the candle on the table, bathing their faces with its warm glow.

'Welcome, sir, welcome, ma'am,' said the chef, escorting the couple to their table and pushing the chair back for Aarti to take her seat.

'Oh my god, Atul! What is this? This isn't a dinner for sure. You are spoiling me, I am not used to this!' exclaimed Aarti, gazing at the ensemble of performers playing light classical music waiting for them to arrive. Atul had already given a choice of requests, a list long enough to last for hours.

'Aarti, I keep the best for my friends, and I can assure you I don't have many. Welcome to my world. You are looking absolutely stunning tonight.'

The starters were brought in dishes with a designer engraving on it that read '*To Atul and Aarti*'. Was this the chef's addition? Whatever, it didn't matter to Atul, it just made the evening even more special.

Aarti was feeling embarrassingly exalted. They conversed about work, Roshni, life, friendship, love, and just about every subject they could touch upon. He even told her all about Shalikram, the laundry, and Prashant's murder, which he explained away as an accidental death. To Atul's surprise, Aarti was practical and did not make much about it. A lot of things needed to be done at work, this was one of them, she thought.

While the music still played with Ghulam Ali and Jagjit Singh compositions in the background, Aarti broke the momentum and killed the excitement. 'Am I leading you on, Atul?' she asked.

'What are you talking about?' he asked warily.

'We cannot have this, if you are feeling anything for me, it is wrong,' she said softly to Atul.

'What do you mean?' he asked again.

'You know what I am talking about, there cannot be anything between us. I like you. You are a thorough gentleman and the ideal person that I could dream of. But you are only like that, you cannot *be* that. That is what I am saying. Whatever happened that evening really couldn't mean anything, could it? I consider you a friend and we should leave it at that.' It was evident that Aarti wanted to set emotions and expectations right before it was too late.

'And why not? Aarti, what's wrong with it?' said Atul, an almost hollow feeling in his heart, which skipped a beat before preparing itself for a long battle.

'You really want me to spell it out? You have baggage I cannot deal with. I am a simple girl with simple dreams. I am tolerant, but your baggage is not something I can deal with. You are married, how can we expect to get anywhere? I feel absolutely privileged about the way you feel for me. But unfortunately, that is where it must stop. We cannot take it further, there can never be a future between us.'

Desperate to change his mind, Aarti had spoken with absolute clarity. She realized that the evening before this had planted the seeds, but she'd never felt that way about him. She did not have the privilege; he was a married man and a father now.

But Atul was having none of it. 'Well, Aarti,' he said, 'let me tell you this. What you feel about me does not change what I feel about you. I love you. I can do nothing to change that. I understand what you say, I am not a fool. I won't ask anything from you. Unless you feel the same, we will remain friends. Within two evenings, I have been able to confide in you and that's something that rarely happens with me. Let's move on with that, we will leave this for another day. I guess I'll eventually accept that my feelings are only an infatuation; I'll deal with it at my end.'

A dejected Atul at least managed to successfully bargain for time to show how much he loved her and to eventually get her to do the same. Aarti did not see anything wrong; she empathized with him as an honourable man with a heart of gold. She even wished he did not have a past to deal with. Did she have feelings for him too? Maybe, but she couldn't afford them, at least not today.

The evening ended in gloom. The only high Atul carried back to bed that night was hope. And hope it was.

Sitaro ko apna banane ke liye,
Chiraago ki roshni dhundhu.
Raah tak raha hun main,
Rahon mein sitaro ki parchayi dhundhu.

Teri aagosh mein jeevan ka matlab dhundhu,
Teri haathon mein apni kismet dhundhu,
Jaanta hun main, hum paraaye hain lekin?
Teri aakhon mein apni tasveer dhundhu.

Teri har baatmein main ek aas dhundhu,
Mere khaabon mein teri hakikat dhundhu.
Tere saayein mein roone ka sahaas dhundhu,
Tere bahon mein jeene ka ek bahaana dhundhu.

Tanhayion mein mehifilon kein roshani dhundhu,
Andhero mein tere dil ka raasta dhundhu.
Manzil saamne nazar aa rahi hain magar?
Vahaan tak pahuchne ka koi fasaana dhundhu.

To make my own the stars,
I search for the radiance of the lanterns.
I keep gazing over the avenue,
In search of silhouettes of the stars in the pathways.

Search for the meaning of life in your embrace.
Search for my karma in your hands,
I know I am an outsider but
Search for my likeness in your eyes.

Search for hope in all you say,
Search for your truth in dreams.

Search for sentiments like weeping in your shadow,
Search in your arms a reason to be alive.

Search in seclusions the radiance of the caucuses,
Search in the darkness the avenue to your heart.
The destination can be seen right ahead but
Search some a romantic fable for to get there.

Back home, Anil had already requested Atul for a meeting. He did not give details, but they never gave any details when it came to situations like these. They decided to meet later that evening, but not before the meeting with Prem and Aarti. Atul had already discussed the agenda for that one with Aarti over the dinner.

When Aarti and Prem walked into Atul's cabin first thing on Monday morning, he kept his emotions at bay, and showed absolute professionalism in dealing with her in office.

They quickly got down to business. 'Prem, we need to become more careful with the laundry activities, we need to bolster everything. It needs an iron hand. Prashant's absence has created a vacuum which needs to be filled,' he said to Prem.

Considering Atul had asked him to call Aarti to this meeting, Prem assumed that Atul would hand over charge to her; he no longer trusted Prem to make that decision. Prem accepted that, because he had made a blunder—he had no excuse to defend his actions. And that's exactly what happened. 'Aarti will take charge of the laundry,' said Atul. 'She will report to me on this. She will continue to report to you on her role in the Vision 2015 programme. What do you think, Prem?' he asked, turning to him.

'Absolutely,' replied Prem, somewhat sarcastically, 'I presume you have already spoken to Aarti about this?'

'Yes, Prem, I did speak to Aarti,' replied Atul blandly. 'I am guessing she is okay as well. What do you say, Aarti?'

'I need to understand the activities there a bit, but I should be fine,' she replied.

'Yes, of course,' said Atul, 'I'll personally take care of that. In fact, I need to review the processes as well. Let's do it post-lunch tomorrow,' and he concluded the meeting.

Come 7 p.m., they all met in the War Room, including Qazi. Rakesh, still horrified about Etawah, had held back his resignation on Anil's advice, and was present as well.

Anil opened the meeting, 'We have a situation. There have been some developments which have disturbed Rakesh and me. We must discuss these and reconsider our options.'

He then looked at Rakesh so he could take the meeting ahead. Rakesh narrated the terrifying scenes he had seen in as much detail as he could. He did not mention his intention to resign at this point. There was pin drop silence, everybody was shocked, at a loss for words—it was all just so unbelievable.

Atul's rage at Shalikram caused his heart to race with anger. Each time, the man had caught him off guard and managed to get the better of him. This time, he had no intentions of letting Shalikram off the hook. But Prem thought otherwise. They were neck deep in this shit and would have to play ball, at least until a better alternative came up. Any kind of exit was just too risky.

Rakesh now voiced his intention of resigning, unless TTL agreed to pay back Shalikram and face the consequences, whatever they might be. Anil was of the opinion that they find a suitable buyer to sell off the company and exit it. The money from the sale could be used to pay off Shalikram. He, however, maintained that none of them should take any decision independent of the others.

Atul looked at the legal head, 'What do you have to say, Qazi sahib. Today, your opinion matters more than ever.'

Qazi looked round the table and finally broke his silence. 'Surrendering to the authorities and confronting Shalikram by ending the partnership are essentially the same thing. In the first case, we hand over evidence on a platter to convict us. In the second scenario, let's say we confront him, he will still bend every rule and turn the same authorities against us. There will be only one loser in either situation.'

He paused and looked at each of them, as though to drive home his point. 'We must still fight him; the authorities will hunt us like hungry dogs. We are innocent until proven guilty, and that may take ages. As a lawyer, I can assure you we still have a fighting chance.'

Next, Atul spoke up, grimly and with absolute authority. 'Prashant Nagarkar was an accident. Shalikram will buy back the factory; I will leave him with no option. We will also return his money. I am already working on that, it will be political money, but not blood money. I will teach the scoundrel a lesson. If we agree unanimously, we continue as I say, else we surrender and turn approvers against the minister.' He was taking a huge gamble by making this proposal.

Atul offered no middle path, it was either kill or get killed. He had no intention of getting killed, and he banked on the fact that nobody else in the room harboured any such desire either.

Rakesh was disturbed at the turn of events, but he would come around soon. Atul knew how to bring him around. Eventually, everyone, Rakesh included, agreed with Atul. With that, the meeting was closed, and Atul had another job at hand.

Qazi wondered which way life was turning for these boys who were so close to his heart. He remembered a few lines from one of his own compositions.

Nikalta hain ghar se sharafat ke irade se,
Phir har roz, har pal, laashon ke malbon se guzarta kyun haeh?

Aaj ka insaan lagta haeh kal ka khuda ban jayega,
Varna gaibh haeh, to kal uska sauda aaj karta kyun haeh?

Aashiyane ki hawa humko bhi raas aayi magar?
Uske yeh pahredaar phir itne pareshan kyun haeh?

Gazab yahan ka khuda bhi haeh, agar farishta haeh,
To har roz, har pal, kuch na kuch maangta kyun haeh?

From out the homestead you emerge with an intent of civility,
Then why each day, each moment, do you pass by the debris of
corpses?

Today's man it seems will become tomorrow's God,
Else if it knows not the concealed, why does he barter
tomorrow's world today?

The ambience of the hearth to me also has become agreeable
Then why are these its sentinels so perturbed?

Outrageous! There is a God of this place, if it is an angel,
Then why each day, each moment, it begs for something or the
other?

Chapter 14

After the meeting, Atul called Mir. 'Mir sahib, I am sure you know about Rakesh's visit to Bharat Pesticides.'

'Yes,' replied Mir.

'Then I presume you already knew about what happens there?' Atul asked.

'I'm bound by duty, Atul,' responded Mir apologetically.

Atul responded in no uncertain terms. 'I am sure, Mir sahib. I don't hold you absolutely responsible, but your minister broke his contract. Trust is the biggest thing in a partnership; you break the trust, and you break the partnership, that's my rule. And I trusted you, can I do that still?'

'You can, Atul. I have the highest regard for you. It will remain that way.'

Atul continued with his mission once he got that affirmation. 'Mir sahib, the partnership with Shalikram is over. You may tell him as well, and don't forget to give him the exact reasons. His money will follow. I have been getting overtures from the big man Shravan Poojari, but want to reach him through known sources. Can you do that for me?'

Mir thought for a long while. Atul had to confirm the call was active before Mir replied, 'I don't know, I never thought he would be interested. Anyway, since he is, let me see what I can do. Can you give me a day or two?'

'Of course, sir, but you know it's a priority.'

'Okay then,' replied Mir, ending the call.

These days, Roshni was busy with the baby and normally did

not bother Atul too much. But she was in a belligerent mood today. 'What held you back the other day when I was taken to the hospital?' she demanded over dinner.

'I told you there was an accident at the office. I needed to attend to it.'

'What accident? Since when did murders become accidents?' she asked boldly.

Atul looked at her, stunned. Where was she getting her information from? This one couldn't have come from Jyoti. 'This is absolute bullshit, Roshni,' he muttered.

'It is not. What have you been doing these days that justifies such ghastly acts?' she wanted to know. 'Atul, you told me you do not love me, I was okay. You ignored me, I was okay. You acted as though you detested me and I was still okay. Even if I were not okay with it, I saw no choice. But how much should be okay? Please tell me, Atul?'

'Roshni, I do not intend to discuss this,' he said bluntly. 'This is business and does not concern you. Everything else you say, we have had a million discussions till date. And I can have a million more until we find a solution, one way or the other.' Then he tightened the screws further, 'I am perfectly fine if you want to spend a few days with your father. It may give you some time to think through all of this. I refuse to have a relationship of compromise any more. I suggest you must not too,' and he stormed out of the dining-room, leaving his dinner unfinished. Roshni rushed after him into the bedroom.

'Fine, if you think this is the way forward, I am good with it, it's over.' She opened her cupboard and started throwing her clothes on to the bed in a heap. Then, she pulled out a few bags and began shoving the clothes and her other belongings in anyhow. She called Babulal and told him to pack all of the baby's belongings as well. That done, she was out of there in a flash. Atul did not stop her. Not once. This angered Roshni even more. Atul had another sleepless night, but this time because he was so relieved.

He missed office the next morning, but reached in time to meet Aarti after lunch to discuss her new role in the laundry operations. The corporate floor of TTL was spread across forty-thousand square feet with eight spacious cabins. Each cabin had a separate dining-room, an anteroom with a sofa-bed, a personal bar and a discussion room.

There were two cabins without the ancillary rooms for the nominated directors, but seldom used. There was also a boardroom for sixty people, and a conference room. There were several waiting lounges near the reception for the VIP visitors.

A vertical waterbody with a soft waterfall made a soothing sound, spreading serenity around. It also provided a fitting backdrop for the boat-shaped reception table in front of it. The floors were covered with white Satvario marble; the walls and ceilings were a combination of walnut wood and white paint. All the enclosed spaces were carpeted and had clear glass partitions overlooking the work areas.

Plush furniture came from the best Italian brands. The walls shone with masterpieces by Husain and Raza, among others. There were open workstations accommodating all the secretarial staff, personal executives, security personnel, and some other personnel handling confidential matters and MIS reports for the promoters.

The laundry had recently been moved on to the same floor, but used a different entry. This was done to avoid unnecessary attention and, at the same time, allow access and control without having to make long trips.

The laundry team had no cabins, just large workstations and a small discussion room. Their office needed fingerprint access to get in or out. Other than the employees working in there, the co-founders were the only ones authorized. That was the case with the other parts of the corporate floor as well.

After Prashant's demise, three people now occupied the room. Shobha Rane generated the fake invoices by programming software glitches. Ramya Apte and Raman Babu managed the banking transactions, bounced off from servers across the world. That way, the authorities could not trace their origins. They handled the movement of huge cash from point to point. The company gave them privileges for their dedication and secrecy.

Now, Atul entered the room with Aarti, introducing her as a manager to the rest of the team. They were happy to see her and, after exchanging pleasantries, they explained their operational responsibilities thereafter. Atul and Aarti went back to his office.

'Okay, Aarti, will you have some coffee before we start?' Atul asked. It was evident to anyone who cared to see that he hadn't slept in the last two days.

'Sure,' she replied.

'Hello, Radha? Could you send up two coffees, one Americano and one latte, and no calls please,' and he disconnected.

'So, shall we start?' He kept his tone purely professional, ready to let her into the dynamics of how the laundry worked.

But Aarti was perceptive, 'Is everything okay, Atul?' she asked, looking him in the eye.

A surprised Atul didn't know what she saw in him to make that comment, how did she find out anything at all? 'Well, except that I miss my love, everything is fine,' he joked.

'Please stop fucking my brains, Atul,' she responded.

'Why should I fuck your brains, I can think of more interesting ways to do that,' he joked further.

Aarti was worried he hadn't slept because of her. The joke didn't go down well, although she wasn't wrong. Part of the reason he hadn't slept was because he was indeed thinking about her.

'Roshni left for her dad's, along with Ananya, last night. Fed up of me, I guess. I couldn't sleep after that thinking about the future,' said Atul, neatly skirting any mention of his suggestion that she leave.

'I am so sorry!' responded Aarti, taking the bait. 'You must take care. Don't be so hard on yourself, Atul.'

'I'm not sure it is so bad. Anyway, we have all the time in the world to talk about my broken relationship, let's get back to work for now,' Atul changed the topic; he didn't see the right spirit and approach in Aarti's summation of the situation.

They got down to business and he said, 'Aarti, I want you to listen carefully. Any questions, please note them down, try not to interrupt me.'

Aarti nodded.

'All the cash we raise needs to be channelized as money attained from legal sources. Bogus profit will attract real tax and hence is not a tenable method. Also, all this money is really a borrowing and eventually needs to be paid back. So we must be able to undo the whole process. Do you have any doubts on the necessity of what we do here?'

'Why are you giving me a lesson, Atul?' she demanded. 'I know all this, for God's sake, I am not a school kid.'

'That's great, but I needed to be sure you knew it,' he responded.

'There are two ways we do this.' Atul continued. 'the first is through offshore funding, where cash is sent out of the country through hawala brokers paid in Indian rupees here. In exchange, we get US dollars in a country of our choice,' said Atul.

Then, he went on to reveal confidential TTL information, 'We have four companies registered in the Cayman Islands. They go by the names Black Investments, Peter Pan Limited, Dynamic Foundries and Label Investments. Don't try to make anything of these names, they mean nothing. The US dollars are deposited in their bank accounts in the Cayman Islands. The laws there do not require us to make any disclosures on the sources of funds. They are tax havens. These four companies are what we call fourth-generation companies. With me so far?'

When she nodded, he went into further and more highly confidential details. 'Different companies with irrelevant names own these four companies, and these are the third-generation companies based in the Bahamas. They, in turn, are owned by another set of companies based in the Canary Islands. These are second-generation companies. It is a web of cross-holdings so complex you cannot untangle it easily.'

He paused for a sip of his coffee and picked up from where he'd left off. 'The companies in the Canary Islands are owned by a Swiss holding company. This is the only company with ownership links to any person who could be in flesh and blood. Those owners are fake too. They exist, but only on paper. I will give you access to the holding data, if required. This, of course, is step one of this maze,' he smiled, and Aarti nodded.

He continued, 'The cash in our bank accounts is moved as fixed deposits to One National Bank and Credit Deposit Group. As you are aware, these are two of the most reputed global banking groups, and through their investment arms have invested about Rs 1,000 crore in TTL. These are the FDI inflows with proper approvals and are 100 per cent legal. These companies haven't invested in TTL out of love but, in reality, our own fixed deposits guarantee these investments.'

Aarti looked a little confused, so he explained with an example, 'Let's say, some day, the laws change and the names are disclosed, we have arranged a web so complex, they will never get anywhere. And let's assume they do get to the Swiss company some day, they will never trace its owner because there isn't one. He is only a figment of imagination. This is how money from the politician travels around the world back into TTL as virgin money. Whenever we need to return the money, it will travel back the exact same route to come back as cash in India. All good? You with me so far?'

When Aarti nodded, Atul said, 'Now we'll move on to the second method, fictional deposits. You are aware that TTL runs a 50 rupee fixed billing scheme. It is pretty popular in the market, right? Actually, about 70 per cent subscribers to this scheme are fake. When we generate one fake subscriber, we generate a deposit of Rs 10,000. A cash receipt is made for this deposit and the cash deposited in the bank here. Also, a fictional income of Rs 50 per month is generated from this subscriber and shown as profit for the company. Now, whenever we need to return this money, we simply cancel the subscription and return the deposit in cash. It is perfectly legal to do this, except that the subscriber is fictional.'

Now Aarti began to see how the laundry really worked.

Atul continued, 'The laundry operates the software and the bank accounts. It arranges deposits across the globe and also a million fictional subscriber accounts in the database. Everything is cloud-based and software controlled. The data will vanish from the local servers at a single click, but will still remain on the offshore servers. The software is designed in a way that it leaves no traces or history. We do not have a single paper that can prove our crime. Shobha will run you through the software.' Aarti nodded. Now, Atul moved on to a deeper discussion of risk.

'Risk emerges at two levels. Suppose any of the eight people with the knowledge of these activities, now nine including you, pukes anything out, it will be only your word; there are no records to supplement it. The other way is an investigation of the subscriber accounts revealing they are bogus. But that can be certainly dealt with as a software glitch. In a country like India, we can drag it through the courts for a couple of centuries. And I guess that is it,' Atul said, concluding his presentation.

Aarti stared at Atul, spellbound and speechless.

'What? Say something,' said Atul, amused.

'What can I say? I have nothing to say. The whole thing seems more perfect than anything real.' Aarti replied. She had just witnessed a completely different side of Atul's intellect.

'Great,' said Atul, 'I guess we are good then. You can spend a few hours looking over the transactions. There are a lot of other things happening at the financing level as well. I will fill you in on those as they happen. I guess we can call it a day now. Let's have a drink before we head home,' and he walked up to the anteroom. They were friends now. She perched herself on the sofa, Atul helped himself to a Black Label and poured out champagne for her.

'So, what are you going to do about Roshni? Get her back, Atul,' Aarti said, sipping her drink.

'Aarti! You know what I feel about everything, you included. Then why would you say such a thing?' said Atul, sounding pained. 'I want you to think through everything I said to you. I am becoming vulnerable. I am trying hard to control my emotions around you, but it is not easy. I am not sure you even understand what I am saying.'

Aarti sat up at once, 'Actually, I think I do, but that is not the right thing for me to do. Not right now. I cannot ask you to break your family to make mine. That would be wrong and I could never pardon myself for that. We could never be happy after that.'

Moving closer to Aarti, Atul took her hand very much as he had on the first night at the lounge. Aarti did not withdraw it, nor encourage him to go further.

'Look, you are not responsible for the situation with my wife. How can you break what is already broken? I had foregone the joys of love. Servitude was the only thing that kept me going, but now I want the joy for myself. I am greedy for love and affection. I feel it for you; I must not let it die. You know what I am saying, right?' he said, gripping her hand firmly now.

'No, Atul, I don't,' said Aarti. 'You are still in a relationship; there cannot be anything between us. Even if we get there, you will have me in every way you can for a few days. What next? Where does it leave us after that? It doesn't work that way.'

A dejected Atul withdrew his hand. He didn't know how else to talk to her, but he did harbour strong feelings for her. He just didn't get the message. All Aarti was asking him was to legally end his marriage. Once that process was truly under way, she would be able to openly accept him; in fact, she already loved him more than he could, but could not say it in so many words. She didn't want him to dump Roshni just because she, Aarti, asked for it. She wanted it to come naturally and without her influencing that conclusion.

Chapter 15

The long-awaited board meeting to conclude the impasse on the public issue demanded by TTL's investors was today. Atul was worried for several reasons. He needed to pay Shalikram his 2,000 crore. And the story of Shravan Poojari he'd planted in Mir's mind was a farce. Shravan Poojari was the Union Finance Minister. Atul had met him a few times at conferences and government conclaves and learnt that he too parked his ill-gotten wealth with corporate groups. But, unlike Shalikram, he was a lawyer by profession and a shrewd statesman worthy of having as a partner.

Atul had a reason for lying. If Mir was not honest to Atul, he would run to Shalikram to tell him about it, and that would keep Shalikram from acting out of haste against TTL. Alternatively, Mir would get in touch with the power brokers in Delhi to get to Poojari for him.

He wanted the word out that TTL was soliciting funding. Even if Shravan Poojari refused, the brokers would get in touch with him with other options. He would never get a worthy deal if he started looking out himself. And if Poojari agreed, he would get a powerful partner, one who could silence Shalikram. But it was three days since he had spoken to Mir, and Mir had not yet called back.

The investor representatives had approved a 10 per cent stake-sale through an open offer. TTL was valued at Rs 9,600 crore and the investors would raise Rs 1,200 crore in cash from this offer. The meeting approved the IPO. TTL would be listed soon.

Atul knew if nothing else worked with regard to raising money, they might well have to offload about 40 per cent to raise Rs 5,000 crore in equity to fund TTL's Rs 17,500 crore expansion plan. This route posed several complications, but was a possibility nevertheless.

About a month later, Mir did call one morning.

'Good morning, Atul, I have some news for you. It took longer than I expected, the minister was busy. How are you placed next Tuesday, can you come to Delhi?'

'Sure, sir, but what are we looking at?' asked Atul.

'Well, I have arranged a meeting with Poojari for you. I will give you all the details later,' said Mir quickly. Obviously, he was not available for a longer chat.

'Thank you, Mir sahib, that is amazing news. I'll be there first thing Tuesday,' said Atul, and disconnected. He was just about to call Prem to give him the good news, when a hoard of people stormed the corporate floor. There were about a hundred of them, and they walked in and occupied every room and computer, and froze the staff in their seats. It looked like an army barging in. They were in plain clothes so he didn't know their identity, but uniformed policemen accompanied them almost one for one.

Before Atul could get a grip on things, two of them barged into his cabin too, and one of them pulled the keyboard away and seized his laptop. Another showed a Government identity card and said, 'K. Ranganathan, Deputy Director, Enforcement Directorate, Central Government. We have a warrant to search your premises. Please sit in your seat, do not move or touch anything.'

As soon as this introduction was done, Atul was asked to hand over his cellphone and his landline was also disconnected. He had no idea what was happening, he was taken aback, given no time even to think. His heart was racing in fear.

The only thought going through his mind was whether Shobha or Aarti or Prem or any of the others had got a chance to delete the data from the local servers or not. It was simple, they needed to press ALT+R and keep it pressed for five seconds and boom! Everything would vanish like a fart in the air.

He didn't get a chance to find out as the moment they got in, they pinned him down in his chair. They created so much panic; there was pandemonium all over. They flung files, books and documents around. They screamed at people, threatened them, froze them in their seats; took over all the computers and cellphones; they had already disconnected the central telephone and access control systems. A team also got into the security room to monitor the CCTV cameras.

They had obviously come in with immaculate planning. They knew every corner of the office and how every gadget worked. All the important rooms, everything. Even with all the contacts TTL had in the corridors of power, they hadn't been able to smell what was cooking behind the Enforcement Directorate (ED) walls. This was an ED raid, pure and simple. They dealt with serious financial crime, such as money laundering, forgery, corruption etc. TTL qualified for all of them.

Atul had no idea if Aarti had come in, or even Prem or Rakesh, or just anyone. There was no way to know. Soon, a squad of hackers took over the server room and started connecting drives to the servers to retrieve data. Ranganathan handed him a document of acceptance to conduct search and seizure of the premises saying, 'Mr Atul, please sign here.' Atul signed it as soon as it was presented to him.

Ranganathan, now scrolling through messages, contacts, recent calls and other information on Atul's phone said, 'You are a smart businessman, Mr Atul, but always remember the law is smarter than you; you can escape law for a while but never evade it.'

'I don't know what got you here. I don't know what you are talking about, this is a huge misunderstanding, there is nothing here that will interest you, and we are clean,' protested Atul.

'Well, you know what we are looking for, don't you? I must say you have a pretty impressive contact list,' replied Ranganathan.

'They are work contacts and a few friends,' Atul said.

'Wait for a while, we will talk about that too, we are not fools, we have all the evidence. If you have anything to say, you must say it now, you won't get a chance later,' said Ranganathan, as he continued sifting through documents lying around the office.

'I want my lawyer here,' Atul demanded.

'This is not the US and that is not your privilege. After we complete our investigation, you can have all the lawyers of the world here, but not until then,' Ranganathan replied, continuing to look around. He picked up a document; it related to TTL's investments in a British company.

'Can you explain this document?' he asked, extending it toward Atul.

Before Atul could reply, an officer came in and asked for Ranganathan's presence. He followed him and had a heated chat just outside Atul's cabin. Atul could not hear the conversation. Had they found the servers? There was nothing in the office that could worry Atul, except the information on the servers. As soon as Ranganathan returned, Atul asked permission to use the toilet. An officer escorted him. Atul decided to use the one near the visitors' area, just so he could get a full view of what was going on.

The scale of the raid overwhelmed him. Every room, every employee had an officer standing next to him or her, they seem to know exactly what they were doing. Prem was in his cabin, he was sure they had reached the laundry too, but he could not see that from where he was.

Atul was told that they had raided the residences of all the directors too. He saw Qazi talking to a few officers in the lobby. He was officially only a consultant to TTL, so they could not detain him.

Atul was kept under constant vigilance and offered lunch in his room. A few ED officers kept popping in to ask him a question or two about some document or other they had found somewhere. He replied to all their questions with composure. There was never a worry. He was still not sure what had happened to the servers, but his guess was that if they didn't come back with that information in six hours, they wouldn't have found anything on them.

Ranganathan came back to Atul's cabin toward the evening. 'Mr Atul, we have searched your office and seized tons of documents. That should give us enough evidence to ensure you do not see daylight for the rest of your life. Unless you cooperate with us and tell us everything you know, we will seize the office along with the belongings. We have already made some arrests and are interrogating those arrested as we speak.' It was a clear threat.

Atul had no experience of being raided and there was no way to verify Ranganathan's claims either. But something he just said assured Atul he was bluffing. Because there were no documents anywhere in the office that were worth even a penny to Ranganathan. Everything was online; he hadn't mentioned anything about the servers, he'd obviously found nothing.

So, Atul was able to respond with confidence, 'What do you want me to tell you about? I don't know what you are talking about, you and your people have asked me this a hundred times since morning. I will reply again. There is nothing I have to say which may interest you. And it is high time you allowed me to meet my lawyer, you are continuously threatening me and I do not take this lightly. There will be consequences, I hope you realize that.'

Qazi was finally allowed to meet Atul in person. An officer stayed on while they talked. Qazi had already met Prem, Rakesh and Anil earlier. Prem was being interrogated by several officers simultaneously in another room, so was Rakesh.

Qazi told Atul, 'Don't worry, everything is all right, it is all a big misunderstanding, they won't get to anything, it will soon be over.'

Atul wanted to confirm about the servers, but couldn't ask Qazi because he knew nothing about how the software worked.

Late in the night, Atul was allowed to meet the other promoters; they had released the pressure at least on their movement within the office. They were now preparing to take statements from all the directors under oath. They had made a seizure list of various files, including investment records, loan-processing documents, investments in subsidiary companies, foreign investments made by TTL, all the data from the servers, even some laptops, but not before TTL was allowed to take back-ups or photocopies of the same, so it didn't interfere with their day-to-day working.

Atul met Aarti too; she said that she had seen what was happening on the CCTV screens placed in the laundry, which monitored all the entrances including the main gate. She knew something was obviously wrong and had deleted the data before they could get to her. The investigative team was no wiser about the business handled by the laundry, despite frisking the employees and checking their computers. For their part, the laundry checked, but gave out nothing. Aarti was questioned, not about business, but about her relationship with Atul and had admitted to Atul being a friend. Atul was surprised, but he quickly gathered that the messages on his phone must have given some idea to Ranganathan.

In the early hours of the morning, Atul was interrogated again. Ranganathan took the statement personally under oath. He asked him personal details such as name, address, relationship with the company, role in the company and related sundry information. This was followed by some difficult questions, the toughest one relating to the investment in Bharat Pesticides.

'Please explain why you invested in Bharat Pesticides, and within months, the investment was sold at an almost negligible price back to its original owner Balchandra Yadav alias Bacchu.'

Atul's feet melted, could they have raided Etawah? But he quickly realized that couldn't be the case, he would be behind bars by now. He composed himself and replied, 'TTL was interested in diversifying into certain other businesses, and pesticides was one of them. Telecom Minister Shalikram Bahujan introduced us to the original owners at a conference in Delhi. We made the investment without a due diligence at our end. We soon realized it was too competitive. Protective government policies towards small-scale industries in the sector led us to lose interest in pursuing the business. So we booked it as a loss and wrote off our investment.'

Atul had taken his chances knowing that involving a minister would ensure that they would not go after him in case they found anything in the future. In fact, they would probably drop the whole thing. Also, he had carefully worded his statement to ensure that he clearly communicated that no due diligence had been done by them prior to investment.

The raid finally concluded around dawn and without any significant find. The ED team realized it had gathered nothing, at least nothing that could justify this kind of action. Rakesh and Prem held fort pretty well too. And soon, it was all over. However, there was a slew of journalists who had been camping outside the compound covering the event live since morning.

Chapter 16

Atul was asked to come down to the ED office several times following the raid. Each time, he was barraged with tons of questions, nothing that really mattered; it was simple harassment.

The ED staffers had not looked where they should have and were now barking up the wrong tree. And Atul was happy to lead them even more astray. He always got them searching for grapes on olive trees. They looked black, so they went for them and came back empty handed each time. He knew the art well by now.

Come Tuesday, Atul was preparing for the big meeting with Finance Minister Shravan Kumar Poojari. He had reached Delhi the preceding evening and met Mir to understand a few things before he went in for the meeting. Atul had been told it was an official meeting, something the minister held, from time to time, with the leading corporate houses of the country.

He also spoke to Mir again about returning the money to Shalikram. They agreed on a six-month timeline. Atul did not give him a choice on that, he knew once the new partnership was in place, Shalikram wouldn't be a problem.

Atul reached North Block, which housed the Finance Minister's office. He was quickly led to a waiting room, while the minister attended a few briefings. Atul eagerly awaited his turn. It came soon, and he was led into a large office with a green carpet and teakwood interiors. It was the worst combination one could think of—green and brown. He figured the minister didn't bother much about it.

'Good morning, Mr Malhotra, I am sorry to have kept you

waiting.' The minister got up from his chair and walked towards the door to receive him.

'Good morning, sir, it isn't a problem, it's so kind of you to say that,' replied Atul.

Soon, the minister and Atul were sitting on a plush white sofa. Leatherette or rexine, thought Atul, this was what competitive bidding did to any sense of quality and design. A bearer arrived with two cups of tea, wearing white gloves, somewhat soiled. He placed the cups on the centre table and walked out of the room. It was just the two of them thereafter.

'So, Mr Malhotra, how is business? I hope you are not facing any issues conducting your business; it is always our effort to increase the ease of business for corporates, the growth of the economy is hinged on corporate performance.'

'Well, things are pretty good actually, except that we had a small issue with the ED recently, but there is nothing for us to hide. I am sure they have understood that by now, and will soon be on their way,' replied Atul, hoping the minister would give him a few words of assurance and comfort here.

'Well, they are doing their job. If there is nothing to hide, why should you worry?' the minister replied, offering no help.

So Atul got down to business and said, 'Sir, we picked up licences for seven circles under the new telecom auctions held about a year ago. We are in the process of building the infrastructure and operationalizing those licences. Those processes are getting delayed in the absence of equity funding. I was hoping you could help me here.'

'Hmm… what is the amount you are looking at?' Poojari asked.

'Well, we are looking at around Rs 5,000 crore really, but whatever you would be able to pitch in, it's your comfort really,' replied Atul.

'I am sure I can put in about 2,500 crore for now, and may

be a similar amount in a year or two, but that's about it for now. We will decide about the next tranche when we get there,' the minister replied.

'What returns would you look for?' Atul asked, 'would 25 per cent be good?'

'What is your estimated net worth and profit after tax for the current year, Mr Malhotra?' the minister enquired.

'Well, sir, we hope to look at a net worth of about Rs 4,000 crore with a profit after tax of about Rs 400 crore this year,' Atul replied.

'Mr Malhotra, telecom is valued at about 25x its profit after tax in the marketplace. Yours is an unlisted company, so we will go by industry standards. I estimate your company to be valued at about Rs 10,000 crore. Therefore my 2,500 crore would be about a 20 per cent stake in the expanded capital base. It is fair that you give us 20 per cent share in equity and profits in the company. Does that sound good?'

'Yes, of course,' replied Atul. He hardly felt he was dealing with illicit money anymore; he was dealing with someone with sound knowledge of financial economics and business ethics. And obviously, Shravan Poojari had already done his homework before Atul got in there.

Summarizing quickly, Poojari continued, 'About 1,250 crore will come in from an offshore company, which will invest in the equity of your company as FDI. These will be preference shares with the option to convert to ordinary equity shares in three years. If we don't like your company, we will withdraw the investment and the shares will expire. The balance Rs 1,250 crore will come in cash. You may use your acumen to pump it into the operations of the business.'

Atul, acknowledging the deal, said, 'Sounds good. I am happy.'

'Good, then,' said Poojari. 'Ms Claudia Augustus is my

consultant and you will deal with her from here on. You will never meet or reach me, and should you need anything, she will be your contact. When you reach her, you reach me, I will know everything you tell her and I will let her know how you must tread. You do not use my name in any conversation anywhere. Just let Claudia know Prince gave you her number and she will understand. Claudia will explain the other mechanics of how I operate. If you ever expose yourself anywhere, causing any harm to yourself or me, I will simply disown you,' he said bluntly.

'As regards your current ED investigation,' Poojari continued, 'I had called for all the relevant records and have gone through the report. They can't touch you with as much as a feather, so you may rest assured. Also, I am presuming you will return any other political funding you may have. Our partnership will be exclusive, and you will not deal with any other funding in cash, other than genuine deals or loans.' He then handed him a typewritten application to sign. It was backdated, and was addressed from Atul to the FM, requesting him to look into the harassment by the ED, and also sought his approval for a TTL investment plan that awaited the ministry's approval.

Atul was impressed, the application would provide a legitimate purpose for the one and probably only meeting he would ever have with the FM. Poojari waited for Atul to sign it and then continued, 'I will be calling in some officials now, before we close. On the way out, please acknowledge the waiting press with some media bytes. Keep it strictly business,' and so saying, he handed him a visiting card which read 'Claudia Augustus—Interior Designer', and bore contact details and an address in downtown Geneva, and closed the meeting. As soon as Atul stepped out, Poojari summoned his Political Secretary and Chief Secretary (Revenue) into the cabin and handed the signed application over to the Political Secretary, and requested him and the Chief Secretary (Revenue) to look into it.

Atul walked out of the room and the office, and on the way out, he saw a group of press photographers and journalists lying in wait for him. 'Sir, what is the purpose of your visit to the Finance Ministry, does it have anything to do with the Enforcement Directorate investigation against your company?' a journalist from a leading TV channel asked on camera.

Atul replied suavely, 'We have nothing to hide, we are one of the most trusted companies in the country. My visit to the FM was regarding some investment proposals stuck with the ministry, and also to request him to appropriately guide authorities in dealing with honest corporate citizens like us. He assured me on both counts. Thank you,' and he walked away without taking any further questions.

On his way back to the airport for his flight to Mumbai, Atul mulled over the meeting. He was impressed by the FM's ways. The man left nothing to chance. Everything had been planned so well, it left him with a thorough regard for him.

The next day, Atul looked at the card the minister had given him. He dialled the number on it and spoke with care as soon as it was picked up, 'Hello, Ms Augustus, this is Atul Malhotra calling from India. Your number was given to me by Prince.'

An irritated person spoke on the other end, 'I don't know any Prince, and I am Claudia, not Augustus, you seem to have got a wrong number.' Atul knew he had dialled the right number, it was still flashing on his phone.

He said again, 'Well, this is the number I have, I am sorry I think there is some error,' and disconnected, not knowing what to do next. He couldn't call the FM, for sure. While he was still undecided about what to do, he received a call from what looked like a Swiss number. 'Hello, Mr Malhotra, I am sorry, I believe you called, this is Claudia.'

Atul replied calmly, 'I thought I had got the wrong number.

Prince asked me to speak to you, did you talk to him?'

'I know, Mr Malhotra,' replied Claudia, 'Prince spoke to me.'

He continued, 'I was wondering if I could see you soon, so we can discuss the modalities related to that discussion?'

'Of course, Mr Malhotra, if you can come here next Monday, we can have a discussion on the possibilities,' Claudia replied.

'Can we make it Thursday, so I can arrange for the necessary travel documents? Also, I need to get a few things done before I can meet you.'

'Very well, Thursday is fine too. You let me know your itinerary; my email id is already with you. I will get in touch with you at your hotel once you are here,' Claudia replied.

Atul disconnected, and asked Radha to get the visa and tickets done for a two-day visit to Geneva.

★

Over the years, Atul had matured as a business leader. A start-up had grown into a billion-dollar company in ten years. Being media shy, Atul had never really looked at any reputed public relations (PR) agency to build an image or reputation. But, of late, he had begun to think this would be important for two reasons: one, the company would sooner or later go public and positive public positioning was very important; and two, in case anything untoward ever happened again, like the ED investigation, a good PR agency could manage media perception well. Perception was everything. He needed to market himself. He had been thinking of appointing a reputed PR agency for a while, but the turn of events had kept him too preoccupied to do so.

Early next morning, Atul got a call from Aarti. He hadn't even got out of bed. She sounded pretty excited, 'Atul! Congratulations, have you seen the news?' A confused and just out of bed Atul hadn't hoped for any kind of good news coming his way, so what could have happened for Aarti to be so happy about, he wondered.

'What's the matter, Aarti, don't build suspense, tell me quick.'

'Wow, you've won the Entrepreneur of the Year award!! I am so happy, it is all over the news, Atul, switch on the TV.' Atul knew of this award. It had been instituted by the Finance Ministry, and he knew exactly what had suddenly qualified him for the award, and it wasn't his hard work.

'Okay, I got it,' he responded dryly, 'I'm switching on the news, and thanks, it is good news,' and disconnecting, he put on the TV. The award night itself was still a couple of months away, but soon, calls started to pour in from across the country from politicians, businessmen, bureaucrats and educationists alike. He answered as many as he could. Roshni did not call.

By evening, all the congratulations and TV coverage had convinced him that it *was* actually his hard work that had finally been noticed. Aarti called again, insisting on a party, and Atul told her he would come to office and see her. Her excitement knew no bounds; she was super elated for Atul.

The same day, Atul learnt of another development, which worried him. He learnt that Ranganathan had summoned Roshni to his office and interrogated her for over two hours. From circles within the department, they learnt that it was in connection with some documents that had her signatures and were found at the TTL office. They had also questioned her about the activities of her husband to corroborate them with the statements given by Atul during his interrogation.

So far, he didn't think there was much to bother about. The ED did not investigate murder, and that was the only wrong Roshni knew anything about. In any case, he was sure she would not spill the beans anywhere. Things were bad, but he was convinced that she would not even think of doing any harm to him.

At office, Aarti visited Atul in his cabin, hugging him in her excitement. Atul was happy to find her so unusually friendly. 'Thank you, thank you, Aarti,' he said, laughing, 'Calm down, it is just an award.'

'Come on, Atul,' she replied, 'it can't mean nothing to you! The whole country is talking about it. I don't care, I want a big party. In fact, I am arranging it, and we'll celebrate with all of TTL and its well-wishers.'

Atul finally caved in, 'Okay, as you wish, my dear, whatever you say. I give up, I know it is an important achievement. We must celebrate, when are we partying, forget the world!'

Aarti quickly responded, 'Tonight, my treat, you tell me where.'

Atul's heart leaped. He said, 'Wherever you want, sweetheart, your treat you choose, my treat I choose. Tell me where and I'll be there.'

Aarti thought for a while, 'Okay, be ready to leave by 8 p.m., let me get everything organized.'

Atul was still at office at 8 p.m., when Aarti walked into his cabin, saying, 'Let's leave, Atul,' and she shut his laptop and dragged him out of his chair.

'Okay! Okay, Aarti! Let me at least tell Radha to call for the car,' said Atul, trying to reach for the intercom.

'No, it's my car, you come to the lobby. And tell Alok to go home.' Now Atul was amused, something had really changed in this girl. He was seeing a completely different side to her. He followed her instructions and got into her Honda City. He volunteered to drive, she happily agreed, then asked, 'Where are we going?'

'I thought you planned everything, that's why we are here,' said Atul, surprised.

Aarti thought for a while and said, 'Hmm... It's your day today, you have won the award, so you take the call.'

'The rewards I seek elude me,' said Atul, 'and in their place, life gives me awards I don't need,' and looked at Aarti as he said this.

Aarti looked at him with a sly smile and said, 'Keep driving and stop cribbing.' They kept going, soon reaching the outskirts of the city and pulling onto the highway.

'Stop the car on the side, Atul,' Aarti said. Atul looked around, there was only darkness, no streetlights, and they were in the middle of nowhere. He wondered why they were here. Nevertheless, he pulled the car up on the muddy sidewalk and off the highway.

Aarti turned to Atul, pushing herself slightly off her seat. She put one hand behind Atul's head and pulled him close, and in a flash, kissed him. As their lips met in a moist embrace, their bodies entwined. Atul cooperated fully, not believing his fate.

Soon, he pushed his tongue into her mouth, the kiss got sloppier, they let out breathless gasps before getting back to kissing. She convulsed from time to time before starting all over again. Atul pulled her closer, pulling her off her seat and almost onto his. The steering didn't allow that, the sloppy kisses now got louder; they let out moans, their joy knew no bounds.

'I love you, Atul,' she finally spoke her mind.

'I love you too, Aarti, I really do.'

After almost about ten minutes of kissing, they broke the tangle to catch a breath. Atul pushed his seat back, lying as flat as he could; he'd got his award. He held her hand like he had before, but today, it felt different, very different. Unlike last time, today she held his back.

It seemed like a new sun had dawned, full of renewed energy and a brightness so brilliant, it blinded them. Aarti had given up her stiffness and surrendered to Atul's charms. Atul was so full of gratitude that tears made their way unbidden into his eyes. He did not have words or expressions to define the moment. His happiness knew no bounds. Aarti kissed his eyes wiping his tears with her cheeks. He was blissful.

Slowly, the euphoria settled and they looked at each other.

The twinkle in their eyes said a thousand words. They just looked into each other; his body wanted to disappear into hers, and she wanted the same too. His mind couldn't get over looking at her, over and over again.

'Aarti, you troubled me a lot,' he said, lovingly. 'You took too much time, you almost drove me insane, you were so rude to me, but I still kept seeking my fate with you,' and he hug her.

'You have no idea how crazy you made me when you said this the first time,' replied Aarti. 'I had no choice, I killed myself more than you, by keeping away from you. You have no idea what you put me through. I couldn't be yours. Finally, I decided to concede. Today, I have surrendered. I have let down my guard, I will love you more than you can imagine, darling. I will never let you be unhappy. You are mine and I am yours.'

Their emotional high wouldn't end. They floated much higher than the ground below and didn't want to climb down. They felt so light in each other's arms, they didn't know of anything that existed but them. Their world had only them, everything else just disappeared, simply disappeared.

After two hours in space without a worry in the world, they decided to return to earth, brought back by their stomachs crying out in hunger. They drove away, and Atul eventually pulled into the Westin Hotel, checking into a suite.

The lift door closed behind them and he looked around for any cameras, there were none. He pulled Aarti close to him and kissed her again, albeit for less than a few seconds, his whole body from head to toe was feeling her presence, and he was drowning in her.

As soon as they were in the room, they intertwined like rabbits, so wild that their hearts raced faster than rockets as they surrendered to their instincts and got to kissing, feeling up each other in every way they could. Caressing the contours of her gorgeous body, Atul's hand roamed unconsciously and kissed every inch of her.

She convulsed in desire to his seditious touch. The armour of clothing was scattered all over the place, as their bodies consumed each other in lust, kissing again.

'Atul, I don't want to make love, I want to save it for an occasion. Let's not get there today,' said Aarti.

Atul respected her and agreed. He wanted this to last as long as he could make it last. He knew he wouldn't hold for long. They stayed in each other's arms for the rest of the night, only to break for the dinner that room service served. Time stood still. Late at night, he dropped her home and drove her car to his house. Atul finally got the life he had been telling Qazi about. It was one of the best days of his life.

Chapter 17

He awoke to see a voice mail message on his phone. It was from Aarti, 'Good morning, love, I couldn't sleep, just been dreaming about you. Didn't want to disturb your sleep, found a new way to talk Muaaah.'

He called her back. 'Good morning, sweetheart. How was your night?'

Aarti replied, 'Didn't sleep for a long while, but when I did, I slept like a log. Dreamt about you all night. Something is happening to me. I can feel your presence in me every moment since you left me last night.' Atul was thrilled.

'Hmm…I didn't dream anything. I don't need to, because I have been dreaming since the day I fell in love with you, and it continues. Listen, honey, I have to go to Switzerland tonight.'

Atul told her about his appointment with Claudia and the meeting with the minister and all of it. Aarti heard him and anxiously replied, 'No, Atul, you can't go alone, I am coming with you. I don't care, I am coming.'

Atul liked the idea even more, what better place to achieve the oneness they postponed for a better time. He said, 'I couldn't be more excited, Aarti, but you need a visa, let me get to that, keep your stuff packed. I'll see you in office in a couple of hours.'

The next call Atul made was to Radha. 'Good morning, Radha, we need a Swiss visa for Aarti; she is joining me. How fast can we have it?'

Radha replied, 'Sir, I can apply today. It generally takes five days, but we have done it in two in the past.'

Atul replied, 'I need it today, please do something.'

Radha replied, 'I can try. Let me talk to them and get back.'

Atul thought for a moment, 'Check and let me know, else talk to someone in the External Affairs Ministry, get someone at our Delhi office on it. I am asking Aarti to hand over her passport to you in a while.' He disconnected the phone and messaged Aarti to give her passport to Radha, and also sign any forms that were needed.

The Swiss authorities wouldn't budge, unless it was a medical emergency, which it wasn't. The visa wouldn't be done for at least two days, he learnt that soon, and called Aarti. 'Let's do it this way, I'll go tonight, let me complete this meeting tomorrow, you join me on Friday, let's spend the weekend together and come back on Monday. Is that good?'

Aarti saw there was no choice on that one. She didn't want to be a moment without Atul. 'Okay, Atul, I'll finish compiling some important data I need for the Vision 2015 presentation. Also, I need to prepare the team for handling the 1,250 crore that will come in soon.'

Atul kissed her forehead and said, 'Okay, darling, that sounds good, I'll finish my stuff and eagerly wait for you. I am dreaming already. Just let Radha know your programme, she will do the tickets as well. Also get mine rescheduled, will you do that?'

Aarti replied, 'Of course, Atul, but wouldn't that make Radha suspicious?'

Atul smiled as he replied, 'Don't worry about Radha, she is family.'

Aarti went berserk, 'What!' Quickly, Atul pulled her closer, hugging her and said 'Joking, baby, but she won't say a word, trust me on that. Just do it.'

Aarti, still wrapped in his embrace, said, 'Atul, remember one thing, we are not an option, I'll cry if we don't happen.' Atul held her tight, he was worried about a few things, but he let that be. He kissed her forehead again and released her.

Atul landed in Geneva early morning Thursday. It was a bit chilly, but nothing that would worry him. He had informed Claudia about his itinerary. He got to his hotel room and sat waiting for her to call. It came soon enough. But it wasn't Claudia, for sure. The voice didn't match up.

'Good morning, Mr Malhotra. I hope you had a safe flight?'

'It was perfect, may I know who is speaking?' Atul asked.

The person on the other end didn't bother to reply and, instead, asked, 'What is the amount Prince asked me to give you?'

Amused by the question, Atul didn't know what to say, but said anyway, '1,250 crore in cash and another 1,250 crore by the way of investments.'

The person on the other end quickly replied, 'Very well, I have left an envelope for you at the reception, can you have it collected? I will see you at 11 a.m. today,' and disconnected, without waiting for a reply.

Atul asked for the envelope, it was a plain white envelope with no markings on it; it wasn't even addressed to him. The hotel had scribbled his name on it. He opened it. Inside was a white sheet with '8, Avenue Rosemont, Geneva' printed on it. Atul reached the place at 11 a.m. sharp, the appointed time.

It wasn't downtown, but a bit on the outskirts. It was a white building, three storeys, with sliding glass windows on the higher floors, hardly fifteen feet wide. There was a door on the ground floor, adjoining it was a showroom space, it was covered with glass façade, it read: 'To Let'.

There was no name anywhere; only a small board above the door with an inscription '8, Avenue Rosemont'. Fortunately, there was a doorbell beside the door, so he pressed it. The door opened with a click sound, it was access controlled and remotely operated.

There was a small staircase, which led to the first floor. The door to the room up there was open. The room was filled with furniture, fabric sofas and a lot of decorative knick-knacks from around the world hanging on all the walls. He entered and waited, thinking he would see someone soon, hopefully Claudia. He didn't see any reason for so much secrecy, but he went along, he wasn't scared or anything, just found it all a bit far-fetched.

Soon, a skinny blonde Caucasian woman, in her late forties, appeared from one of the rooms to greet him. She was almost 5'8" tall, had neatly trimmed nails and polished manners. 'Good morning, Mr Malhotra,' she said, 'I am Claudia Augustus.' She spoke in a sharp German accent.

Her handshake was firm, typically Swiss, he thought. But there was a problem, her voice didn't match any of the two voices he'd heard over the phone, and he didn't know what to make of it. He decided to proceed cautiously and simply said, 'Good morning, Ms Augustus, how are you doing? I am sorry, but I haven't spoken to you before, have I?' He wanted to clarify his doubts and didn't see a better way to do it. He needed to know what and whom he was dealing with here.

'Oh, don't worry about that, Mr Malhotra,' she replied, 'we have our ways. We do a lot of things to keep our customers safe. All I can say is I am the person you were asked to meet by Mr Poojari. I hope that puts you at ease.'

Atul knew he was meeting the right person, she knew things which only he and Poojari knew. He had quickly come to rely on Poojari's sense of handling matters; he had seen a few trailers and those were enough for him. He felt safe all the way.

Claudia and Atul spoke about Swiss customs for a few minutes, before Claudia got to business. 'Do you have the card Mr Poojari gave you?'

'Of course, Ms Augustus, here it is.' He fished it out of his coat pocket and gave it to Claudia. She took the card and put it in her pocket. Atul didn't ask for it back either. Then, Claudia picked up what seemed like a bunch of stapled sheets that had been lying on the table when Atul had entered the room. Atul picked up and read the first sheet, 'Agreement for Investment between Transmech Telecommunications Limited and Luxor Investments'.

'This is the draft agreement based on your discussions with Mr Poojari,' she said, 'If you agree to this, we will conduct a small due diligence of your company and get this executed. That would only be a formality, however, just in case it is ever necessary to prove our caution. Wouldn't it be odd that anybody invested 250 million dollars in a company without verifying it even exists?' They both smiled.

Atul looked at the documents briefly and replied, 'Looks okay to me, we will need a board resolution to get this executed, we will take care of that.'

Atul showed exemplary manners to impress her. Claudia was impressed. The respect was mutual, and Claudia opened up as well, knowing she was indeed dealing with someone who was worthy of her time. A thorough professional at heart, Claudia continued, 'With that behind us, let us now concentrate on the 250 million that we need to give you in cash. We have that amount in Switzerland right now.'

Atul thought about it for a while and said, 'Well, we need that money in India, but it can stay here for a while. I have an account here, you may transfer the same into that account for now, does that work?'

Claudia replied, 'Works for me, email the details to me and consider it done.'

There was silence for a while, before Claudia continued, 'I believe we are done then, is there anything else I can help you with?' Atul was hoping she would mention the precautions to be taken, because Poojari had specifically said Claudia would explain the mechanics. But he did not want to get too nosy about it, maybe there were no mechanics. No noise is better than less noise.

'Well, Ms Augustus, I guess we are fine. It was great meeting you,' said Atul, as he got up from his chair to conclude the meeting.

'Same here, do send me the account details on the email address you have. How are you spending the rest of your time here, would you wish to join me for dinner tonight?' she asked, as he got up to leave.

'Thank you, it would be a privilege. I am going to join my girlfriend for the weekend and will be back in Mumbai by Monday.'

'Is she Swiss?' Claudia asked, inquisitively.

'Oh no, she is joining me from India,' Atul replied, with a smile.

'Oh, that would be very nice, the weather has been excellent for the past few days, you will enjoy your time. You are staying at the Hotel De La Paix, there is a wonderful restaurant there. It goes by the name Vertigo. We can meet there at 7 p.m., if you like,' she responded.

Atul didn't think much about it, but he was pretty intrigued and would love to explore the mind behind the woman. He was sure she was shielding too much, that probably was her job, but still...

He needed to know more, he was not comfortable, or maybe he was greedy to learn a few ways of the new world he was witnessing. So he jumped at the invitation, 'Thanks, Claudia, I'll see you there'.

'I will take care of the bookings then,' she replied. 'See you in the evening.'

He drove back to his hotel after the meeting with Claudia, and after reaching his room, spoke to Aarti to ensure everything was in place. The excitement was building.

That evening, he met up with Claudia, both were punctual and neither had to wait. The restaurant itself wasn't much to talk about—it was a small, quiet fine dining restaurant that overlooked the waterfront. It had about twenty seats dimly lit by large lamps hanging from the ceiling that gave just enough light to brighten up the tables below.

Atul and Claudia were led to a corner seat that had been reserved for them. There were no other customers. Claudia broke the silence saying, 'I believe you run a telecom company in India? How is business in your country? I am told you are one of the most amazing first-generation entrepreneurs!'

Realizing Poojari had briefed her already, Atul laughed and said, 'Well, I do run a growing telecom business. India is growing, the future is bright.' Claudia was listening to him while going through the menu.

'That's true,' she said, 'we hear about it all the time in this part of the world. What would you like to drink? They have a lovely selection of champagnes, if you like.' They ordered a bottle of Bollinger and continued to converse.

'So, how do you know Mr Poojari, if I may ask?' Atul asked Claudia.

'Well, I do not have the privilege to talk about customers, I am sure you can appreciate that. Thanks to a few laws that still exist in my country, I manage funds for some customers whom I can trust; they come from various parts of the world.'

Atul nodded appreciatively and said, 'So I guess I could request your services too, if I ever required them?'

Claudia looked at him, 'We will see as it goes, we will get there soon.'

The rest of the evening they spoke about the weather, places to go for the weekend, Indian culture and Swiss customs, while Atul tried his best to steer Claudia towards a question which he had already asked once earlier and had failed to get a reply. He tried again, 'We haven't spoken before today morning, right? I am guessing you don't work alone.'

Claudia looked at him and replied, 'Mr Malhotra, I understand your concern and appreciate it. I have already disclosed more to you, on the first day, than I disclose to most in a lifetime of business acquaintance. And that list includes Mr Poojari too. Hope that puts your mind to rest.'

Atul chose not to probe any further. They were now acquainted well enough to easily conduct the business they sought with each other. Some people are mysterious, and one has to live with that.

On the way out, Claudia gave another card to Atul. It read 'Elisabeth Gustavo' and bore an address '8, Avenue Rosemont, Genève'. It also had a telephone number. Claudia said, 'There is no Claudia Augustus. Have a good night.' They were by now outside, in the crisp night air. Claudia shook his hand and went on her way, and he went on his.

Atul felt at complete peace with himself. The sort of peace that only comes when you win the trust of another person. That is what had just happened.

Back in his hotel room, he went online to check out some of the places Elisabeth had recommended for the weekend. Atul already had made the bookings at a resort in Interlaken, but he wanted to see if there was anything better. A 20-acre resort property nestled in the Swiss Alps, about sixty kilometres from Geneva looked promising. It was made up of twenty independent chalets and looked perfect for the kind of holiday Atul was looking for. He immediately called Aarti to find out if she was okay with going there instead. Her phone was switched off. She must have already taken off, he presumed, and went ahead and changed the booking anyway—the place seemed just too perfect.

The next morning, he could hardly wait for Aarti's plane to land, and spotted her almost as soon as she came out. Hugging her, he asked, 'How was your flight, honey? I called you at night, I guess you must have left, hope everything was okay?'

'Everything was just perfect, love. Who cares about the journey when the destination is so beautiful.' Atul kissed her before they proceeded to the waiting car—an Aston Martin convertible. Aarti was dazzled. 'Wow!' she exclaimed, 'what's wrong with you, this is so amazing!!!'

Atul, on a high, put her bags in the boot, got into the car, and said, 'There's been a change in plans, sweetheart. I won't tell you about the new place I've booked us, we'll just drive there.'

Until she had landed at the airport and met Atul, Aarti had been gripped by the apprehension that she never would be able to match up to him, in terms of all that he was giving. She'd felt, sometimes, that he did just too much for her. But the strength of his feelings for her was so palpably evident that she was no longer worried.

That drive up those beautiful roads with Atul, through the misty morning in an open top Aston Martin, with the gorgeous icy peaks of the Alps in the distance, seemed all too short and, before she knew it, they had reached the gates of the resort.

It was perched on the top of a hill, with not much ice at this time of the year. Atul handed the car to the valet and they went into the warm and beautiful reception area to check in. The desk clerk handed them the keys and wished them a pleasant stay. They accompanied the bellhop, who escorted them and their bags to their chalet, which was one of twenty on the large property, with enough distance between each to ensure complete privacy. The restaurants and bar were in the main reception building, but room service excluded the need to step out unless one wanted to.

The chalet itself was breathtaking and had superb views. Built of beautiful oak, the aroma of which permeated the walls, floors and ceilings, it was a treat to view from the outside, and would be a dream to live in, on the inside.

The living-room had one wall made of oak, and two walls of

floor-to-ceiling glass windows that overlooked a spacious garden attached to the chalet, with the snowclad Alps beyond. There were comfortable looking chairs and a table placed near a beautiful flower bed. Inside, the living-room opened into a dining-room, and from there, through a solid oak door, into the bedroom. All the rooms looked spacious yet cosy, thanks to the clever use of colour and the eclectic mix of furniture. Atul and Aarti were thrilled.

Atul tipped the bellhop and carried their bags into the bedroom, with Aarti following. The bedroom was huge and done in white, with the exception of coloured throws on the king-sized bed. There was a love-seat placed beneath a window that ran the length of the wall. The attached bathroom was very well appointed too. The shower sat above and beside heated plunge pool, large enough for two, carved from sandblasted grey stone. There was no ceiling, just the sky above seen through a sheet of clear glass. Frosted sliding glass doors separated it from the bedroom.

There was another set of frosted sliding glass doors at the far end of the huge bedroom. Atul and Aarti opened it to find a heated private swimming pool, almost twenty feet long, connecting to the garden outside, separated by a four-foot high hedge to give enough privacy to the guests.

Atul looked at Aarti and sighed, 'A dream, isn't it?'

'Heaven,' said Aarti, and embraced Atul. Neither moved, not her, not him. They just held each other as tight as they could, fearing they would be torn away, and when enough heat had passed from one to the other, they felt each other up and their mouths fused again. Finally, still holding each other, they went back into the bedroom and drew the curtains. It was almost midnight, in the room that is. They got on the bed fully clothed, rubbing their legs against each other, as if to confirm this wasn't a dream, holding their heads close to each other and kissing, only parting to catch a breath.

Atul unbuttoned her top, he nibbled her bosom, tickling her and igniting her passion. Her erect nipples excited him no end. Convulsing and exploring every inch of each. Time passed, yet stood still; they held each other and felt the other's bodies, they ripped off any clothing that remained.

'I cannot wait anymore. You are making me mad. Come inside me, Atul,' she said.

'I am not done, sweetheart,' Atul went lower, smelling the musky odour of her love-spot. He savoured it to his heart's content. Aarti reciprocated too. Not able to hold out anymore, he thrust himself inside her in a missionary position. They exploded together and it was bliss. Their thoughts stood still. They experienced a peace from another world. About an hour later, and still in that position, they drifted into sleep, to get up only after a few hours.

Aarti awoke first. She spent about ten minutes gazing at Atul asleep. She observed every feature of his face, his lips, his nose, his closed eyes, his forehead, his body features, and watched him sleep peacefully. Then, still with a smile on her face, she got out of bed quietly and went into the dining-room and picked up the menu, lying on the table alongside a basket of fruits, and perused it. Having called room service and placed her order, she wandered over to the minibar fridge and pulled out a bottle of champagne she found lying within, and picked up two champagne glasses from the tray on top, and carried it all into the bedroom. There, she carefully placed them on the table in front of the love-seat in the bedroom.

Then, she lay down on the bed again and softly rubbed her cheeks on his in an attempt to wake him up. Without opening his eyes, Atul kissed her lips, held her close and refused to let her go. They stayed that way till the doorbell rang.

'It must be the food, let me get it,' said Aarti. The food was brought in and duly arranged alongside the champagne. They finished eating, and spent a few hours sipping champagne. Atul didn't get wasted, he didn't need any more highs, and he thought he would die of contentment if he got any more of it.

Towards the evening, she said, 'lets take a plunge.'

'On the bed or here?' he asked.

'In the pool, you idiot,' she replied.

They took themselves and their champagne glasses to the plunge pool, skinny dipping, observing every mole on the body of the other for the first time.

When the euphoria of this episode of love settled, Aarti said, 'Atul, we have a long journey ahead to fulfil our dream. I know what you feel about Roshni, but feeling separated and getting there are two different things. I will wait for you till the end of time until you get there. I will hold on to you while you finish that page of life. For a long time, I thought I must let you do that without me, but I now know I cannot wait for you till you get there. I love you, Atul. I want you for us. Please make this happen. I am depending on you,' she said, with absolute sincerity.

Atul listened, knowing in his heart that the journey thus far was probably the easiest part. Dealing with the Roshni aspect of this triangle was a job far from done. He did not want to plunge into that today, but he knew he soon would. To Aarti, he replied, 'You think I don't know that, honey? It was a concern when I pursued you, and today, it is my only concern.' Aarti hugged Atul and left it at that.

True bliss is an experience you can feel when it is happening, its identity cannot be mistaken for anything else. Spending hours in each other's arms, just lazing around and experiencing the bliss, skinny dipping in their private heated swimming pool, with the mighty Alps in the background—these were unforgettable days.

'Aarti, we have to make promises to each other.' They were holding each other so tight, even water couldn't pass through.

Looking into his eyes, Aarti replied, 'We got here against all odds, we know we have to fight the world to make this happen.' Atul knew the days ahead would prove challenging, and that Aarti knew it as well.

'We must promise to hold each other from slipping away, we have to be selfish, very selfish to make this happen,' he replied, very unsure but equally emphatic. He had surrendered, so had Aarti. 'Let's make this promise, and promise to make sure either won't slip. It's our responsibility to remind each other of our promise today. Each time we falter, every time we are weak, till we make this dream real for the rest of our lives.' It sounded like a pledge, a pledge it was.

Atul's eyes welled up with tears of joy, washed away by the water they were floating in.

Chapter 18

Back home, folks were preparing for TTL's 11th AGM. It wouldn't be anywhere close to the 10th in grandeur. But it was a year TTL had done—and 'done' doesn't mean necessarily achieved—when TTL had done more than it did in the first ten put together. Its geography of services had expanded from a few hundred square kilometres to a few thousand, laying the foundation for five-fold growth over the next five years. They had as partner no less personage than the Finance Minister of the country. The CEO had been honoured with the Entrepreneur of the Year award. They had even managed to commit a murder.

The AGM events would consume the whole day, starting with the board meeting in the morning, followed by a presentation of Vision 2015, concluding with dinner. The arrangements were in order. Aarti had contributed greatly to the vision statement, sitting with Atul for hours on end to craft the vision of the company for the next four years.

The TTL board had already approved the Public Offer to be made by the investors at the last meeting, though Atul had never wanted the IPO. He knew no way to reverse that decision. It was not his decision to make. However, during the board meeting, he made a stunning offer.

'Members of the Board, we are aware that at the last board meeting, we approved the IPO of your company, the shares to be sold would come from the holdings of the private equity investors. I now propose that instead of a public offering, the company arrange to sell that equity, valued at 1,200 crore, to another fund. In fact, that source is willing to fund 1,250 crore. Also, the investors can realize their monies immediately, and also save the huge costs and risks of running a public offering.' Even the other promoters didn't know what he was talking about, as in who this fund provider was who would buy the equity from the investors.

Actually, Atul was proposing that instead of issuing new shares to Luxor Investments, the private equity investors sell their shares to them. This way, he could avoid the IPO. But there was a problem; they would still be short of enough equity to complete their expansion, and also the shares had to be changed from ordinary equity to preferential equity, as needed by Poojari. There were no clear answers to these problems in his mind. But he knew he could place additional shares with new investors, who would not jump for an IPO from day one and would wait for a three-year period before they could get one. This way, he could make good the notional loss of cash for the company.

The idea was in fact Aarti's brainchild. She had proposed this to him whilst they were working on the Vision document. It seemed like a perfect plan. The plan flew, given that the investors would save about 125 cores in IPO costs, and also the new buyers were willing to shell out 50 crores more for their stake, they were looking at a neat 175 crore more as returns for their investment.

They accepted it, and with that, the board meeting ended. Atul was elated. He ran the plan by the other promoters and they liked the idea as much as he did. It was a win-win for all. However some technical issues ensued and TTL still had to buy back the equity from the investors and allot it back to Luxor.

This AGM had been designed as one big party with emotional speeches, and it was emotional, with the Vision 2015 programme generating a lot of excitement. Aarti presented it—Prem had insisted on it—since she was the dominant force behind the document.

It covered everything—skyrocketing turnover and growth,

mind-boggling subscriber growth, robust recruitment plans, investments, incomes, profits and social welfare initiatives. All presented with a lot of charts giving statistical information about the economy, industry, competition and company.

Aarti enjoyed the importance the opportunity gave her, presenting the slides with her natural flair, and almost sounded like she was the next CEO. Unless one knew what position she held in the company, it was easy to mistake her for one already.

Atul had not yet managed to speak to Roshni about what had happened during her visit to the ED. Busy with Aarti and the forthcoming AGM, he had not felt any urgent need to follow through either. But now his mind was getting noisy about getting closure on that chapter of his life; it was a necessity now.

That evening, he reached home late and found a letter marked for his consideration. Usually, Radha received all the incoming letters and sent emails to company personnel, seeking information or action based on what they contained. She also made a short summary email of communications she received each day, along with an action-taken report. Atul would glance through it to know what had come in and what had been done about it. Some important communications were directly put in a folder and handed over to him for personal reading. This letter was one among them.

It contained a proposal sent by a Mumbai-based lawyer, headed 'Draft Application for Divorce by Mutual Consent', and thereafter listed the many terms of the divorce, including Roshni keeping Ananya and Atul being allowed visitation rights. It also asked for alimony of about five crore a month, with about 500 crore worth of Atul's holding in TTL.

This was not Roshni's idea, thought Atul. In fact, he pretty much knew it. He was thinking Jyoti, but that didn't matter. Also, he was surprised at the timing; he wondered if the knowledge of his relationship with Aarti had been outed more than he knew, and if that had anything to do with it. It didn't seem probable; the relationship was hardly a few weeks old.

He loved Aarti, but somewhere in his mind, he also felt that things were happening too soon, too fast. Even for Atul's brilliantly quick mind, this was way too fast. He needed to talk to Roshni, not for the notice, but he needed to know what was going on. All these years, he had not taken any steps towards a divorce, out of concern for her; he never thought she could be happy without him; and today, he was really concerned for her. He could not just let her be. He chose to keep the letter with him for now, and did not respond to it. He hoped to be able to talk to Roshni soon. He was perfectly fine with her demands, but something stopped him from accepting the document the way it was presented to him.

★

Things went on as they were for a few months, there wasn't much that happened during that period. The folks at TTL spent most of the time in operationalizing the licences Shalikram had bestowed upon them, overseeing infrastructure developments and appointing personnel.

Atul and Aarti got busy looking at finances, and, of course, nurturing their newfound love. She also worked with Prem on getting in a new private equity partner, and they injected a fresh investment of 1,000 crore as planned, so that was behind them too.

Another development worth noting was that Shalikram had been moved out of the ministry in a cabinet reshuffle and was reduced to being an ordinary MP. He was toothless now, which worked very well for Atul, or so he thought, until one morning, when he received a call from Mir. 'Good morning, Atulji, you never called me to tell me what happened about your meeting with Poojari.'

Atul thought quickly and replied, 'It wasn't that, Mir sahib, I was bound by duty as well, terms of non-disclosure...'

Mir laughed it off, knowing Atul was taking a jibe at what Mir had disclosed, or rather had not disclosed, a few months back. He understood the result anyway. 'Atulji,' he said, 'there is a problem we must talk about, I cannot do it on the phone, I am coming to Mumbai tomorrow to meet you.'

Atul quickly responded, 'In fact, I am going to be in Delhi the day after. If it can wait for a day, I can meet you there.'

But Mir said urgently, 'Atulji, there may be a threat to your life. That is all I can say now. I have just heard some murmurs. I know more and I will tell you when we meet, but just stay safe and don't go any place that may be insecure.'

Atul's mind only thought of one thing, Shalikram. But he would rather hear the whole story. So he said, 'Thanks, Mir sahib. Let's meet tomorrow, I want to know what is all this about, do you think I need to arrange security?'

'I am not sure,' replied Mir, 'I am not even sure I have the right news, but being safe is never a bad idea, let's meet tomorrow evening around 5 p.m.'

Atul replied, 'Fine, I'll wait for you, sir,' and Mir disconnected the phone.

Atul told no one about this conversation except Aarti. She was extremely scared for his life. He moved out of office at his usual time, but took an unusual route and chose to go in Aarti's car. He told his driver Alok to drive Aarti home and he reached his house without incident.

However, when Aarti moved out with Alok, two helmet-clad men on a motorcycle appeared alongside just as the car reached an isolated bend on the road, and opened fire with assault rifles, stopping only when they realized it was a woman and not a man in the passenger seat. The whole incident was over in less than thirty seconds. Needless to say, Aarti or Alok had no time to gather their wits and read the number plate.

But thanks to the fact that Atul's BMW was bulletproof, they escaped unhurt; the bullets had just dented the glass and made some holes in the metal body. A scared Aarti asked Alok to drive her to Atul's house as fast as he could. Alok, still scared for his life, did just that. She did think of taking the car to the police station, but there would be a lot of questions, and Atul's house was just ten minutes away. She reached there without any further incident and ran into Atul's arms, who cursed himself for letting her use his car; he should have thought about the consequences. But now that she was safe with Atul, Aarti soon regained her composure. The police, meanwhile, having heard reports of firing in the area, had rushed to the spot. They found nothing but a few used up bullets. There were no witnesses to testify to anything at all.

As soon as he settled Aarti, Atul called Mir to let him know what happened. On Mir's advice, he did not leave home the next day, nor did Aarti. As decided, Mir came straight to his house from the airport, and Atul introduced Aarti to him, adding, 'Mir sahib, Aarti almost took the shots meant for me.'

Mir nodded seriously and said, 'I hope you are better now, Aarti? Maybe we better go in.' Atul ushered them into his den. Babu brought in tea and snacks and set them out on the centre table, in front of the plush leather sofa set where they were seated. Once he had left the room, they got down to the reason behind Mir's, visit.

'The fellow has gone mad,' began Mir, 'The search conducted by the ED was his mischief. He wanted to pressurize you with evidence, so you would need to go back to him and he could save his investments. When they found nothing, he couldn't do much. Also, when he learnt that Poojari was backing you, he had to step off. But your cold approach to him really angered him; you should have handled him more diplomatically, Atul,' he said, shaking his head wryly. 'He is not used to this kind of treatment you see. Anyway, his ways angered those at the highest levels of power and, before he could be much of a problem to you, he was moved out. After that, he just became desperate, I think.'

Atul couldn't quite understand what Mir was getting at. It didn't need too much brain to understand the sequence of events that had led to Shalikram's actions today. Atul had always thought he might have had something to do with the ED action, but had never enquired, because he never intended to get back at him in any way based on that information. He only wanted Mir to tell him about the attempt on his life, and discuss future actions related to that. Aarti was intently listening to what was being said as well. So, he asked Mir outright, 'What does he want?'

'I told you the guy has gone insane,' said Mir. 'His ego occupies so much of his brain that there is little room for anything else. How does one reason with a person like that? He moved out of the ministry, so I don't have a good connect any more, though I keep hearing things. I heard this yesterday and was duty-bound to inform you. I made one mistake in the past, but that was business.'

Atul heard him out carefully, and then asked, 'What do you think I must do?'

'Atul, the first thing is to plan for your safety. It's a good thing you didn't approach the police. It would have worsened the situation. You need to secure yourself. Second? I don't know, maybe talk to him. What else do you think we can do?'

Atul thought it over carefully, then asked Mir, 'Does he fear anybody, somebody who can control his actions?'

Mir shook his head, 'Sorry, no one. With his ministry gone, he does not even fear anyone in the corridors of power, they cannot do any more harm to him than they already have, so he has nothing to lose there. There were some major fuck-ups he was involved with, an exposé on that was averted by his resignation. I hear he was involved with some prostitution rings and drug rackets as well.'

Seeing Mir at a loss for ideas, knowing he had no ideas either, it suddenly struck Atul that there might be someone who could help. He told Mir, 'Let me talk to someone, I think there may be a way,' and he called Elisabeth Gustavo.

'Hello, Elisabeth. How are you? This is Atul Malhotra from India,' and having introduced himself, he came straight to the point, 'There is an emergency I need to talk to you about.' He narrated the entire sequence of events—Mir informing him, the attack on Aarti, and the story he got from Mir.

Elisabeth heard him out, without interrupting, and said, 'Mr Malhotra, I advise you to stay put at home. Let me make a few calls and get some advice for you.' Atul was glad to hear exactly what he wanted to hear. Although Mir maintained that Shailikram feared nobody, Atul refused to believe him.

Later that day, after thanking Mir and seeing him off, Atul decided to work from home for a few days. He knew some solution would come along soon. He also arranged for security cover for the house, but didn't like it one bit. Aarti, scared and worried, stayed with him throughout. Even the ringing of a doorbell sent shivers down her spine, and she broke down often, still traumatized by the attack. But they needed reassurance. They had a mini holiday of sorts at home. Lazing around, making love, dreaming.

Atul also informed the other promoters of what had happened, and they came over for a meeting. A whole day passed without any call from Elisabeth. The next day, Atul called her again, but all she said was, 'Things are being looked into, as we speak. Once we are sure of everything, anything that needs to be done will be done to resolve the problem for good. Please follow my earlier advice until I tell you otherwise.' And with that, Atul had to be content.

Three days later, Aarti and Atul had just retired to bed. It was past midnight. The phone rang and it was Elisabeth. 'Good evening, Mr Malhotra. I have some news for you. Your former minister will not be a problem any more.'

Atul couldn't buy that statement, even if it came from Elisabeth. She was a lady of very few words, but he wanted to know how the truce had been achieved. He asked again, 'Are you sure, Elisabeth, has anybody spoken to him? And honestly, his assurances are of little value, the man simply lacks ethics.'

Elisabeth replied after a few seconds, 'You need to be human to have ethics or lack them. I doubt he qualified, just let him be in peace. He won't ever come back to bother you, that's all I can say.'

It was late at night, he didn't know what to make of it. He told Aarti about what Elisabeth had said, and she simply said, 'Look, Atul, let her say what she has to say, I am not letting you leave home, it is okay to work for a while from here. Let's be safe. It doesn't matter. Please listen to me, Atul; I am very scared for you, I love you Atul, I don't understand what is happening.'

Aarti woke early next morning and saw the newspaper headlines. 'Ex-Telecom Minister Shalikram Bahujan shot dead.' She felt numb, grabbed the nearest chair to avoid collapsing, and sat on it. She was shocked, not because of what had happened but because she kind of knew who had done it. She quickly flipped at least a dozen other newspapers lying on the table. They all ran similar headlines. Finally, she picked up one paper and read the whole story.

'Former minister Shalikram Bahujan was found shot dead in his car, along with his driver and secretary, on the highway near Etawah, around 11 p.m. last night. All three were reported dead on arrival by the time they were brought to the government hospital at Etawah.

The minister was returning to his constituency from Delhi when the incident occurred. The police have launched a manhunt for the assailants. The incident happened on an isolated stretch of the highway and the police are hunting for evidence.

She rushed up with the newspaper to Atul, shouting, 'Atul, wake up, they have shot the guy!' Atul woke up, shocked, read it and quickly switched on the television. All the news channels maintained the same thing—the police were investigating, had launched a manhunt, but had no clues yet. There was no point in calling Elisabeth again, she wouldn't say a word. He had little doubt that Elisabeth and Poojari were behind this. They'd done this for him? He was unsure of it, but there seemed to be no other reason behind it, if indeed they were the perpetrators—which he felt quite sure they were.

He turned to Aarti and said, 'Let's not talk about this to anybody, we'll keep it to ourselves like we did the secret of the laundry, just forget about it as a bad dream.' Then he called the other co-founders and asked them to come to his house as soon as they could. They resolved to remain silent, as Atul wanted. There could be repercussions, so they needed to secure themselves and their establishments.

Rakesh took the responsibility to put up extra security cover for all the directors, and for Qazi and Aarti. Security was also increased at all the offices and homes. They needed to be ready for any fallout of this incident. 'What about Roshni, Atul?' Anil asked, 'She is your wife, we must inform her also. She too must be secured immediately, and she is an easy target.'

Atul had a different problem there. Roshni already knew about the Prashant Nagarkar murder, and if she learnt about this, it might just cause even more hair-trigger responses from her. As it was, she hated Atul for his ways. So Atul said, 'Let me speak to her,' and reached for the phone, but Anil interrupted, 'Atul, that may not be a good idea, let me handle it.' There was a moment's silence and then, Atul agreed. So, Anil called Roshni in the presence of all in the room on a speaker phone. Putting her on the speaker phone was Atul's bright idea, in case he had to guide Anil.

'Hello, Anil here, Roshni bhabhi, how are you doing?' said Anil.

'I am fine, Anil, how are you?' came the reply.

'Bhabhi, there was an attack on Atul's life day before yesterday...' Before he could complete the sentence, she replied, in anguished tones, 'It was not on his life, it was on that bitch's life, why didn't she die?'

The room was stunned for several reasons, the least of which was Aarti being referred to as a bitch. The first question on everybody's mind was how had Roshni got to know before they told her? At that point, all the people who knew about this were very much in that room. How had the news leaked? Anil quickly asked Roshni, 'How do you know that? The attempt really was on Atul's life, not hers. She was an accidental target. At this moment, we need to make sure you are safe. You are his wife.'

Roshni replied bluntly, 'Look, Anil, I don't care about what you people are doing. I am not a part of all this any more, I can take care of myself. If Atul feels so much for me, tell him to throw that bitch out of his life and call me, I am willing to talk about everything.'

She disconnected the phone without expecting any answer. Atul listened to every word, analyzing and trying to read the intent behind them; only embarrassed that Aarti had been party to the conversation. He was even embarrassed about what Prem, Anil, Rakesh and Qazi must be thinking about it all. Prem, Anil, Rakesh and Qazi were even more embarrassed than Atul, and felt bad because they had never seen him this helpless. As they all stood about in an awkward silence, Qazi quickly stepped in and said, 'Atul, we are down in the living-room, we will see you there,' and walked out of the room, with the others trooping hastily behind him.

Chapter 19

Atul did not know what to say to Aarti as she sat looking utterly dejected. Her whole resistance to Atul all along had been because he wouldn't come clean with Roshni, and the call had just confirmed that. Finally, he broke the silence, 'Aarti, I understand what you are going through. It was never going to be easy. If the love we have for each other is strong, nothing else must matter. What she feels, what anybody else feels, we did no wrong, you know that, I know that. And once we know that, there is no reason for your mind to be troubled.'

'Atul, you need to end this, and fast,' she said. 'I am patient, I don't feel anything about what she said. I can promise you that for now, but I cannot say the same for tomorrow. The faster we can gain closure on this, the easier it will be to move on with our lives. I say this for Roshni too. She is a woman and I understand her emotions. She is not entirely wrong. Even now, if you want to reconsider your decision, you are free to do so, I will not hold you responsible for it.'

Atul did not reply, but simply put his arms around her. The urgency of resolving the situation had been sharply brought home to him. He couldn't even begin to consider any of the options Aarti had just offered him, in a voice filled with such anguish and pain. Anguish and pain he had caused her, he realized. The intensity of her feelings had been building up from the day they got to know each other, but Atul had just got a glimpse of it for real, for the first time.

The day Atul got back to office, he spoke to Radha, 'I had

this driver Shashi who drove me when Alok wasn't around, where is he now?'

'Sir, he is on duty for one of the executives in the HR department.'

'Shift Alok there and ask Shashi to take my car, make sure that happens now. Let Alok know it is for security reasons.' The news about Prashant Nagarkar's murder could have reached Roshni from no other source but Alok. Still, he hadn't been completely sure. But now, with the news of this attack having reached her so quickly, he knew there was no one else who could have told her. Mir wouldn't leak information to Roshni. Other than all of them in the room that day, Alok was the only person who knew the whole story. And given that Alok knew too much, Atul did not want to sack him, not now.

A couple of days later, Atul's wedding anniversary came up, and he picked up the phone and dialled Roshni, 'Hello, how are you?'

'Okay,' came the flat reply.

'How is Ananya?'

'You haven't seen her since she was a week old, I am glad you even remember you have a daughter,' came the disgusted reply.

'Look, Roshni, I don't think this is the right way to deal with our problems, sending divorce notices and then telling Anil you are willing to discuss everything. It doesn't work that way. I need to know what's on your mind.'

'What choice do you leave me, Atul?' asked Roshni bluntly, 'I have no options left.'

Reading between the lines, Atul realized this would need careful handling, 'Let's go for a quiet dinner,' he said, 'I'll listen and you tell me what you must. We'll keep it light, let's understand each other, we must do what is right for our future. I'll make a booking tonight at the Dome, can you come there at 8 p.m.?'

There was no reply. Atul continued regardless, 'I will be there at 8 p.m., it's your choice if you want to join, that is all I can say. I am okay that we separate, in fact, that's what I want, but not with you unsure in your mind.' After waiting a while, when he still got no response, he disconnected the phone.

That evening, he reached the restaurant at the appointed time, ordering a Black Label for himself. He had no idea what he would say to Roshni or what she would reply.

On the one hand, he loved Aarti, but that was love. On the other hand, there was something on his mind that would not let him forget Roshni? Did he feel responsible for Roshni? Was being responsible a form of love too? If yes, then did he still love Roshni? If yes, why did he detest her then? He waited for her, his feelings in complete turmoil.

At 9, an hour past the appointed time, he was still waiting and knocking back Black Label. It was their wedding anniversary today, a fact that he'd thought best not to bring up in the conversation. He thought of all the good times and wondered where they had vanished. Why could those memories not light a fire in him now with Roshni? His thoughts moved to Aarti and how she had entered his life. Why had she happened? Just why had Aarti happened in his life? Was Roshni the reason why Aarti had happened to him in the first place? Was he still not ready to choose? Not ready to even decide whether to make a choice or not?

He wanted the divorce, but more than on paper, in Roshni's mind. He was ready; she wasn't, he knew that. But why should Aarti bear the brunt of his mess with Roshni? She had done no wrong and deserved better.

He loved Aarti; he was sure of that—then why was this decision a hard one? Maybe what Qazi said was right. Love was an illusion. When enough time passed, all illusions would be revealed for what they were, just illusions. Maybe illusions were necessary to keep the demons out. Maybe his love for both was nothing but an illusion, so was he trying to choose between two illusions? That shook him, and so, for a while, he stopped thinking. But just for a while. Then, back he got on the bandwagon again.

Aarti was a whiff of fresh air, but so was Roshni when she entered his life. And he loved her for that. But once body gets accustomed to fresh air, then it ceases to charm, to be a miracle any more. How could you keep any choice fresh long enough? How did one stop things from becoming stale? How does one stop seeking fresher environs when one's own environs became stale? Thoughts ran rampant, aided by a free intake of Black Label. He couldn't bring himself to hurt anybody, not even his own wife, who he detested yet perhaps loved, thought Atul sadly.

It was now three hours past the appointed time and Roshni had still not come.

Just before midnight, Atul left the restaurant and told Shashi to drive to Aarti's place. Once there, he rang the bell. Aarti opened the door in her night wear. He hugged her in silence. She closed the door behind them and saw he was almost wasted, and guided him to the sofa and sat beside him.

'What's wrong, Atul? What happened?' she asked. He lay down, rested his head on her lap and broke down, saying nothing, just crying, the tears pouring down like thick raindrops. Aarti pulled his head closer to her and calmed him, but let him cry. His sobs became muffled after a while. He turned his head and kissed her stomach, held her close. Finally, he pulled himself together and apologized.

'I am sorry, Aarti. I really am.'

Aarti, confused as it was, said, 'What did you do? What happened? What are you talking about?'

All Atul could say was, 'I love you, Aarti, and that is all I know, nothing else matters, please hold me, I don't want to part from you.'

He seemed so complex to her that night, she didn't know what to do.

'Atul, please tell me what's happened. I am getting worried, what happened?' He did not reply but got up, went and washed his face. Aarti followed him. Turning, he hugged her, then kissed her. His palms roamed her back, feeling her hourglass shape with his hands. He pulled her closer, got past her gown and guided it off her body. She unbuckled him. They dropped onto the bed. Fiery passion erupted. Soon, the energy of his hyperactive mind was drained.

'Please hold me,' Atul begged, 'don't let me slip, I can't let us drown, I need you now.'

She asked no more. He said no more. Desire consumed the questions of the night. Atul was finally wasted. The night passed.

The next morning, Aarti said nothing about the previous night, she understood that Atul needed answers not questions. She was a very intelligent girl, at times more intelligent than Atul. Atul knew that too. She didn't have the answers, maybe he had them already, she only had the questions, and putting her questions to him wouldn't help their future. Her love for Atul was steadfast. She let him seek his answers, and hoped she had the patience to wait and see him on the other side of his pandemonium.

That day, Atul received an unexpected call from Elisabeth, 'Good morning, Atul,' she said, 'how are things now?'

'I am good, Elisabeth, and I am surprised you called,' replied Atul.

'You asked the other day at dinner if we could do business together,' she replied, 'I have a customer who wishes to invest US$500 million. I wanted to recommend your company to him. May I?'

Atul was cautious, he did not want any more political funders. One was enough. In any case, he was bound by the agreement he had made with Poojari. So he said, 'That is nice of you, Elisabeth, but I cannot accept funds in cash. This is my agreement with the customer whose funds you have placed with me already.'

Elisabeth replied, 'This is a fund from a Trust, they will do their due diligence and invest only if they find you worthy, there is no cash here. I can only recommend you, the decision is theirs.'

Atul quickly understood that he was talking real world investment here. 'You are welcome to recommend us then. I would be glad to meet them. And I thank you for your gesture.'

'I will let them know,' said Elisabeth. 'If you do get the investment, please confirm it with me once you close the transaction. However, please remember, I never called you with this offer.'

In another month, after a full-scale due diligence, a Luxembourg-based fund invested another US$500 million in TTL, at extremely healthy valuations. Atul called it 'miracle money'. Sometimes, problems solve themselves like an act of God. It solved a lot of equity issues TTL would have faced; they could easily raise a debt of another Rs 6,000 crore, almost erasing any money worries, at least till 2015.

Around a month after that investment, one morning, there was a notice waiting for him at office. An ED inspector had served it personally. It asked him to be present at the ED office the same day at 3 p.m. It said nothing else. It had been months since he was last called. All the questions and answers were done, he'd thought the chapter had been closed. What had they found now? Atul summoned Qazi to his cabin. Reading the notice, Qazi said, 'We already have the closure order for the search they conducted. This should have nothing to do with the earlier search.'

'That is bad news then,' Atul replied, 'Could they have got on to some other trail?'

Qazi thought a bit and replied, 'Yes, it is possible. Since it can have nothing to do with the raid, it is something else they have got which they want you to answer for. You are not going. Let our lawyers attend it, let them find out what is going on.' He also immediately made a few calls to people in the ED who supported TTL, and after the raid, there were quite a few. No one, however, seemed to have any information about the cause for this development.

Nevertheless, Atul insisted he would go; not going would only strengthen any doubt they could have. 'It is best we face it straight, we cannot avoid it for long, they cannot touch me. I know that, why do you worry?' But though worried, Qazi didn't argue after that. Beyond a point, he knew it was futile to insist anyway.

Aarti said she would accompany him, and Atul agreed. They reached Ranganathan's office at 3 p.m. and were told he was busy. They were asked to wait on the bench outside the office. It was a small wooden bench, the polish long having worn off, long enough to seat three people. It had no back, like the benches you saw in schools or jails.

It was over an hour now that they'd been waiting. The bench was very uncomfortable. Atul sat down and, when it made his back stiff, he walked up and down the corridor and returned in a while. Aarti did the same too. The wait was testing his patience. Finally, at 6.30, after making Atul Malhotra, the Chairman of the Board and the CEO of a billion-dollar enterprise, wait for three and a half hours, Ranganathan called him in. Atul went in with Aarti and politely said, 'Good evening, Mr Ranganathan.'

Ranganathan, standing in one corner of the cabin with another officer, looked up and said, 'Who is she? The summons was for you, please ask her to stay out of this room.' Atul turned to Aarti and motioned her to wait outside, while he moved to the chair and sat on the seat.

'Did anybody ask you to sit?'

Atul stood up and the blood rushed to his head, much to

Ranganathan's amusement. He felt like murdering the guy right there, but plastered a fake smile instead and asked, 'I hope I am not under arrest?'

Ranganathan continued to ignore him, looking instead into the file in his hand. Finally, after a minute, he looked up at Atul and said, 'Please sit, Mr Malhotra.'

Ranganathan took his seat also, and the other officer who was with him sat next to Atul. Then, glancing through a few documents in his hand, Ranganathan spoke, 'Mr Atul Malhotra, you are under oath, we will record your statement and whatever you say will be permissible as evidence in a court of law.'

Atul replied, 'I understand and accept the same.' Atul had been through this part of the drill several times before today, this wasn't the first statement he was giving the guy.

Ranganathan continued, handing over a document to Atul, 'I am handing over a document which is an agreement between Transmech Telecommunications Limited and Luxor Investments, can you identify this document?'

Atul looked at the document, it was a copy of the share sale agreement, which his company had executed. He replied calmly, 'Yes, it is a share sale agreement between my company and Luxor Investments.'

Ranganathan continued, 'How did you come to be in touch with Luxor Investments?'

Atul was now perplexed, he hadn't met any of their executives, he could not name Elisabeth, and he did not even know what connection she had with Luxor.

He thought for a while and replied, 'The process of identifying partners, including Luxor, and all the negotiations were taken care of by our Executive Director Krishna Pandit, who heads our international operations out of London. I am personally not aware of the answer to this question.'

He named his executive from London, knowing well that the ED could not reach him or question him at that moment, and he could be kept out of reach till he was informed to maintain the same line, if questioned.

Ranganathan further questioned, 'You visited Switzerland between 18 August and 22 August this year. Can you tell us the purpose of your visit to Switzerland?'

Atul's heart started to sink, Ranganathan was getting too close for comfort. He somehow maintained his composure and responded, 'I visited the place for a holiday lasting three days.'

Ranganathan showed him a photograph of Elisabeth and asked, 'Can you identify the person in this photograph?'

Atul looked at the photograph and quickly replied, 'No, I do not know this person.' Now, his heart was really racing. He knew something was wrong, really wrong.

Ranganathan showed him another photograph taken just outside the restaurant, after the dinner he had with Elisabeth, that showed Atul shaking hands with her, and asked, 'Do you wish to change your answer?'

Atul's heart missed a beat. Several questions raced across his mind, had she been arrested, had she spilled the beans already, what could have happened here? They had presented him with a photograph, he instantly realized he had been under surveillance in Switzerland, but still kept calm.

'I maintain I do not know her. I did meet someone at the restaurant of the hotel, from the photo you show me now; I can recollect it is the same person that was in the earlier photo. The acquaintance did not last more than a few minutes, there is no reason for me to remember her face, I never met her before or after that occasion.'

Ranganathan asked the officer sitting next to Atul to stop writing the statement for a while. Now, Atul got scared, real scared.

'Look, Mr Malhotra,' Ranganathan began, 'if I asked you so much, you must be a smart man to know that I know a lot more than that. I also know that this lady runs the funds for some politicians in India. I also know that she arranges the funds for your company. I also know that she runs and moves drug and mafia money across the world.'

Ranganathan's way of asking questions was to usually put questions that he already knew the answers to, and then go on to hedge the unknown, using that as a threat. Atul could make out when he bluffed. Atul decided this was a bluff.

'Are you placing me under arrest?' he asked.

Ranganathan refused to answer that straight, 'Well, the evidence we have is enough to nail you, right here and right now. You can make that choice, would you like to cooperate or should we make the arrest?'

Atul was way too smart for him. What was he offering here, toffees if he spoke out? He knew he could never cooperate with the authorities, whatever happened. Also, there was no way Ranganathan would have made such a long-drawn-out appeal if he really had any more evidence. If he had enough on him, he would make the arrest first and talk later.

So Atul calmly replied, 'I do not know what you are talking about, I have no investments from any minister, or from anyone, including the person whose photo you showed me. All my investments are legal, with proper government approvals, and perfectly tenable under the laws of this country. I am a law abiding citizen and unless you are placing me under arrest, I would like to leave.'

What Ranganathan said next only confirmed Atul's take on him. 'We know the facts, and you know very well that we are on the right track too. Let's not fool either of us here. I even know you will run to your friends to tell them about what happened in here. If you can testify against the minister, you will do your country a big favour, and I may be able to plead for a lenient sentence from the courts for your association with all of this.'

Atul didn't lose any time in replying, 'I don't know what you are talking about. You are wasting your time asking me the same question again and again.'

Nevertheless, Ranganathan continued to question Atul in several ways about the same thing, over and over again, hoping Atul would slip up; just one mistake and he could trap him. Ranganathan was smart, Atul was a couple of years smarter than him. Atul's statement was concluded and he was allowed to leave the office at 2 a.m.

Aarti had waited all along outside the room. Atul drove her to his house. They spent the night together. A worried Atul knew Ranganathan would not stop here. He called Elisabeth too, but her cell was switched off. That worried Atul even more. Ranganathan was incorruptible; did he even realize he was trying to nail the FM? Atul was not so sure of that. But he did know that though he himself was under surveillance, nobody could tap his phones, they needed TTL to do that. Nevertheless, he had still to be careful, very careful.

Later in the day, Atul reached out to Qazi and invited him home. He came late in the evening, and as soon as he was comfortably seated, Atul said, 'I am tired, Qazi sahib, internally broken. Honestly, the business does not worry me. I will handle it all. All the investigations, growth plans, funding worries, everything. I have all of you to help me there. What worries me is my personal life. I need to make a decision there. I don't want to do it alone, though I know I am the only one who can do it.' Then he narrated the whole story of his inviting Roshni to the Dome and the final emotional outburst at Aarti's.

'Qazi sahib, I am not able to decide why I go through what I go through. I love Aarti, then why do I even want to think about Roshni? Why cannot I make the decision simple in my head?'

Having heard him out, as the father figure that he was to all of them, Qazi replied, 'Atul, your paranoia is very complex but not impossible to resolve. You may probably never find the right answers for yourself. You have been telling me for years you never loved Roshni. You shared all the reasons and the emotions, but you still hung in there, and you would have continued, but now, you have the reason to make a decision, and that reason is Aarti.'

He waited, while Atul absorbed what he was trying to say. Atul said nothing but waited to hear more. Qazi continued, 'I'll tell you a small story. It's from a film called *Conspiracy*, but it's totally apt here. May I?' Atul nodded.

'There was a boy who got all the love in the world from his mom. He loved her dearly too. On the other hand, his dad was a drunkard who beat the boy black and blue each time he was drunk. When he was still very young, his mom died. At her grave, the boy stood gazing but didn't shed a tear. The tears just didn't come. His father, on the other hand, died living his life in full. At his grave, he cried inconsolably. He just couldn't control his tears. You know why?'

Atul had no answers, he simply shook his head. Qazi replied, 'Because the boy's father had been the object of his hate all his life. With his death, there was no objective or purpose left in his life. His loss left him completely devoid of purpose and empty.'

Atul looked at him, thinking hard as to whether he really hated Roshni. He did not love her, that was a foregone conclusion. But was it hate then? He detested her, he had remorse for her, he never liked to be around her, but his mind never visited hating her.

'In your case, you are giving her pain because of that hate, but will not give her enough to let her go, and thus, relieve her of her pain—that is hate,' pointed out Qazi. 'Hate is a conscious emotion, but we rarely express it openly. Identifying hate in oneself is probably even more difficult than identifying love. Hate must not be confused with anger. It is very different. Hate has no reasons. Often, it just sits deep in our body, rarely expending itself in a way that we can identify. Hate must be dispensed with periodically, when the object of hate is no longer there, hate cannot thrive, and the mind becomes hollow and without purpose. I suggest you must now decide where you stand, and then stand firm on that decision. Accept it and move ahead.'

He said no more after that.

Atul was left to take a decision. He acknowledged he needed to decide. Qazi had indeed made the job easier for him.

Soon, their conversation drifted to the ED questioning earlier in the day. They discussed several measures that must be taken; Atul was emphatic in his views and decided there was nothing that could get them in trouble really. The authorities could search all they wanted; they would have to give up in the end.

Chapter 20

Aarti visited Atul that night, as she usually did, very often, of late. They sat in the balcony of his bedroom, an apartment on the 38th floor of a plush housing society facing the sea. A ship or two sailed in the distance as they sat there on a lounger clinging, as usual, over a few drinks, talking about things galore. Time travelled faster in that balcony than anywhere else in the world, and they were always left wanting more.

'Aarti, I've made up my mind about a few things and I need to share them with you.'

Resting her head on his strong shoulders, Aarti turned her eyes to Atul and caressed his cheeks, waiting to hear him speak. 'I have accepted the divorce with Roshni; I made some corrections in the draft and sent the notice back to her lawyer today.' With tears in her eyes and relief in her heart, she hugged him, then kissed his forehead, eyes, and ended with a messy kiss on his lips. Atul was happy she was happy, and they both sat blissfully in silence.

It was quite some time before Atul saw that Roshni was standing inside the bedroom, staring at them. Completely embarrassed, he got up and opened the sliding door of the balcony and said, 'When did you come in, Roshni?'

Not having gone to the Dome that evening because Jyoti told her not to, Roshni had decided to meet Atul at home today, hoping its familiar environs would give them both a chance to recall better times, and discuss their issues in a less impersonal atmosphere. It had taken her days of preparation to make up her mind to reconcile with her husband and drum up the courage to return, but all of that had been overturned in a fraction of a second. Not by her, but by an outsider.

'I didn't know you were fucking this bitch here,' she said, blazing with rage, 'I shouldn't have come. Jyoti was right, I was mad. You continue to screw her and be happy with her, I am gone for good,' but before she could leave, he grasped her by the arms and pushed her onto the sofa.

She used all her force and finally managed to get up but Atul quickly closed the door to the bedroom and stood there. He wanted to close this chapter today and make his stand forever known to Roshni. Now that she had walked in on it, she knew the unvarnished truth. It saved him a lot of the difficult explanations he would have had to make otherwise.

'Let me go, Atul,' she shouted, 'I cannot stand in this place for one more second, my breath is choking, the place is stinking of her.' But Atul wouldn't listen. Aarti cringed in the balcony feeling guilty about being there, though Atul's promises gave her enough confidence to face Roshni. Now she slowly got up and edged her way to the other side of the bed, and stood there uncertainly.

Roshni looked at Aarti standing brazenly in her bedroom, possessively next to her and Atul's bed, and raised her hand and slapped Atul hard. The power of that slap shook Aarti. Atul didn't say a word, he simply stood still and Roshni collapsed into a chair.

Then, she sat up straight and looked at Aarti, 'What did you get by doing this? You must be the happiest woman on earth today. You finished my family, and are happy. What kind of slut are you?'

Aarti said nothing, just listened; this time, it was Atul who was enraged by his wife maligning his girlfriend. He grabbed Roshni by the arm, opened the door, dragged her down the stairs to the main door, shouting, 'Get out!' Aarti followed a few feet behind.

Roshni stood up to him, 'I am not the one who should leave, I am your wife. Ask this bitch to leave.' Blind with rage, Atul opened the main door and tried to push her out; she resisted. But as he continued push her away with all his might, she suddenly realized the futility of it all and walked away forever.

She was gone. There was silence. Atul shut the door and went back upstairs and sat on the sofa. Atul said nothing, just gazed at the ceiling. A while later, Babulal came to ask if they would have dinner. They had a quiet meal. Atul called Roshni's driver to confirm she had reached home, before getting to the table. That night, Atul felt like a winner.

Chapter 21

Life was on a new course. Another year had passed. The change he asked in the divorce notice was the custody of their daughter. Roshni did not accept it. They went to court; it had all been very painful for Atul. The final hearings were in progress. Aarti continued to date Atul, they were more settled now. Atul asked her to move in with him; she insisted that could happen only if they got married, and they had to wait for the divorce for that to happen.

Ranganathan never got anywhere with the information he had on Elisabeth, and one day, Elisabeth herself reached out to Atul. There was nothing wrong at her end, the leak had happened because the ED was following Atul. He continued to grow his business unabated. The launch of the new circles was just around the corner. TTL got all the loans they needed, there were no issues anymore. He never met Poojari again. The need never arose; however, he did call once for a donation for the national elections, which were to happen soon. TTL contributed about fifty crore. Atul reflected on the past year, but never thought much about the evils that passed with it.

Today was 7 October 2012, an eventful date on the TTL calendar. This was the day they would launch the services in all the new circles on the same day. The event was planned on a grand scale. It was to be witnessed by over 2,000 TTL employees, along with their families. About 500 VIP guests, including ministers, CEOs, technocrats and bureaucrats, would be hosted at the event as well. The Telecom Minister himself would make the first call on the new network announcing the launch of the services. Atul did deserve the best entrepreneur award when one saw the effort and result of this massive exercise.

Every member pitched in. Rakesh spent endless hours meticulously planning and detailing the colossal infrastructure requirements and painfully selecting from available technologies, to bring the best to the market.

Anil virtually lived on the road, understanding the competition, devising a marketing strategy for each market, and going through endless options for media campaigns and sales locations before deciding on the perfect one. He came up with several new service and package offerings for the prepaid and post-paid businesses to beat the competition. TTL now claimed to offer the fastest service in the market and even advertised a lifetime of free mobiles to bolster the claim. Anil stunned the markets with his new schemes; the competition was really on its knees even thinking of their prowess, and therefore the threat this enterprise now posed to them.

Prem worked with the bankers, planned finances in the long- and short-term with Aarti. Together, they ensured there never was a hitch, they craftily ensured that the speed never dipped or slowed down at any time. They met their delivery schedules to ensure everything was up in time.

Qazi dealt with operationalizing the licences, and approved various drafts for thousands of agreements required for offices, transmission cabling, infrastructure, properties, licences and leases. For a man of sixty-two, he worked as though he was still forty-five. It was difficult for him to keep pace with the speed of things, but he hardly let anyone see that. He had decided to retire after the launch, but had not yet let the other promoters know of his plans.

The markets were hoping TTL would come up with an IPO; they were amazed they managed to stay private with all the investments they managed from private funds. The promoters now owned a little less than 60 per cent of the company, still enough to come up with a massive IPO, probably the biggest in the industry. The markets were looking forward to the day.

The fears of the past receded in Atul's mind. He had settled in with Aarti, relationship-wise, and he was happy with her. Aarti was happy with her decisions too. Their dream was still a while away, but she never thought about it. It was a done deal for her, like waiting for a kind of technical glitch to be sorted. The divorce would be decided in a few months. She looked forward to her marriage with Atul in the very near future. She saw no obstacle in that path any more. There were none, really.

Mir came closer to Atul that year, moving beyond the corridors of power and turning into a friend indeed. Atul would never be able to thank him enough for his help. Atul was also in touch with Elisabeth, though she hardly spoke to him for more than a minute ever, but he knew she was there for him.

Aditya remained close to Atul as well, though they hadn't met in the past year. He spoke to him on a few occasions to let him know how things were, but he never took Aditya's advice any more. Nevertheless, Atul was longing to meet him. Aditya was present today, along with Sapna, to grace the launch function. Roshni, of course, was not invited.

The fanfare that ensued was a spectacle to witness. TTL had finally launched its services in the new circles, moving on to the national stage as the third largest company in the telecom services space.

Atul addressed the gathering which had been enthusiastically waiting to listen to what he had to say: 'Good morning. I welcome the honourable Telecom Minister, respected bureaucrats, fellow entrepreneurs, members of the TTL family and their families present, friends from the Press, valued business associates, ladies and gentlemen. Today draws to close a massive exercise of setting up infrastructure at an investment of over Rs 15,000 crore to create the world's fastest implementation of a telecom service in this kind of time.' He paused for effect.

'I congratulate one and all for their contribution to this amazing feat we were able to pull off in an incredible period of eighteen months. There was so much done in this period— putting cell sites and towers over 2,500 square kilometres, laying millions of kilometres of new cables, employing and training over 12,000 new employees, massive campaigns over TV, print and other media, setting up over a thousand new retail stores in the allotted geographies, several call centres and subsidiary offices, seven new corporate offices and as many operational control centres with equipment from around the world.' The venue rang with applause until Atul put up a hand requesting them to let him continue.

'In a while, when the honourable Telecom Minister makes the first call on this network, all these will be put to the test. I hope it will be a happy call. Come tomorrow, customers will experience this service, which I assure you will be the most reliable and economical telecom service anywhere in the world. It will be our endeavour to take customer experience to a new high. We have worked hard to build this, we now wait to hear from our customers how they rate us. I thank you once again and hope you have a wonderful day with us. And now, I hand over to the honourable minister. Thank you.'

The short speech drew a standing ovation lasting over a minute. Atul waited for the applause to stop before he handed over the proceedings to the minister, who unveiled the service to the world.

'Hope everything went well?' Atul asked Aditya.

'Oh, excellent; when you are the boss, how can things go wrong!' replied Aditya, smiling.

'Did you have lunch?' Atul asked, looking at Sapna. 'No, we were hoping to have it with you,' she replied.

'Of course, but I cannot see Aarti, I need to introduce her to you guys, she is dying to meet you.' He soon spotted her among the crowd and called her. 'Guys, meet Aarti, the apple of my eye; Aarti, my great friend Aditya and his beautiful wife Sapna.' Aarti hugged them both.

'Atul talks so much about the two of you, he just cannot stop,' she gushed, 'I was so hoping to meet you today, I am so glad to see you.'

'So were we, you think you don't figure in every conversation we have?' Aditya laughed, as he said this to Aarti.

Sapna was taken by Aarti's beauty; she was looking exceptionally beautiful in a bright purple saree she wore for the occasion, and which made her the centre of attraction. She didn't need much make up, she was naturally beautiful. Though only Atul knew she was more beautiful than that, only he could see the inside beauty of his miracle girl.

Knowing Aarti was there to take care of his dear friend, Atul said, 'So guys, you will have to excuse me, Aarti will take care of you, you guys have lunch. I have at least a hundred people I must personally acknowledge and thank for being here today, I hope you can understand, I will see you in a while,' and so saying, he vanished into the crowd.

★

Over the months, the services were monitored closely, and Atul spent his days and nights at the famous War Room of his corporate office. He personally overheard calls being attended at the various call centres—complaints, service issues, sometimes even compliments. He received painful statistics of the issues at hand, and ensured they were systematically dealt with by the other directors and senior executives in time.

It did become one of the most reliable services in the country.

People swore by the TTL brand. Soon, it was business as usual but at another level. But Atul could never rest on his laurels. In a review meeting in the presence of all the directors, Atul said, 'Prem, I think it is time to think of our next steps. Our Vision 2015 is almost a done deal, we merely need to steer the ship, there is not much to be done. Do you think it is time to think ahead? Maybe, Aarti and you can start working on the next vision plan?'

Rakesh quickly snubbed Atul, 'I think we must wait, Atul. We surely have the infrastructure and services in place, but we must wait a while for stability and new customer flow to come to a threshold level before we can jump into newer ventures.'

Anil intervened, 'Rakesh, look we have beaten our own estimates for subscribers in the first month itself by 20 per cent. In fact, in the second month too, growth has been higher than estimates even with a broader baseline. The revenue per subscriber is also strong, the best in the industry actually. I do not see any reason to believe we are doing anything wrong or there will be any mishaps.'

Rakesh said, 'Me neither. In fact, customer complaints have dropped to half in less than two months; by then, we can safely say we have managed the start-up glitches also pretty well, but we must wait a while before we take on new ventures. We won't have operational break-even for another year; we should not deploy finances meant for emergencies to any expansion till then. Any failure to meet estimates in the first year will need cash from the reserves, if that cash is committed elsewhere, we could be in trouble. That is all I am saying.'

Atul, hearing his point of view, said, 'Guys, I am sure we all know that. All I am saying is start planning; we will invest after a year if that suits us, but any plan now will be very large, it will need a year's preparation at the very least. Also, I am thinking acquisitions; let us identify targets that are a quick ticket, since organic growth could take years to kick in. Keep a plan in hand. The moment we make operational profits in the current venture, boom, we startle the markets again.'

The directors unanimously agreed to the suggestion. Qazi also agreed without any comments. Who could dampen Atul's excitement? The excitement of an achiever could only be fed by more excitement.

At the end of the review meeting Qazi decided it was time to make his farewell speech as well. 'People, I have a thing or two to say, and I hope you will agree. I am getting old, my health does not allow me to do justice to my job. I wanted to do this earlier, but the launch did not let me. But now, I need to rest, I want somebody to take up my role. I have a couple of trained lawyers in my department who will do as good as or even better than me. I'm sure you will allow me a long holiday; what do you think, people?'

Atul replied, 'Qazi sahib, I think your contribution to the company has been more than exemplary. I cannot imagine anybody else in your place. We will never feel safe without you. As much as that is true, you know we will never place our word ahead of yours. This is your company, you can come in whenever you feel like. But we cannot let you go, we would all like you to continue, if not as regular as you do now, as a guide and a mentor. We will leave the decision to you and respect that. But please do not remove your hand from our heads, we will feel orphaned without you. And I mean it.'

Qazi's eyes were moist in gratitude when he heard this. 'Thank you, Atul, I can never imagine a world without all of you. I will be there whenever you need me or whenever I can come and spend some time, but for now, you must let me go.'

Atul got up from his seat and hugged him respectfully. He could not put the acceptance of his decision in words, he could not muster the courage to let him go, but he had no choice to what was being asked. He accepted it with grace and respect for the old man.

★

One morning, Elisabeth reached out to Atul by email, in connection with some opportunities in South Africa. A medium-sized telecom company was on the block. The proposition interested Atul. It needed a small investment of about 250 million in equity. Elisabeth wanted to meet Atul to talk about it, if he was interested. Atul accepted and a meeting was arranged in Cape Town. Elisabeth also agreed to get some of the promoters to meet Atul for some initial discussions.

Elisabeth met Atul at his hotel at Cape Town. Unlike last time, there were no secret parleys; she called and they agreed to meet over dinner at Atul's suite instead of a restaurant. The meeting was cordial.

'Good evening, Elisabeth. It is indeed a pleasure to meet you after such a long time, how have you been?' asked Atul, shaking her hand and showing her in.

'Very well, Atul, I am indeed good, and you?' replied Elisabeth, dressed in a long light-gray woollen overcoat that perfectly set off her blue eyes and blonde hair. They met like the old acquaintances that they were, though Elisabeth refrained from divulging any personal details even now. It was okay with Atul. It didn't matter. Soon, they got to the subject of the meeting.

Elisabeth said, 'There is this company, I have shared the 'white paper[3]' with you already, I presume you have read it. They are a listed entity; we propose that you initially buy the entire promoter's stake, we can also help arrange any equity funding you may need,

[3] Short summary of an opportunity or proposition.

but that would be in your primary company in India, you will need to re-route the funds from there.'

'I have read the white paper, but I need to know a lot of details though. I need to visit them and meet the promoters to know how things are. But the opportunity provides an excellent entry into a growing market like Africa. Also, I did have a small funding issue, your help would be necessary and welcome too. One more thing, we would have to delist the venture, at least for now. Let's be safe, we don't want public questioning on the source of funds. So we may make an open offer post the acquisition to buy the stake. I will need my lawyers to look into the exact laws here to do that, but it would be a necessary requirement.'

'You are a sharp man, Atul,' Elisabeth nodded. 'I was sure it was a perfect fit, I wouldn't have proposed it otherwise. I rarely bring any proposal to the table that may be rejected. I hear about your great success back home. I am happy to partner with a gentleman like you.' Soon, they concluded the discussions relating to the opportunity. Atul agreed to make a blue print after getting the necessary legal ticks and the upcoming meeting with the promoters.

'I had a small question, if you are comfortable talking about it,' he said to Elisabeth, as though asking her permission. She looked at Atul, kind of knowing the nature of the question.

'Please go ahead, I will do my best to answer.'

Atul asked, 'Who killed Shalikram?'

Elisabeth had anticipated the question. 'Well, Atul, in our business there is no scope for chances, that is also the secret of our success. The man was not worthy of a life. God almighty chose that fate for him. The question you ask doesn't concern us any more; if I were you, I would never seek answers to questions which do not concern me any more, let us pray his soul rests in peace and leave it at that. Some people seek their fate faster than others, he was one of them.'

Atul quickly knew he would never know the answer. He also agreed with Elisabeth, he should never seek it either.

★

The divorce arguments had concluded and the family court would give its verdict at the next hearing. Atul's lawyers had made fierce arguments for Ananya's custody. In return, they had been offered a monthly visitation for their client, pending the final decision of the court. Atul ensured he spent the first Sunday with Ananya; over time, he was getting very fond of her. He had begun to thoroughly enjoy the routine. She was almost two now. He loved the way she kicked his face when she walked over his stomach in play. He never failed to notice how her high cheekbones, broad jawline and crown resembled his, more every time they met.

Atul was deeply pained by the arguments and affidavits filed in court by Roshni's lawyers and his own. Fighting a contemporary in business is one thing. If that contemporary was family and the fight wasn't for business, it was a sorrowful thing. Win or lose, it would be painful either way. Was marriage invented to cage love? And if it was, could it be love then? These and similar questions got him to damn the institutional future of marriage, if separation left you so scarred in the end. He had promised Aarti he would marry her, and he loved her more than anything else. However, he was beginning to believe that marriage as an institution did more harm than good to a couple. He was beginning to build very strong opinions against it. But he left that for another day.

The judge was to pronounce his judgement today. Aarti accompanied Atul. Roshni was accompanied by her sister Jyoti and brother-in-law Jignesh. She couldn't understand why Atul had insisted on custody of their daughter. For his part, Atul had initially wanted to delay the divorce—he liked being sure about where life was taking him, and preferred to hold on to all his options as long as needed. Asking for custody ensured he got a couple of years. That is exactly what happened too. He was a strange man, he kept his cards close to his heart and options open all the time.to take that call. Over time, he became fond of Ananya, which just added to his reasons. His lawyers fought the petition overwhelmingly, even accusing Roshni of horrific things she had never done. Atul didn't like any of it, but he had to accept it in the end; besides, equal muck was being thrown from the other end as well. Today, it would all end.

Soon after the court resumed, Case no 432/10-11 was called out, Roshni Sinha v/s Atul Malhotra. The court pronounced the order. The judgement was at least four pages long, the divorce, of course, was granted. The judge gave his views while pronouncing the judgement.

'Mr Malhotra is not a faulty parent, he is fully capable of providing for maintaining their daughter Ananya. However, his primary shortcoming in relation to maintain their daughter remains his continued relationship with Ms Aarti Mathur. Also, the defence could not establish sufficient cause for the court to believe that there was any disability in Ms Roshni, which would disable or restrict her ability to maintain her daughter. Considering Ananya's age, the court maintains the custody remains with her biological mother, Ms Roshni Anand Sinha.

'However, the court grants visitation rights to Mr Atul Shyamlal Malhotra for one Sunday every month. If the biological parents are not able to mutually decide on that, it shall be the first Sunday of every month for a continuous period of eight hours during daylight. Further, annually the court hereby grants Mr Atul custody for a continuous period of fifteen days. This will coincide with the school vacations for the daughter, from time to time, as may be mutually agreed. Also, in case there is no agreement on the timing, it shall be the first fifteen days after the official vacation. The petition is put to rest.'

Thereby ended a major dilemma and chapter for Atul. He was remorseful in court as he met Ananya and hugged her for the last time before he could meet her again, before she was handed over to Jyoti, who was waiting eagerly behind her. He did not even greet her. He knew what she had done to his family life, right from planting ugly seeds to this day, when the court passed this order against them.

That evening, Aarti and Atul went out for dinner, but Atul was unusually silent. 'I understand what you are going through,' Aarti said, taking his hand and saying softly and soothingly, 'but aren't you also happy today? The darkness has ended and it's daylight for you and me. Finally, we have closure that we waited for so long. I understand the court did not grant you custody, but that was expected, wasn't it? See the brighter side of it, please.'

Atul was unmoved. He heard her out, knowing she had no idea what was going through his head. 'It isn't about the custody, Aarti,' he said. 'Whether the court finds me guilty or not guilty, I know I am not innocent. It takes two to destroy a marriage. We managed that and well. Divorce is a bitch and marriage is the mother of that bitch. During these months of the court battle, I learnt one thing. I married once. I lived the marriage. The bonds it created killed its soul, its very purpose. Eventually, we lived together only because of the bond we had signed up to; more of a bondage than a bond, an institution reduced to an agreement of servitude. And today, I am in another relationship. I wonder why I'd want to jeopardize it with another marriage,' he said honestly.

'Why are you even thinking anything like that will happen to us!' said Aarti, shocked, 'We have just started.'

But Atul wasn't to be deterred. 'You don't understand, honey, it isn't about anything happening. We are happy, nothing changes. Whom do you want to prove anything to with a paper signed in court? It just lays the foundation for a divorce. Breaking up is hard enough, why the paperwork? Love doesn't need certified true copies. Marriage mutates the love into something else. One marriage, one divorce, and I know that.'

Aarti saw her dreams rapidly perishing. 'Atul, I didn't wait more than two years to hear this. Marriage is an institution where families are built. I want babies, I want respect, so we can walk with our heads held high in a bond that's socially recognized and respected. I have trust and faith in us; if I didn't, I would simply have moved in with you. You cannot ignore my feelings; it is your responsibility to make me feel at home too. It cannot be you all the way.'

Atul said flatly, 'Society institutionalized sex. The same society institutionalized marriage too. Aarti... let's not make it about man and woman. I promise to be faithful to you, but think about it. Is it necessary to cage us? I cannot get around the thought that marriage was invented for the deceitful, so that they remained monogamous; at least in the other partner's mind, if nothing more.'

Aarti said nothing. She didn't know how to convince Atul on this. She was deeply aggrieved; her forehead wrinkles spoke loud and clear. She could see the future she dreamt about so long now slipping away for real.

'And Aarti, let's not make this a man and woman thing. Look Aarti, this isn't about you. Let's think about this. Let's enjoy our meal now. But I really want you to consider this.'

This was a total turnabout and had caught Aarti completely unawares. She wasn't willing to change her views suddenly to fit in with this change. 'Don't take me for granted, Atul,' she warned, 'this is a subject we discussed time and again over time, and you never told me any of this. It is unfair of you to take this stand now.'

'...But I'd never been through the pain of a divorce earlier,' said Atul, 'I know it now, so do you want me to ignore what I feel? I love you, isn't that enough?'

'It isn't,' said Aarti, in a tone that brooked no argument. 'I am very clear. We cannot deal with this, we will leave it at that for today. But it's best that you know I cannot accept this.'

'Let's eat,' said Atul, agreeing, 'We will deal with it another day.'

Having pushed the issue under the carpet, Atul breathed easier. Life moved on for now. Aarti was not ready to give up, but Atul knew he was done with marriage.

★

The results of the national elections were due, and pollsters were predicting a hung Parliament. Atul was hoping Poojari would return to power. But the results were a complete surprise to everybody, including Atul and the pollsters. The opposition National Democratic Party (NDP) won an absolute majority. Poojari lost the election in one of the worst drubbings he'd ever had. He lost his parliamentary constituency too. Atul called him and realized that the tables had suddenly turned. Poojari needed Atul more than Atul needed him.

On his next visit to Delhi, Atul made it a point to visit Alam Shaikh, treasurer of the NDP. TTL had funded them as well for the last two elections, hedging their bets, giving them five crore in the last one. He needed to let him know TTL was willing to switch alliances. It was business.

On the relationship front, though, it had began to wobble in the wake of his newfound distress. Each time Atul and Aarti met, they would somehow manage to drag themselves to the question of marriage, and since he kept speaking his mind on the subject, their opinions never converged. Their dates became quarrels—Aarti would persist and plead and Atul would insist. The inevitable arrived one day when Aarti said, 'Atul, I've been wanting to tell you something but managed to gather courage only now.'

'Since when did you need courage to talk to me about anything?' said Atul, stunned, 'What are we doing to our relationship!'

Aarti quietly spoke her piece. Over time, it had become slowly clear to her that this relationship would eventually challenge all areas of her life, possibly scattering the focus that she had built up. And so, she told him, 'I don't think I am doing justice to my talent, Atul. It has been a while since the launch, but my mind is always consumed by us. I have not been able to get satisfaction from work; even there, all I think about is you. I want to do something independently. I want to prove to myself that I am worth something without you. I need time.'

'I don't see it that way but...' said Atul, and asked straight out, 'Are you wanting to opt out?'

'No, honey, its not that,' she replied, 'just that I want your opinion. I feel I need to join another company, just for a while, so you and I can think through the options. Also, it will get me back to what I was. I don't think I am enjoying my work; I am hardly working these days. At work, all I think about is us. And really, I need to think about other stuff too. I think you must also do the same.'

Atul took a minute to respond, and when he did so, it was in neutral tones, 'Look, Aarti, you don't need my permission for anything. You haven't understood me if you ever thought that way. It is sad that you should even talk this way. I wouldn't stop you from pursuing anything professionally. That decision would always be yours. And let's not mix us with the job; they are two different things, I would like to keep it that way.'

The relationship dynamics had shifted for both, and perhaps

irrevocably. The evening ended on a polite and superficially friendly note, and the next morning, Atul found Aarti's resignation in his mailbox. He accepted it immediately, though he didn't want to, but could do nothing about her decision. She felt almost betrayed when she saw it had been accepted; it was a loosening of ties. She now saw their relationship only going downhill, and Atul couldn't see it any other way either. His views on marriage were hard even for him to comprehend. But he would not compromise on them, not even for Aarti. Not at least now. He soon would, but it would be too late then.

Chapter 22

Around six months passed peacefully, and within a couple of months of her resignation, Aarti had drifted completely away from Atul. They hardly even spoke, let alone meet. She joined an NGO working for spastic children and loved her job there. Initially, she and Atul met every week, but as the bickering continued unabated, work and deadlines started popping up as excuses so as to avoid another confrontational meeting.

Ranganathan, however, remained faithfully attached to Atul. He had simply been silenced by Poojari. Now, the winds of change had blown him into Mumbai as Deputy Director, Enforcement Directorate, and he had launched a full investigation into the doings of erstwhile political bigwigs. He didn't take long to summon Atul and also hauled Poojari in, showing the latter incriminating documents with regard to his family's association with Luxor. Poojari somehow found it convenient to blame it all on Atul, and attempted to hang Atul using the few strings he still had in Delhi. The ploy didn't work beyond a few hours.

Atul was summoned again, and Ranganathan said, 'Mr Malhotra, all your friends in the corridors of power are now worrying about their own well-being. I think it is time for you to name them lest you get into trouble.'

'Mr Ranganathan,' responded Atul, 'I have built this business on hard work and prudence. I don't know what makes you feel TTL is a charity which survives because some politician funded it.'

'Look at this,' said Ranganathan, showing him shareholding documents relating to Luxor which clearly indicated that some family members of Shravan Poojari owned almost all the shares in the company. 'Is this TTL's so called FDI?' he asked. 'Please tell me what I must do with this information. I can place you under arrest right now. I also know I won't be able to keep you in jail for long with this, but I am sure there is more evidence out there against you and your prudent company. It won't take too long for me to get there,' and Ranganathan wasn't bluffing.

Atul was unnerved. For the first time, he was seeing the real chance of a problem here. Getting Ranganathan off his back now seemed impossible, but he still refused to give in. But he was very aggrieved by the whole episode. He called upon Shravan Poojari at his residence in Delhi and said, 'Mr Poojari, you need to sort this mess out, I cannot let my company be tainted by your mess.'

The ex-minister did not like his language and retorted sharply, 'Look, Mr Malhotra, I did not give these documents to Ranganathan. I was questioned too, I have denied anything to do with Luxor or its investments. In fact, they have moved the international courts to freeze the assets of the company, which holds over 1.2 billion dollars in holdings with various companies. This includes 250 million in TTL.' Poojari had neatly extracted himself; now Atul did not know what to do. He was really worried, and the next day's headlines proved him right.

Ranganathan had gone to the media with the story, because he did not want any shutdowns from the power corridors in Delhi. The media called it the Luxor Scam. A national daily ran it on the front page, 'Former Finance Minister Shravan Poojari owns billion dollar Swiss-based Luxor Investments'. It opined funds had been moved there through hawala transactions and invested back in companies in India. It also gave a list of twenty-three companies with investments from Luxor—TTL topped that list with US$250 million. The news also gave the names of TTL's shareholders and the relationships of those shareholders to Poojari. The writing was on the wall. If Ranganathan really had evidence, Atul knew he was in serious trouble.

That morning, there was a huge police deployment outside the TTL Head Office because NGOs, opposition parties and public interest groups across the country were agitating against TTL. There were reports that some TTL showrooms and offices had been stoned, glass broken. There was rage against the company across the nation. An executive director based out of Pune had his face blackened, was made to sit atop a donkey and paraded on the city streets.

Atul announced that all offices and public touchpoints be shut down for the day, and then called the PR agency they had recently hired. He also summoned Rakesh, Anil and Prem. Qazi was in office and was called in too, but since he was busy creating a legal net for the company, he said he would not sit through the meeting but come in when he could.

Atul opened direct fire on Baig, the PR agency's CEO. 'Who is this chimpanzee we have employed in the name of PR? Baig, I want to know what you are doing about all this. If this continues for a couple of days more, we are doomed. We cannot have this continuing, I need this situation sorted.'

'I understand, Mr Malhotra,' replied Baig, unflustered, 'but this is a serious situation. There are no easy answers.'

Just then, Qazi walked in, asking Atul to sign a few papers. Atul asked him what they were. Qazi replied, 'Anticipatory bail applications. I am seeking this for all four of you. We have no choice, the next natural step for the ED is to pick you up. There is pressure on the government to hand the case over to CBI. If that happens, it is a surety.' Atul signed it and got back to Baig.

Suddenly, there was so much happening but he knew he had to save the business before himself. He knew arrest was imminent as far as he was concerned, but there was no proof that TTL knew about Luxor's owners, so the authorities couldn't eventually prove anything, at least that was the consensus in the room. There was no clinching evidence of wrongdoing here. At least, that's what Atul and Qazi believed.

Getting back to the discussion at hand, Atul reeled off instructions, 'Damage control. Arrange a press conference, we will talk to the press; that will send out a message to the media and the public at large, it may calm some nerves, I will handle that. Anil and Prem, you guys go live tonight on all media channels, Baig, I need you to arrange this. Pay what you need to get positive coverage and maximum visibility on prime time. Let us also release a press notification. Run advertisements in every newspaper in the country tomorrow giving a clarification from our end. Get in touch with all the NGOs, start with those holding black flags outside, pay them double of what our competition has paid them, get them off our back.' He stopped and looked around, 'Right. Is there anything else we can do at this moment?'

Rakesh spoke up, 'We need to increase security cover at all installations. I have already asked the Chief Security Officer to look into that, even a rat won't be able to enter any of our locations.'

Qazi walked in again, 'I got off a call with some people in the ruling party; they are not interested in pursuing this because if it blows up, some of their leaders will also be in trouble. It's a bloody mockery of democracy, they are all involved in this mess.'

'Can they help us in any way?' Atul asked.

'There is too much public outcry,' said Qazi, 'They will not do anything, at least not now. They have handed over the case to the CBI, the announcement will come within the hour. We have filed for an anticipatory bail, it will be heard tomorrow. Also, I suggest all of us operate from one of our guest houses, it is not safe here, just in case.'

But Atul refused, 'No, Qazi sahib, we are not gangsters, we are businessmen. Let us hold our head high, they won't be able to get at anything, all we did was take money and do business with it. We paid our interest or dividend from time to time, we didn't care where the money came from, but when it came to us and through legal routes, we did what every honest businessman does with money. We did business with it. At best, they can arrest us, but we must always stick to our ground. Also, make sure we do not do or say anything negative at any time. Let's not give them anymore ammunition than they already have.' Qazi accepted Atul's point of view. He couldn't agree with him more.

The boardroom was set up for a press conference in fifteen minutes. They didn't have to wait long, the press was thronging the gates of TTL for bytes anyway. The room was filled to capacity. There were representatives of at least fifty media houses barraging them with questions. Qazi addressed the media asking them to remain quiet, when Atul walked in, head held high. His natural flair undisturbed, he faced the media with poise. The shutterbugs took snaps of him, as if he was a thug who had walked in or maybe a celebrity. There was so much chatter; it was impossible to get the questions correct, there were at least ten people talking at the same time. Atul still got the most important ones and started to address them, they all wanted to know the same thing.

'Mr Malhotra, please tell us what links you have with former Finance Minister Poojari?'

Atul replied, 'We have absolutely nothing to do with him. I haven't even met him in the last two years.'

'How did your company agree to take investments from Luxor Investments? How could you not know who the owners were?'

Atul calmly replied, 'Investments are sought through professional arranging agencies like merchant bankers. We rely on their expertise and experience, and the onus of due diligence is on the investor. We only received funds, we have the necessary Foreign Investment Promotion Board (FIPB) approvals for all the investments in our company. There was no way for us to know their ownership structure. Indian law does not even require us to know that.'

'You are lying, Mr Malhotra. How could you not know Poojari owned Luxor Investments?'

Atul quickly replied, 'I still don't know that, it is the media that is saying it. Please let's not jump the gun and pass judgement. It is the prerogative of the courts to decide on that, and we will wait for them to pronounce a decision on that.'

'Is it true that you had a relationship with Aarti Mathur and she has now resigned from your company?'

Annoyed at the question, Atul replied, 'The question does not concern the company or public in any way. I refuse to respond or comment on that.'

Among so much chatter, it was difficult to gather who was saying what, and even what Atul was saying in response. Atul had to appeal for silence, so he could hear them and they could talk as well.

'Everybody is saying that the rapid growth of TTL was achieved by corrupt practices and a trail of dirty money that flows here; what would you say to that?'

'TTL is an open book, our growth is a result of best practices in business. Our financing is open to any scrutiny and it goes through several audits. There is absolutely no dirty money in here. There are government regulations in place to scrutinize the source of funds, it is not our business to look at that; we pay our interest and dividends for the money we borrow or bring in as equity from time to time. We are ready for any and every investigation to prove our point.'

'Mr Atul, do you think you will be arrested?'

Atul replied, 'I don't believe I will. TTL has done no wrong, so we have nothing to fear.'

'There is also a story that you are the victim of a political vendetta?'

Atul replied again, 'We have nothing against any political party or union; our business is based on sound principles. We have nothing to do with the politics of the country.'

'It cannot be coincidence that the money from Luxor flowed into TTL, it must surely be political money...'

Atul reiterated, 'I have already explained how Luxor came to invest with TTL, there is nothing more to it. If the ownership does belong to people who amassed that wealth by illegal means, it is for them to answer that and not for TTL. There are rules set by the administration for investments, we followed every one of them.'

'How would you address the public outrage against your company?'

Atul replied calmly to that one, 'I grew up in poverty, and rose to make a future with the opportunities provided by a resurgent India. I would appeal to the aggrieved people of this country; we are as much a victim of corruption and political crimes committed all the time. As a company, TTL has always subscribed to ethical business practices. In our twelve-year long history, there has never been a single investigation against us. We are innocent. Please be patient, let the authorities handle this. I respect our citizens and know they will not do anything to damage the peace.'

They issued clarifications, press notes, advertisements, went live on air on multiple media channels, paid off NGOs, media houses, even bloggers and tweeters, to generate positive chatter or at least to kill negative chatter. They did everything they could to mute the chimes. It helped to a large extent, but Atul knew this wasn't the cure; it was only a stop-gap remedy. Within a day or two, operations resumed.

Knowing that the real problems were yet to begin, he called another meeting, 'We've got to get ready for the CBI and the investigations. It's going to be long-drawn-out, with arrests and investigation. I don't see a way out. I still believe we have done no wrong—does anybody in here believe anything else?'

It was a rhetorical question, too late to ask. They all knew that. The question was irrelevant; any answer would be completely devoid of value.

Atul continued, 'I will lead the investigation, I will take responsibility, at least, for the investigation, we cannot all get arrested if they must arrest us. I want the business to run; I will see to it from the other side as well. I have run too long too far, I need some rest too.'

Anil intervened, 'Nothing of the sort is happening, and if it does, we take joint responsibility.'

'Don't be an emotional fool,' snapped Atul. 'We need all of us at work. No one would believe any of you signed up for anything, all the documents are signed by me. If you volunteer, you will go under, but they won't spare me anyway. So, let me handle this. You trusted me till today. Trust me now. This phase will pass too.'

In another completely unrelated development on the morning of August 21, 2012, the Mumbai Police arrested Prem from his residence. Atul learnt about it within minutes of the arrest and rushed with Qazi to the police station.

Prem's arrest, it turned out, was the unfortunate outcome of an unrelated police raid on Bharat Pesticides and the subsequent arrest of Bacchu. A truly unlucky coincidence for Atul, Prem and TTL. Without Shalikram in power, Bachhu knew he had no other godfather and confessed all, giving the police a trail of hundreds of criminals, Salman included. The court gave police remand to Salman, who named Prem in the Prashant Nagarkar case since Prem had spoken to Salman, allowing access to his goons into the TTL compound.

It turned out that a day earlier, the police also had visited the

TTL security gate, seized the entry registers for the period and taken statements of the guards on duty. The gate entry confirmed that Prashant Nagarkar did enter the premises, he signed in, but there was no exit entry. It also marked the entry of the two men who were arrested later the same day; the person they came to meet, as per the register, was Prem. The news did not reach the management as they were busy handling the other crisis.

There were fourteen murder cases against Salman alone, all the bodies having been cremated at Bharat Pesticides. The police had clinching evidence at hand. The court granted the CBI police custody of Prem for seven days, for further investigation—the Luxor crisis pyre was still burning and another inferno had hit TTL. Atul just didn't know what to do now. This was a criminal case. The evidence was too much, not enough to convict Prem in any way, but enough by itself to ground the company for now.

Atul met Prem briefly and told him, 'Look, brother, I cannot change what happened. Just sit tight, don't talk, say you know nothing. The only thing they have against you is a security entry saying the guy was coming to meet you. There are at least twenty Prems in the company, there could be a mistake. That entry can at best keep you in for twenty-four hours. I will put all our might behind you, just hang in there till then.'

On the way to office, Qazi made a few calls appointing the most prominent lawyer in the city, in tow with whom came a battery of solicitors and counsels. They had only one task, get the man home.

Just as he was about to walk into his cabin at work, Atul saw a missed call from Aditya and called him.

'Hi, Atul, what's wrong between Aarti and you? You never told me it was over.'

'It wasn't,' said Atul, wondering why he had to deal with this now, in the middle of the worst crisis TTL had ever faced. 'We just took a break, she needed to think about things, so did I... he let it trail knowing his friend would not have called him just because of rumours of a problem with a girlfriend. Something else was up. So he asked him outright, 'What's the matter, Aditya?'

'Atul, I got a pre-invite for her wedding, she is getting married!'

Atul felt the walls closing in; it was a blow so deep that all the problems he had faced in the past few days paled into insignificance. Somehow, he pulled himself together and said, 'Look, Aditya, she did what she had to. I don't have the time right now to discuss this because we have a real mess to sort out here. I'll call you later, at night. Also, catch India's news, then when we talk at night, I'll tell you all about what's happened; Aarti may not be so important a discussion then.'

There was no time to mourn, think or express any emotion; there wasn't enough space in the mind left to fuel the emotional pain he felt or to allow it to take any form of expression.

Within minutes of that call, Qazi visited Atul's cabin, 'Atul, they are on their way.'

'Who, they?' asked Atul.

'The CBI. I just got a call. I'd put some minnows there knowing this was coming.'

Atul was scared, 'So, what do we do about it?' he asked.

'Nothing, I guess. Just wait.'

It wasn't a long wait either. A few minutes later, six men walked into the room, handcuffed Atul, and arrested him in the Luxor Scam. He was taken to the CBI's local headquarters to be presented in court later that evening. Qazi had a job on hand again. He had long forgotten about his retirement plans. Anil and Rakesh were the only ones left to handle everything else.

Chapter 23

At the CBI office, Atul was made to wait in a room with grey walls. There wasn't much else in the room; just a small square table in the centre, with a chair on either side. There was a large one-way mirrored glass window beside the door, for investigators to watch proceedings from the outside. The room was air-conditioned. He waited, hoping someone would come soon.

Soon a small man, about 5'2" in height, thin, with a French beard, arrived. But for the beard, he would have passed off as a college kid. He was wearing an over sized white shirt and black trousers. He came over and extended his hand, 'Hello, Atul, I am Madhavan, CBI. I am the investigating officer for this case.' He spoke in heavily accented English. Atul got up and shook his hand.

'Please sit, please sit,' said Madhavan courteously, seating himself in the chair opposite. 'So, Mr Atul, I have gone through all the things you have said to my good friend Ranganathan, so I won't waste your time asking you the same again. I want to know what you haven't said yet.'

'I doubt you've gone through everything I said to Mr Ranganathan,' replied Atul, 'because I also said I had nothing more to say, other than what I had already told him. You should have read that too.'

'Very well, Mr Atul, we have our means. You are an honourable man, I would not like to go there.'

Atul looked at the man thinking he couldn't be serious. Just then, another officer came in and handed over a document to Madhavan. Madhavan read it for a minute and walked out of the room.

Outside, Madhavan spotted Qazi was preparing the bail documents; the CBI couldn't take Atul into custody unless a CBI court granted permission. They should have taken him straight to court to request custody before any kind of interrogation. So Qazi served a notice to the CBI office, warning them of any action against his client without appropriate court custody.

Soon enough, Atul was taken out of there in a police van to the CBI court. There were at least a hundred journalists waiting to take one picture, one photo of a handcuffed Atul Malhotra; a picture that would make national headlines the next day. A handcuffed Atul was smartly photographed by a few on the way from the CBI office to the car. There were at least five police vans behind and ahead of his car in the cavalcade going to the court. The journalists with their hundred-odd vehicles followed this cavalcade.

The prosecution explained the charges against Atul, including destruction of evidence, violation of the Foreign Exchange Act, connivance and offering bribe to government officials, and demanded fifteen-day CBI custody for interrogation. They also showed the document of ownership of Luxor Investments and proof that TTL had equity from Luxor.

The judge asked the CBI lawyer, 'Why do you need custody? Is the accused not cooperating?'

'We fear the accused will not cooperate and will run away; he is also a very influential man,' he replied.

The judge then looked at the defence lawyers. There were so many, the courtroom was full with them. It looked like all the lawyers of the country had been employed to rescue one Atul Malhotra. The senior counsel, a national celebrity himself, rose and presented his case.

'Your honour, the prosecution has no case against my client. They accuse him of destruction of evidence, violation of the Foreign Exchange Act and promoting corruption—with no documentation to prove any of it. The only case they have is a document suggesting that Luxor Investments, the company which has invested equity in my client's company, is owned by an ex-union minister. There is no evidence this document even exists, the document they present as evidence of ownership is not even verified. My client is a reputed citizen of this country and has never missed a single date when he has been called upon for interrogation. My client is willing to surrender his passport and will present himself on every occasion, when requested. Without any admissible evidence tenable in the court of law, we request your honour not to accept their demand, we fear they will harass my client.'

The prosecution interjected, 'Your honour, the document has been issued in a foreign land, we have already requested verification. In the meanwhile, we fear the accused will move to destruct evidence if allowed to roam free. We need time for verification, we are also building the case on the other charges, and we need custody to interrogate.'

The court heard both parties. 'Do you have any documents to back up any of your other charges?' asked the judge, and waited for the prosecution to say something. They were silent. He continued, 'Merely on charges suggested without any evidence, the Court cannot grant custody to the investigating agencies. The Court does take cognizance that documents issued in foreign soil need time for verification. This Court grants the bail. However, the Court instructs the accused to remit office till such time the Court passes an order otherwise. The Court also bars the accused and any other promoters from sale of shareholding in the company where they are directors. The accused is also instructed to remit his passport and is barred from foreign travel without the permission of this Court. This Court also directs TTL to deposit an amount or provide a bank guarantee of Rs 1,250 crore within thirty days of this order; this being the entire equity Luxor Investments has invested in

TTL. The Court hereby grants bail to the accused in these cases till the next hearing.'

The CBI had hurried to arrest Atul without any preparation, thanks to pressure from the union ministry, because the government needed to calm public outrage and show action. They didn't care if the court discharged him. Atul drove straight home, along with Qazi and Anil. Rakesh was in office handling other matters of importance.

On the way, he asked, 'What's happening with Prem's case?'

'That comes up for hearing tomorrow,' Qazi replied, 'The police have twenty-four hours to present an accused in court, CBI must present immediately. We are prepared in that case. We were, in fact, worried about your case.'

Anil was handling the PR and media, and doing a good job. Now, he immediately changed the company positioning and played the victim card. The court discharge had given Anil the teeth to plant that story and he used it well. He claimed they were being made scapegoats in a larger political battle between the government and the opposition. It was an easy sell.

Late that night, Atul called Aditya, it was about 2 a.m. 'Atul here, Aditya, tell me now.'

'Atul, I am so worried for you, we haven't slept and have been watching the news. I heard about your bail, I was waiting for your call, but I knew you must be busy. I hope you are all right.'

Atul replied, 'I am fine, Aditya. Soon, this will be over, it's a phase; they are on a wild goose chase, there is nothing they can get from me. What were you telling me about Aarti?'

Aditya replied, 'I received an email from Aarti, it was a pre-invite; she is getting married on 18 November 18, the invite will follow later, it said. Some guy in South Africa, I am not sure. I was wondering what happened, you told me nothing.'

'Well, Aditya, there never was time. I guess it is fine, good wishes to her, what else can I say. I will also message her to congratulate her. I will accept that as the fate of things.'

'Atul, what is happening there? Things were so good, we met hardly a few months ago, what suddenly happened?"

Atul broke down on the phone, 'Aditya, can you come to India? We must talk, I need help, I am all alone in this battle; I cannot fight all these demons.'

Aditya immediately said, 'I'll be there in a day or two, just hang in there. Everything will be all right, we will set everything right. Be a man, you are the last person I can imagine crying.' They spoke a while longer, until Aditya was sure Atul was stable. After that call, Atul messaged Aarti, 'Congratulations. May you have a lovely married life and a wonderful future.'

The reply didn't take time, it arrived in a couple of minutes, even though it was 2 a.m. 'Thank you Atul.'

A tired Atul thought about Aarti for a while, his heart began to break with distress as he thought of his times with her; soon, he was so tired, he drifted to sleep for the night.

★

Much to Qazi's disappointment, the Sessions Court granted the police fifteen-day custody of Prem and he was sent to the city jail. Atul could do nothing to change that; they appealed in a higher court. Three days later, the Mumbai High Court granted bail to Prem. It was unconditional bail, which was good because Prem could now walk free till the case was settled. Qazi knew that would take at least twenty years. Though he did spend three nights in the city jail with hardened criminals, as one among them.

Atul also called Elisabeth. There was something he needed to do. 'Hello, Elisabeth, I am sure you are aware of all the developments,' he said.

'Yes,' she replied, 'I hope you are well.'

Atul quickly continued, wanting to make this very short. 'Look, you deposited 250 million into my account. The amount Poojari asked you to give me. I want to move that money, just in case they get their hands on my account.'

'I don't know,' was her hesitant reply, 'That will not be easy. The Indian government has moved the Swiss authorities to freeze the accounts of Luxor Investments. But unless the Indian government can prove money laundering or drug links, the bank is not obliged to share the information. I never deal with any drug or terror money, so I guess we should be safe. However, in case your government is able to prove anything, your account will be exposed too, since the money was wire transferred into your account directly from Luxor Investments. The best I can do is move the money out in cash and keep it on me, but I cannot guarantee that either. I will try.'

Atul suddenly saw a new problem. If the Indian government did get hold of the direct bank transaction between Luxor and Atul, he would be sealed for good. There could be no legal explanation as to why Luxor would give Atul US$250 million in his individual capacity. Setting that problem aside, he requested Elisabeth, 'Please do your best, please keep me informed, and thank you.'

Next, Atul called a board meeting, the last he would attend. The court had restrained him from holding office on the board of TTL. So Anil chaired the meeting and was appointed the new Chairman and CEO of TTL, as Atul stepped down from the board and all other positions he held in the company. Prem did the same voluntarily, pending the police investigation against him in the Prashant Nagarkar case. Anil and Rakesh insisted he stay, but he wouldn't agree.

Atul's shareholding and that of all the other directors would be frozen; they would own the shares, but were barred from selling or transferring them. The resignation calmed the general public's nerves too. Anil would have the uphill task of building TTL's lost reputation. They would need all their reserve cash to fill the losses. Thankfully, they hadn't made any of the new investments they had spoken about.

A number of circles began to show sharp dips in sales, day by day, and much-needed additional subscribers in the newly launched circles were hard to come by. Customers were not willing to trust TTL any more.

Anil called a meeting with Shobha Rane, Ramya Apte and Raman Babu in the War Room. 'You have done us a great service, held your nerve even in these times, and shown absolute dedication in delivering as per your role expectations. However, we do not need the laundry any more. With the turn of events, it is an unnecessary exercise.'

He paused a bit before continuing, 'I want the three of you to resign. I don't want you to continue in this company, I don't want to put you in any kind of risk now or in the future. I hope you understand.'

He continued, 'The company will give you three years' salary as compensation. I am hoping this should be enough to take you through the transition with ease. If there is anything else I can do to help you in any way, I would be glad to do so.'

The three were filled with gratitude. Anil hugged each one of them as he personally escorted them to the door of the War Room, and finally closed the door on a dark chapter in the history of TTL. The company would start with a clean slate once again.

Late that evening, Anil visited Atul, he knew Atul needed help. Atul received him at the door, already a few drinks down. They hugged for a good minute, which gave Atul much needed energy and warmth, something he missed acutely at this time. Anil knew Atul might be down with all the problems that surrounded him, but he was definitely not out.

'So, how is work?' asked Atul, as he and Anil went to the

den and made themselves comfortable. 'Are things showing any signs of settling?'

'You did a good thing by not letting all of us get involved,' replied Anil. 'That isolated us, we could simply say we knew nothing and that you handled everything. If you hadn't done that—not isolated us—TTL's management would have changed hands.' He paused for a moment, struggling to control his emotions, then said, 'Thank you, you took care of us like your younger brothers. We are all very sad at what is happening. Work will fall into place sooner or later, I don't see a problem there. But when we reflect at all the things we did to get here, I don't think it was worth it, do you?'

Atul finally spoke, 'Well, nothing is really wrong, you think they can prove a thing against us? It is really a matter of time before things will be normal. The evidence they have can never get them any convictions; you and I both know that. Public memory is short; they will soon forget this even happened. I still maintain we must not do or say anything wrong. Keep your head high and you will float, we are all the best fuckin swimmers around here, aren't we?'

Then he asked, 'Do you know anything about Aarti?'

'I know she is getting married,' said Anil, looking at the carpet, 'I heard that, she called me last week to tell me that.'

'And you didn't tell me?'

'Where was the time! Also,' he said, looking up at Atul, 'I didn't want to disturb you any more than you already were.'

'What do you think made her take this decision all of a sudden, you don't think she should have spoken to me once?'

Anil didn't know what to say. 'Look Atul, after you parted with her, what choice did she have? And you don't go around asking exes when you start a new one. That's not how it is done.'

Atul said nothing. He continued to sip his whiskey. 'Thanks for coming, Anil, I really appreciate it. I don't know how long my freedom will last; I am sure the CBI will knock again when they have verified the documents and put a few more fangs on the other charges they have made out. I am enjoying my time till that happens.'

'Atul, please don't say all this. We are standing by you, every step you take. You are not alone, so don't feel alone.'

Atul smiled and raised his glass, saluting their friendship. 'Life was so simple at General Mobiles,' he reminisced. 'We were so carefree, never took a problem home. All the girls we flirted with, all the time we spent over the pool tables after work, ...the beer challenges. ...Even making those small tweaks in our reports to impress the bosses. And once we were out of there, our crazy parties where we smoked up, drank like fish and danced like mermaids, without a worry. I miss those days now...'

'Yeah,' said Anil, laughing, 'remember the one time I fell for that chick, what was her name, Neha or something. And I asked you to talk to her for me. You know how shy I was, and I remember that chick told you, "I don't love Anil, I love you Atul." Rakesh and Prem couldn't stop laughing for weeks over that one,' he recalled, adding, 'and the bastard that you are, you actually banged her. I got so angry, you have no idea, felt like killing you. Even now, I feel like that when I think about it.' Atul laughed, his first hearty laugh in a long time. Anil smiled, he had brought up that memory just to improve his friend's mood.

Atul said remorsefully, 'Can we get those days back, Anil, the Rs 30,000 a month we made then? It was a happy 30,000; the race to add so many zeros behind those four has brought us here. Our poison is still the same, and even now, we need just three pegs to get to heaven.'

Anil looked at Atul and picked up both glasses, giving one to Atul, and then raised his and said, 'Cheers to those times,' and they drifted along in a nostalgic reverie for hours, remembering times that they had left so far behind.

The next day, Atul waited for CBI officials and Aditya to

show up. Both were due. He wasn't sure who would come first. He hoped it would be Aditya. However, he did make one fatal mistake, he dialled Aarti. 'How are you?'

'I am fine, Atul, how are you?' she replied.

'How do you think I am?' he asked.

'Well, I know things are hard on you, I am sure you will come out of it soon,' she said.

'Do you know why things are hard, Aarti?' he asked. Even before she could respond, he continued, 'You should have spoken to me once, Aarti? I mean we made so many promises to each other, how could we just part and forget them all? I made a few mistakes, but they were mistakes.'

'Atul, what do I tell you. I respected every decision you made, you decided we must part, without as much as telling me goodbye and putting an end to our relationship. Can you imagine what I went through? Feeling completely discarded, as though I was an obstacle. Just taken for a ride when I was easy. I still respected your decision, never interfering with your life. Went through the pain in silence and built my life again.'

'My guilt has killed me enough, Aarti. I'm paying a heavy price now,' replied Atul. 'Almost as though I cheated on you. And from the moment I heard this, I really don't know why it is affecting me, but it is. Lost chance, wasted life, cowardly thinking, misuse of your trust, all of it, and only me to blame for everything. I am so mad at myself. I can't think of anybody more patient than you in my life. I know I made a mistake, an unpardonable one. But one pardons loved ones. I realize my mistake, and that it was of an unpardonable proportion. But our love was real. You know that and I know that. No one can question that love. I want you to reconsider your decision, it is not late, I don't want to let go of our dreams for us.'

There was a short silence at the other end, and then, Aarti

spoke, 'I know you are in pain, but there is nothing I can do about it.' She took a deep breath and said, as gently as she could, 'I don't love you any more. I cannot help but believe that and I want to have nothing to do with you any more. There were a lot of dreams we built, there was a time for us and that time has passed. You moved on, so I moved on. Today, you've rebounded because you're in misery. Once that is gone, I will be gone from your mind all over again, then what? When I was with you, you never cared for me.'

'No. Aarti, my rebound is not situational, yours is... To myself I say, "One way or the other, suffer you will," but that suffering is an outcome of hope and love that I truly wanted to experience with you. Within your subconscious self, you believe you have buried our love, which is why you could shoot your new love out.

It is born out of the seed of your old love that you chose to bury. It was born out of the situation, necessity, need, experience and pain.' He paused, Aarti was quiet, so he continued. 'You gave fictional birth to a new aspiration. I call it fictional, because your love is born out of the necessity to bury your past love. And even as the new seed sprouts and grows ever deeper roots, you will feel me screaming as those roots strangle me below. Ignoring my cries and trying to look the other way seems your only option. But remember, just as we blind ourselves to a past we wish to forget, we also blind ourselves to the evils of the future. Our mind shows us just what we want to see, just so it can carve the path it has chosen for the self that it embodies itself in. This is rebound... And you are right; you cannot *help* but believe that you do not love me any more.'

Aarti remained silent for quite a while, she did not know what to say, she really had moved on. She loved Nikhil, her fiancé. She could not do anything to relieve Atul of his pain. He must find his way. She had little emotion for his distress now. The time was gone. She had tried to pacify him and give him the strength to fight, but now she was the worst person to do that for him. Broken love was painful. She knew it way better than him.

After they disconnected, Atul spent the rest of the day mulling over times gone by. He had all the time in the world to think about his two broken relationships. He felt responsible for them. As if the pain of that regret wasn't enough, the guilt, the severe guilt of having pained Aarti so much, tore him apart. At times, he broke down and cried, then would calm down a bit, only to cry again.

Aditya did not come, nor did the CBI, though Aditya called to say he would be there in another couple of days. Atul spent his time in solitary confinement. He wasted himself when he couldn't handle it, got some energy, did some positive things, thought of things, even called or messaged Aarti. She was getting fed up with his stupidity, she had so much to do in life and Atul had nothing else to do.

Finally, Aditya did come. Atul went to pick him up at the airport and hugged him. It lasted long, very long. Atul could have stood all day with that hug. Aditya broke the hug, 'Enough, brother, let's get home.' They got into the car and Aditya spoke in concerned tones, 'Atul, you are facing arrest, even that doesn't seem to bother you as much as Aarti. Get your priorities right, I'm really surprised at a businessman like you getting this emotional. Life is all about being rational.'

Atul started the car and said, 'This is what it is. I know I am not thinking rationally, I even know she doesn't think about this at all.'

'So take a cue and move on,' replied Aditya, 'It will pain you for a day, maybe a week; you'll get over it sooner or later. You are strong, you cannot go on behaving like this. So, what's up with work?' he asked, trying to bring Atul's focus back to what really mattered. Atul gave him all the details of the court order, his resignation and the impending CBI arrest.

'Now *that* really worries me,' said Aditya when he finished, 'and honestly, that is what must worry you too. Wake up, Atul, there is more to life than lost love. She is planning her future, you should be planning yours.'

Atul said nothing, but felt more balanced than he had in a long time. Aditya had shown him anew to tilt the scales of balance in favour of rationalism, and against emotion. Soon, they reached home.

Chapter 24

After a wash, Aditya and Atul sat in the infamous balcony of Atul's bedroom, where Roshni had found Atul and Aarti embracing. Atul picked out a bottle of whiskey and two glasses from the closet, while Aditya stood at the balcony watching the setting sun as it changed from a radiant yellow to a bright orange, then shimmered down to a hazy magenta. He waited to see what hue nature would dazzle him with next. But Atul, least interested in any of this, pulled him down to a chair and perched himself on the couch.

So, Aditya took up from where they had left off in the car, 'You are acting insane. What's come over you? You must realize that your love for that girl was always an infatuation! Don't you realize that?'

'So that's what you think I am, insane. So does Anil. Even Aarti gave me doses of sanity assuming I was insane. You know what I have concluded?' he asked Aditya, who was by now holding his head in his hands, 'I am the only one who is sane and thinking straight, and I am dealing with the collective insanity of people around me.'

Aditya started to respond but Atul hadn't finished, 'Insane people, and in my definition that means you, just want me to agree that your insanity is the sane way to be. Because your insanity will bring stability to my environment, make me content with what I have. But being content means killing desires and aspirations and settling with the status quo. So….,' said Atul carrying on with his thesis, 'if I rebel against your insanity, the stability caused in the environment will start to collapse. Too many people turn like me, and the order of the world will be questioned. That's what you don't want, because it will destroy generations of rules, written and coded and brainwashed into kids and adults alike. You are the coward and not I.'

Aditya, more than a little alarmed at the way his friend was carrying on, said, 'Calm down.' This was a side to his friend he didn't know existed. He cautiously added, 'I don't subscribe to what you say, at least not in this regard, and there is no point getting philosophical about it.' But Atul wouldn't relent.

'Why do we need to perish under the burden of responsibility of sanity and balance, which is the order of the insane world,' he asked passionately. 'Just so that we can join the ranks of the billions of insane people who have already sworn allegiance to perceived interest before their real and larger quest—to be unique, to be more than just ordinary, to be extraordinary? These are the people who stop to seek, and start to desire. Very few even experience the urge to move toward such a destiny. For most, moving away from the security of civilization becomes just next to impossible.'

'Snap out of it,' said Aditya, with the bluntness of an old friend. 'I am sorry I brought up the subject of insanity. I'll tell you what is happening to you.'

While Atul was deciding whether or not to get offended, Aditya asked him, 'When did you start thinking so intensely about her again; you and she quit months ago.'

'When you told me the other day that she was getting married,' said Atul. 'For a while, I was okay, maybe even happy for her, but after that...'

Aditya hit his head and said, 'Damn me. I told you that. In any case, I guess you would have known. But tell me something, did you feel anything about her when you first decided to move away?'

Atul thought it through and said, 'I guess not.'

'So, until what I told you the other day, you weren't really obsessing about her. Okay, now listen to me, I've known you for years now, probably better than most. What you are seeing in yourself is nothing but pure ego,' and he waited for that to sink in.

'You forgot about Aarti when she went away, it didn't bother you. The reason for that was somewhere in your mind, you believed she was out there for you. She never rejected you, you rejected her. Suddenly, when you learnt she had moved on, it hurt your ego no end that she could actually love anyone other than you. The same ego now was ready to do anything to overturn that. Get it?' he looked at Atul, who nodded.

'You still don't need her. Your ego does. You know what she has done is right. You even know where you stand today—in no position to hold on to her. You could be in jail in a few days, what kind of a life can you promise her? The ego can make us do insane things, Atul, including calling the whole world insane. If you don't believe me, please convince me why did she not haunt your thoughts until the moment I told you about her engagement?'

Atul had no answer to that. Nodding, Aditya carried on, 'For a woman, marriage is the most important event in life. Now that she's taken that decision, don't expect her to return. She will turn back only if she feels the way that you feel. I know it is very hard to believe things are the way they are. But unfortunately, they are the way they are.'

Aditya was right, and Atul had no choice but to accept it. Nevertheless, over the next few days while waiting for the CBI to move court again to cancel his bail and arrest him, he mostly thought about what he could do to convince Aarti that he loved her and get her to be by his side. Neither the CBI nor Aarti dropped in.

Finally, about a week later, late in the evening, the CBI knocked on his door. Atul came out of the bedroom hearing the hustle bustle below. Two CBI officers with at least twenty police officers entered the house. As soon as one of the officers spotted him, he said,

'Mr Atul Malhotra, you are under arrest, you must come with us.'
Atul had been anticipating this for so long that he simply asked for
a couple of minutes, changed into a plain white shirt and trousers
and walked down the stairs and gave himself up.

He was presented in court. They did have the verified copy of
the ownership of Luxor Investments. Their other charges had also
acquired fangs. The court, however, only granted judicial custody.
The defence still argued his fresh bail plea, but in vain. Atul would
go to jail that night.

Qazi immediately applied to the High Court for a review of
the order of the CBI Court. But that could happen only the next
day, it was very late that evening for courts to hear the petition.
In any case, that would turn out to be an inconsequential exercise.

The media was abuzz and every channel was talking about
nothing but the arrest. Anil sat in office all night monitoring
developments. The TTL team even made a four-point programme
to attack the administration using neutral media such as social
media platforms, independent speakers who visited the debates
that evening, they even influenced anchors to ensure Atul was
given a fair representation.

The four-point defence revolved around the following facts:

1. TTL was only an innocent beneficiary, as it had received the
   money from Luxor through perfectly legal channels.
2. Also, now that the ownership of Luxor was verified, why was
   only Atul arrested while the former minister and his family
   sat in the safety of their homes?
3. If charges of corruption were alleged, there must be someone
   who had received the money given by TTL—why was only
   one angle of the story being investigated?
4. Were bureaucrats and politicians above the law? The
   administration had dropped all charges of violation of the

Foreign Exchange Act as they never found anything on it after making the charges. What did this prove? Maybe the other charges were false too.

They also suggested that this was trial by media and that TTL was being victimized to guard the real culprits behind the scams and frauds. TTL had absolutely nothing to do with any of it.

They highlighted inconsistencies like these and various other smaller stories like why the other companies in the scam were not being investigated. Slowly, these things began to neutralize the negative opinion against the company. Some channels even slanted their reports to show Atul as a hero, running stories of his history and his rise to fame.

Nonetheless, even after all of this, Atul would still go to jail.

A journey that started with repulsing the devil, continued when he jumped into the sea; the devil was there too. He befriended it, it took him deeper. Soon, more devils came along, now he would live with the devils. He left himself no choice!

One thing happened the next day as an outcome of the media roar. The CBI, in a disproportionate assets case, arrested former Finance Minister Shravan Kumar Poojari. He was jailed too.

★

As Atul Malhotra wrapped up his story, Qasim and Krishna did not know what to say. The last few hours had left them spellbound. They could not come to terms with what they had heard. How could a man of his calibre and honesty come to do the things that he had done?

Atul completed the rest of his jail term without much ado, and was finally released on 14 July 2014—two months before he completed his eighteen-month term. Qazi and Anil came personally to take him home.

Chapter 25

Though the world outside hadn't changed much in two years, nothing was the same. He was a changed man, and most of that change had happened in the first few days at prison.

Anil took his friend to his own house; the huge fine ordered by the court had knocked off all Atul's assets, and even after that, there was a lot left to pay. Atul had a shower followed by some home-cooked food. Anil told him to rest for the day, and stayed on to try and cheer him up, but soon realized Atul wanted to be alone.

Atul spent most of the day either lying down or standing on the balcony, looking at the fast-paced life below. In two years, he had lost seven kilos. He looked frail and tired.

That evening, Anil knew he couldn't keep the news from Atul any longer, and after dinner, once they were sitting comfortably, he said, 'Atul, there is something I need to tell you.' Atul looked at him, puzzled, and he continued, 'Two weeks ago, Roshni met with an accident. It was a terrible one, and unfortunately, she did not survive.'

'What!?' asked Atul, in complete shock, 'When? Why was I not informed? Why would you hide something like this from me?'

'Atul, this happened only two weeks ago, they were travelling to Pune…'

'Who is they? Who else was there?' he asked, worried.

'Ananya, Roshni's father and their driver,' Anil replied.

'How is Ananya?'

'She's fine. She only received a few bruises. An oncoming truck struck the driver's side and Roshni was sitting right behind him. The impact killed them both on the spot. The old man and Ananya got away with a few stiches, nothing major. I visited them last week; they are fine, Atul. Nothing to worry.'

'I want to meet Ananya,' Atul said.

'Sure, Atul, I'll talk to Sinha sahib, he'll understand.'

The only decision he had made in jail was to reason with Roshni and correct his mistakes. He'd wondered for hours every day if she would forgive him. Unfortunately, fate had denied him even that chance.

'Is there anything I can do, Atul? What's happened has happened, we have to face it.'

Atul silently stared at the floor beneath his feet, his mind trying to take it all in. 'I'll take a while. The time spent behind those walls silences the mind in any person. All this is too fast paced for me now, Anil. I just want to meet Ananya; I want to know she is well. That's all I want now.'

Ananya was almost five years old now. Atul was desperate to find a way to keep her, but no court would allow a convict to take custody, even if she was his daughter. For his part, Anand Sinha did not want Atul to meet Ananya. Anil tried to put some sense into him, Roshni's death had weakened the old man a lot, made him more vulnerable emotionally; but he was still very angry at Atul's actions and did not want him in Ananya's life. Nevertheless, after much convincing on Anil's part, Anand Sinha agreed to let Anil take Ananya to meet Atul. Ananya got into the car with her maid and they drove to Anil's house.

Atul saw Ananya. She looked like a doll. She had a Band-Aid on her head from the injuries. She resembled Atul in so many ways; her nose, high cheekbones, big black eyes, even her broad forehead. The impact of the pre-birth conditions had not affected her; she was among the fortunate few. Atul mentally thanked Roshni for not agreeing to the abortion. His heart had melted as soon as his eyes fell on his daughter.

Anil introduced them, 'Say hello to papa.' She said nothing of the sort. She just stared at Atul and announced, 'He is not papa, my papa is at home.' Anil did not know what to say. She was talking about her grandfather. Since Roshni called him papa, she too called him the same. And she had no other papa, so it made sense. Roshni always thought she wouldn't feel isolated among peers this way.

Atul held her close, wanted to hug her, but Ananya wasn't comfortable. 'I am your papa. Papa had to go far away, so he couldn't meet you all this time, but now I am back. You want to see baby Ananya?' he asked, and showed her a photo of him holding her, which had been taken the first day at hospital. Her mother was in the photo too and Ananya started crying.

'I want to go to mamma,' she wailed, and wouldn't stop. Anil had been told by Mr Sinha that she must not be reminded about Roshni, her sudden demise had left the child very troubled and traumatized. Atul tried to divert her, 'Let's play a game, you want to play a game?' and he brought out a Barbie playhouse that he had bought for her earlier that day. He set it up for her, a house, a Barbie; it also had Margaret and George, the fabled doll's parents, but Atul made sure to leave them in the box lest she remember her mother and start crying again. The little girl was soon involved with it all. They played for a while, trying to make Barbie sleep, bathe and change clothes, and all of that. They laughed, played; he experienced fatherhood for a while.

Anil finally said, gently, 'Ananya, it is time to go home, Nana is waiting for you.' Atul looked at him; Anil told him, without expression, 'He told me maximum four hours.' He continued looking, said nothing. Atul went to the car to drop her, carrying the playhouse and other gifts he had bought for Ananya and handed them to her maid.

'Can I come with you?' he asked Anil, 'I will sit in the car while you drop her off.' Ananya sat in Atul's lap. Atul kissed her and hugged her all the way. Finally, they reached the apartment. Atul handed her over to the maid.

'Wait, aunty,' said Ananya to the maid. She looked into the bag and removed the box containing George and Margaret. She handed over the dolls to Atul and said, 'I will put Barbie in my room, papa doll does not live with me and mamma doll left me too, so I am alone now; you can keep them both.'

Ananya had finally accepted Atul was her daddy indeed. And not only that, she also accepted that her mother was gone for good. Tears rolled down Atul's eyes. Ananya had become an accidental casualty of his divorce. He was sure of that; the only thing he was unsure of was whether it was accidental. A helpless Atul walked back to the car while Anil took her away. He cried like a baby.

Aarti and Roshni roamed his conscience; Ananya had shaken it completely. His being was shattered by the turn of events. But, as they say, life must go on, and it did. Atul couldn't shake off the death grip that guilt and remorse had on him though, nor was he able to come to terms with how life had changed for him in the blink of an eye.

One evening, Anil decided to talk his friend and partner out of his misery. He wanted Atul to take up something and keep busy, but what? The court had restricted him from participating in any business. The huge fine had knocked off all his assets, and even after that, there was a lot to pay. It would never be enough. 'What do you want to do, Atul? I mean, have you thought of something?'

'I don't think that is something I need to think of now,' replied Atul, 'except that I need a place of my own, I cannot be a burden on you much longer.' Anil waved that away and said, hoping to cheer him up, 'There is an invitation if you want to take it up.' Atul looked at Anil, wondering who on earth would invite him now.

'Bombay Management College has instituted a case study in their syllabus on you. It is named "The rise and fall of Atul Malhotra". They want you to speak to the students.'

Atul looked at Anil. 'They have already written my obituary, now they want me to come to my own funeral?'

'It is not that; on the contrary, they have extremely good things to say about your management acumen and business strategies. But they cannot ignore the other part of the truth. In fact, it may be an opportunity to talk about it and get them square; we have to do that some day. You spoke about public relations all the time,' said Anil, trying to convince Atul.

'When is it?' Atul asked Anil, after thinking about it for a while.

'Let me set it up for you,' Anil replied.

'I spoke to Elisabeth a couple of days back,' Atul said, 'I have been thinking about it. US$250 million is lying with her. It is TTL money really. The amount Poojari gave us. The South African telecom opportunity is still there for the taking; you think I can do it again? I cannot do anything here, I was thinking if you are okay, I can try there and start a new life,' and he looked at Anil with anxiety and hope. He knew it would not be an easy answer. And it wasn't.

'Who would be happier than me to see the vibrant you back in action? But Rakesh and Prem would never agree to TTL using the money anywhere. We have forgotten that money, we can never have anything to do with it. But I wouldn't mind if you used it to do something good,' Anil replied. 'I will not let you die until you have erased the scorn of taint life gave you.'

Anil set up the lecture for Atul at the college. Atul reached the college. It was the largest management college of the city. Famed. For the first time in his life, he was unsure of what he would say. Would it even make sense, did he have the moral authority? He was at a loss as he waited in the conference room until he was escorted to the auditorium.

It was packed to capacity with two hundred students who applauded as he entered the room. Atul stood there, no emotion; a smile for a second or two. Nothing beyond that. Soon, the room fell silent.

'Thank you,' said Atul.

'Good morning. I am told you invite speakers to this podium based on a student poll. I am surprised how I got that vote. I never got it when I should have, why now?

'Would anyone want to answer that?' he asked. The students, all two hundred of them, waited in silence. Then, a girl from the middle of the auditorium raised her hand.

'Yes,' said Atul, acknowledging her.

'Good morning, I am Rita Sharma, 2nd Year MBA. I am guessing we wanted to know what is your story, your version of the truth,' and she sat down.

'Anyone else?' Atul asked, and waited for a while. No one responded.

'Okay, so I guess we do have a starting point. My version of the truth!' he said, and thought about what to say next.

'You know the story, my story. But I don't believe in stories, all stories are different, but they are, after all, just stories. We can't get anywhere with stories. So we will not talk about the story. You already know it. No two stories are the same, but behind every story, there is a truth. Let's talk about the truth. Let's make that the topic of discussion today.

'I started my career coming out of a college like yours; my ambitions were similar to yours, and my hopes and anxieties too were no different.

'I joined one of the largest telecom companies, ended up founding one myself, making it one of the largest telecom companies around, all in a span of fifteen years. Even went to jail for doing that. Even today, my ambitions are similar to yours, and my hopes and anxieties too are no different. But there is a difference and that difference is I have a version of my truth.

'In the literal sense, truth is merely a stated fact. The versions are in the mind. My version cannot be your version, so you ask me mine, and rightly so. So what then is my version? Versions of truth are always arguments.

'Life may throw devils on your path to success. Disgusted, you may take another path. It may not be the best path, not the most honourable path, but it is a lesser evil to choose that path, because to achieve success, succeed you must. So you take this alternate path. Not too far away, you see another devil; once again, instead of confronting the devil, you opt for an alternate path to success. The decision is the same as the last time. It even comes faster this time. It's easier this time, for you've been there and done that.

'The devils continue to come, only they seem slightly bigger each time. Soon your mind succeeds in fooling you that the path you take is the path that must be chosen. Honour takes the back seat in your mind. Do it all the time and, soon enough, you forget to question your actions and caution ceases to exist. But on the path of devils, one more devil is all you will ever see.

'Unless you are faced by compelling needs, needs rising from inequity and consciousness, you will never need to confront the devils. All you do is avoid the devils you face and switch to the alternate road ahead. Passing these devils and forging ahead of them soon becomes the road to success. The more you win, the more you start to love it. A time comes when all you want to see is more devils and win over all of them.

'Enough time passes at this game, you become the devil. But you still don't realize that. It takes you too far, and when you need to look back, you realize how far you have come while also seeing all the devils you crossed along the way while forging ahead.

But they do not look any different. They look like you. Infact, they were like you before they too become devils. Almost clones of you. When this reality dawns, you know the devil was always in you. You are the devil, and depending on how far you have moved down that road, you are only bigger than the ones you left behind in the race of life.

'This is my version of the truth. Thank you.'

The audience rose as one to applaud the man for a full minute. Atul stood modestly all that time, waiting, and out of shame, he thought. The kids out there hoped to get a story of his defence and a juicy one; instead, they got a lesson for life and without any garnish, straight and simple.

*

Atul felt regret, guilt and remorse. His life was moving slowly, but his mind raced with thoughts of destruction. His present could no longer fathom the things he had done in the past. At times, he did pick himself up to think positively. He wanted to lift the broken pieces and rebuild again.

One day, he got a call from Elisabeth and booked himself to go to South Africa to meet her. He knew Aarti was there too. He hadn't planned on meeting her, but he had never got a chance to apologize to her; not enough of a chance, he thought. A large part of his guilt also arose from that episode of his life.

He met Elisabeth at a hotel room, just like last time. His decision to buy the company was driven purely by the necessity to start all over again, not by hope or ambition. He discussed the option of purchasing it with her and asked for time to think over it. He was not ready for it. Elisabeth agreed; it wasn't her choice really.

Back at the hotel room, he sat thinking about Aarti, whether he should make the call or not? Whether he should meet her or not? He couldn't even decide that. He was a devil after all, a large one at that.

'How are you, Aarti?' he finally made the call very late at night.

'Atul?' she asked.

'How have you been, Aarti?' he continued.

'Where are you calling from?' she asked.

'I am in Cape Town, staying at the Table Bay hotel,' he said.

'Oh,' she said. 'How are you, Atul? I learnt about it. It was in the news here. I was happy to read it was finally over.'

He didn't reply.

After a pause, he said, 'How is life with you?'

'Well,' she said, 'It is how life is, never easy. I work for an NGO here, they work with spastic children, and I handle fund-raising for them.'

'That is really noble work, I am happy for you,' said Atul. 'I am sure you like it, you always did. How is Nikhil?'

'He is good. He is busy with his own software development company, he started it recently,' she said.

'That's nice,' said Atul, before continuing, 'Would you like to meet me?' he asked.

'Sure, why not, let's meet. I have work during the day, but I will try and finish by 4 p.m., let's meet after that. How long will you be here?'

'I don't know,' he said, 'but I will wait for you tomorrow,' and he disconnected.

Atul did meet Aarti the next day. She hadn't changed much. The same face, the same manners, only the flair was mellow. She wore a white salwar kameez; he had mostly seen her in T-shirts and jeans outside work and in suits at office. Even today, her beauty didn't cease to appeal, thought Atul, as he looked at her approaching the lobby.

They greeted each other and Atul asked, 'Where do you want to sit?'

Aarti looked around, 'Wherever,' she said. 'Okay, there is a lounge at the first level, Casimma or something; lets sit there, its pretty tranquil.'

It was tranquil, in fact it was a pretty silent place. It overlooked the inner harbour, had dazzling views and one could see the boats pass by. It was a quiet afternoon. Except for a few bearers moving around to serve guests on some other tables, it was mostly isolated. The place was bathed in natural light reflecting off the painted white interiors.

They each sat waiting for the other to speak. It took a while before Aarti could muster some courage to break the uneasy peace, 'You have lost a lot of weight. You haven't been taking care of yourself,' she said.

'Have I?' he asked, 'I guess you are right. But I've lost much more, and weight comes last in the list of my losses. How is life with you, Aarti? You didn't sound convincing last evening, I could read your mind, I still can, at least I believe I can,' he said.

Aarti saw the bearer approach and said, 'An Americano for the gentleman and café latte for me.'

Atul intervened and said, 'Make that two café latte, no Americano please.'

Aarti looked at Atul, surprised, but didn't comment on it. Atul never had any latte; in fact, he despised it, his coffee had to be black. 'I still know how you think too,' she smiled. 'Honestly, I don't know what to tell you or even whether I need to tell you. Anyway it doesn't matter now, things happen and we are responsible for our own choices in life. There is no one else to blame. I guess it's the same everywhere.'

'We did what we did,' said Atul, 'I erred, you moved, and then it didn't matter. I did what I thought was right, and you followed up and did what you thought was right too. We are square, I guess.'

'Atul, we always live our relationships with an exit option. I did that. You did that. I don't know where you stand with Roshni, but I still continue to do that. I guess everyone does. Even during those days, there were occasions I thought about a rehash; I guess I didn't have the courage to face your mess. I couldn't tell you then but I can tell you now, the love never died. Yes, I guess that was it.'

Aarti was not happy. A conclusion Atul drew from that one line. But would she be happy with him? He guessed not. Still, he needed to talk. 'I had to visit the inside of a jail; I couldn't do much to put my life together again. I tried to pursue you, but I guess, after a while, it didn't make any sense to me either. I simply let you do the thinking and assumed that was the best way forward. I am guessing you are not happy with your choices. It doesn't mean making another choice today will make you any happier, will it?' he asked, as though he were ready to try again even today, and he was. But what he said and thought did not match.

Aarti thought again before replying. 'I guess yes, I have to agree with you.'

'Every person we meet on our journey leaves a memory. That memory leaves an imprint on us for the rest of our lives. I have learnt that the only objective is to keep that imprint a happy one,' said Atul.

Aarti smiled, 'Did I leave a happy imprint?' she asked. He sat there and said nothing. 'You haven't replied, Atul,' she said.

He finally said, 'Well, let me tell you a few things I felt, I still probably feel those now. You never saw me in love with you. It happened later, long after you left. The time we were together, I was still deciding, it was just too short and so much was happening then. I also harboured a lot of confusion. By the time I realized it, you were long gone. When I could not stop loving you, I simply tried to chuck the emotion of love out of me. I found no other way. Whether that is a happy imprint or otherwise, I leave to your judgement.'

He calmly observed Aarti fidgeting with the linen and the spoons; she was still structuring her mind to say something. She didn't know how or what.

'Do you regret it, Aarti?' he asked.

'Regret what?'

'You know what.'

She waited for a while before she replied, 'The regret will never leave me.'

They sipped their drinks before Aarti continued, 'I believe I got into the relationship in a hurry; I went with the flow. That is who I am, it was more like a rebound relationship, though I never wanted to think of it that way. By the time you came back to me, it was too late, I had begun to like my new life, and I never thought we could make a happy life anyway, even if we tried. I was also angry with you about a lot of things.'

Atul did not want to pursue that chapter of his life. He had buried the mistakes he made. He had probably got to Aarti in an attempt to rekindle that part of life that he missed with Roshni. He had never really missed Aarti while they chose to take the break from the relationship. When the realization dawned upon him that he had played with her emotions all along, he had felt guilty about it. So much guilt that it almost consumed him, even when in jail. Guilt for playing with her emotions and regret because he had not been able to see her love, losing her in the bargain.

Thankfully for him, he did eventually fall in love with Aarti, and with that love, the guilt and regret had simply disappeared. Until he had to let her go because he had no future to offer her. That was then, but even today, it seemed no different to him; even today, there was no future he could offer her, or perhaps was reluctant to offer her. But he wanted to know more from her about her new life, so he asked, 'What's up with your life? You want to tell me something about it?'

'There is nothing to say really. He is nice, takes care of me, I don't see anything that one could pick up to make good enough reason to believe otherwise. Except that I just could never love him. He is different, he always was. In fact, that's what I liked about him in the first place, it was something aspirational. As time flies, we start to question, why is he not like me? Why can't he think with me? Why cannot he identify with my mind and ways?' She paused for a second or two before she continued, 'Also, he is possessive and I am simply tagging along. How do I tell myself that not being in love in an otherwise perfect marriage is enough of a reason to give up on it?'

'There you go,' said, Atul reminding her about why he did not want that bond of marriage, a bond that had troubled him for so many years. The bond he did not want as much as she did. The same bond that now troubled her. So, he had been right.

They didn't talk much after that; there wasn't much to talk about. He wasn't ready, he really wasn't. He didn't want to offer anything that he could not promise. Not again. They were on very different paths. Atul waited to see her off as she waited for her taxi to arrive. 'See you soon,' he said, 'and, well, I never got back to Roshni after that, I never could. I still couldn't love her, the burden of serving a responsibility was a burden after all. I couldn't carry it for long. To my misery, she is no more, and worse still, I didn't have the opportunity of apologizing to her either.'

A shocked Aarti did not know what to say. Then she said, 'I am sorry to hear that.' Her waiting taxi didn't leave much time to offer any more condolences.

Her veiled tale had a lot to say, thought Atul, though he couldn't do much about it. Not because it was too late, he never thought that way ever, but because he didn't have much to offer even now. He felt absolutely remorseful. Not for anything else, but for the pain her story brought up within him all over again. It wasn't the pain of parting or a break-up. It was a pain of helplessness for someone you love but can do nothing to help relieve him of his misery.

Soon, he returned to India. His mind was still unsure of what to do. He kept to himself most days thinking about things, recounting his regret and guilt by events. The more he counted the more appeared. Regret occupied most of his day, leaving little time for anything more meaningful.

He tried to keep his mind busy, distracted. He didn't like being preoccupied with regret and remorse. He donated a very small amount of his money that lay with Elisabeth to some charities, mostly those linked to children, but not under his own name—he wasn't looking for publicity or appreciation. One such charity, the King Edward Memorial Trust, invited him to visit their orphanage. Atul accepted the invitation under the name they had sent it in.

He felt nice being welcomed. In the outside world, everybody looked at him with suspicion. But that was outside. Inside here, the innocent children had only one feeling for him, gratitude. The keepers of the place took him around to the classrooms, the hostels and the facilities. They had about three hundred children in their care. It was a pretty large place. Enclosed in a compound surrounded by some of the most expensive real estate were many small single-level structures with thatched roofs. The internal roads were wide but muddy. Every cottage had something or the other for the kids. They even arranged a small event in Atul's honour.

He sat in a classroom where a group of students gathered. They were all sitting on the floor, while Atul and the few teachers accompanying him were given chairs to sit on. The walls had representations of work done by kids, including drawings showing seasons of the year, timetables, a world map tattered around the edges, and collages of photos of kids.

The children were between three to seven years of age. Their innocence and charisma did not reveal their sorrow. Or maybe they were indeed happy there. Children are like water; they don't much care where the stream takes them. They do nothing to avoid or follow the contours.

Some kids recited some poetry to Atul, some showed him paintings, and a boy even showed some acrobatics he had learnt; each child was more eager than the other to show his skills. Their eagerness gratified Atul, and at the same time, he was sorrowful they needed to do that, as if to prove his charity was being put to a meaningful purpose.

One of the girls from the group, about eight years of age, got up when her turn came and announced, 'I have written an essay and I would like to read it.'

A little more than three feet in height, dark complexioned, she had an unusual glow on her face. Her lips and nose had sharp outlines, distinct. The glow on her face outshone her paltry attire. She wore a pink school frock with thick white stripes on it. The dress had outlived its life, one could see from the wrinkling treads and patched holes at places, and it wasn't ironed but washed clean. She had an unmistakable twinkle in her eye, cute and innocent. Her hair was neatly oiled, tied with two pink ribbons. The little girl started reading aloud from a page she held in her hand, taking deep breaths at intervals to gain energy for the high-pitched recital.

'My Father'

'My father is a very beautiful man. I love him a lot. He loves me too. I miss my father. He sends me my food and books. Madam Verdi tells me my father will send me a doll soon. I am waiting for it. But father must be busy with God. So I must wait for it.

'Madam Verdi also tells me father will come back. But I know she is telling lies. My father cannot come back. Once somebody goes to God-house, he never comes back. I miss my father every day. I promise I will be a good daughter to my father.'

Atul was touched by her story and called her closer to him

and hugged her, asking her, 'And what would be the name of a beautiful girl like you?'

The girl looked at Atul, wanting to impress the guest, raised her pitch again and, with a sharp accent, said:

'My name is Jayna Prashant Nagarkar.'

The words hit his ears like thunderbolts. His world collapsed all over again. Here was an abyss he had never visited before. The girl stood still in his arms; he was still perched on his chair. His guilt rose to a level of indescribable proportions. He hated himself so much he wanted to meet death. Right there, right now.

He did nothing of the sort. He simply walked away. The only thought that came to his mind, other than abject hate for himself, was how could he have never thought about her all these years? He knew she existed.

Atul's mind raced faster than a rocket in descent. And as if the nausea from the rapid descent wasn't enough, it now oscillated too, spinning his brain like a whirlwind. His illusions made it even more difficult. It was absolute pandemonium or at least that is what his mind made it out to be. He looked around, there were no devils anymore, he had passed them all he thought. The devil in him too vanished in a split second, but not before growing roots that would freeze him in time. He could see the dead end ahead, but he wouldn't even be able to make it to his death on that dead end. Dead end it was.

Itna uncha ude ke laut ke na aa sakey,
Aasmaan chune ke aaib mein wapas na ja sakey.

Ashkon key har samandar se nazar chura kar chalte rahey,
Khabar kahan thi, har baar, thodi thodi insaaniyat peeche chod chale.

Kal tak sang-e-marmar ka Taj Mahal dekha karte theh,
Aaj magar usme daba Mumtaz ka makhbara yaad aaya.

Jawaan dil ko kisi ka khauf lautana paaya,
Maut ka yeh mod aaisa aaya. Saara maajara phir samajhaaya.

Flew so high that there was no coming back,
The desire to touch those skies could never let me back.

Continued walking with eyes shut to every tear,
Little did I know at every turn a little humanity I left behind.

Till yesterday would see the Taj Mahal of marble,
But today I remembered Mumtaz' sepulcher buried therein.

The young heart could not be backslid by any trepidation,
Death's turning came such that then the whole story unfolded.

That was Atul Malhotra. Soon after this, Elisabeth invited Atul to move to Switzerland. The last that was known about him was that he placed the Rs 1,250 crore lying with Elisabeth in a Trust. The money now belonged to Jayna Nagarkar, and would be given to her when she turned eighteen years of age.

Acknowledgements

Destiny of Shattered Dreams was only a couple of chapters when I shared it with a very close friend, Vinod Agarwal. It was on his persuasion that I decided to write the rest of the story. Hence, the first person I must thank is Vinod.

To Pooja Joshi, Priyanka Bhanushali, Rachita Shah and my dear friend Shraddha Goenka, my gratitude for their valuable insights and contributions to the book. Subhadra Devi for ironing some of the flaws in my writing. My childhood friend Preeti Sancheti for introducing some of these individuals to me. My cherished friends Divyush Goenka, Manoj Agarwal, Rajesh Panjwani, Rakesh Reniwal and Vishnu Agarwal for believing in me. Always. Mrs Machado, my schoolteacher.

My editor Dibakar Ghosh for his guidance, and Rupa Publications India for accepting to publish my work. Nyla Daud from Pakistan who penned the English translations of my poems.

My son Shloak who was more excited than me. A budding poet, he also has plans to write a book. My wife Preeti for whom no words are enough. My brother Vikas for being so supportive and managing the business while I was away writing the book. Last but not the least, my parents for everything I am today.